ANGEL'S KEEP

BOOK 1

AN ARMANI INVESTIGATION NOVEL

KELLY KATA WINFREE

ISBN-13:

Angel's Keep | Ebook : 978-1-968700-10-2

Angel's Keep | Paperback : 978-1-968700-23-2

Angel's Keep | Hardback : 978-1-968700-25-6

Angel's Keep | Audiobook : 978-1-968700-26-3

First Edition: 2026

Book 1 of [?] Series

Cover Design: KL Thorne: www.klthorne.com

Formatting: Refine and Format

For everyone who was told they couldn't, but did anyway.

TRIGGER WARNINGS

Kidnapping, violence, guns, cussing, dead parents, ACAB representation, corrupt police officers, betrayal, breaking and entering, addiction/sobriety, past abuse (referenced), character involved shootings, ADHD, religion and religious talk, religious jokes, cancer, car accident (referenced), on screen character death (implied), mental health issues

ONE

Research is my bitch! I think to myself as I leave the courthouse parking lot. *Research is my bitch, even if professionalism is not.*

My body feels heavy, and my head is pounding. The defense attorney took great pleasure in trying to rip apart my business, looks, and life–not that his vicious words helped his case much. The outraged glint in his eyes at my simple responses will fuel my daydreams for weeks.

The Ivermans' attorney wasn't much kinder, even though I was her star witness. Then again, I spent two hours arguing with her prep team before I even took the stand. They wanted to change everything about my carefully curated outfit, and I refused every single suggestion.

Yes, I looked especially young in my low-rise jeans and graphic tee; that was the whole point. It may have been more professional to look my twenty-five years, but I purposefully dressed younger than I am. I purposefully mimicked the youthfulness of the Ivermans' daughter–bringing the jury's attention to the age difference between her and her attacker.

To the difference between me and the man I caught spiking my drink.

I'm lucky, really. As a Private Investigator, I have no boss to report to, no official dress code, and no chain of command. I work for myself–my own company, Armani Investigation Services–and I get to live by my own definition of *professionalism*. Any client who doesn't like my jeans–or attitude–is free to hire someone else.

If I want to let a suspect ply me full of drinks and talk about himself, with a recorder in my pocket, I have no supervisor to tell me no. Alabama is a one party consent state–even if there is no expectation of privacy in a crowded bar.

I'm not an idiot. I showed up to that bar early enough to introduce myself to the waitstaff and make a request that any drinks made for me be virgin, without letting anyone buying those drinks know. I also set my recorder to sync with my laptop every fifteen minutes, saving all files to a folder titled 'Ivermans' Case'.

Besides, the Ivermans certainly didn't care if I dressed like the young adult I am. My results speak for themselves. They even offered a bonus for my testimony–not that I would have taken it. They paid more than enough for my billable services, anything more would just be obscene. Instead, I asked them to donate to their local woman's shelter. I mean, since they wanted to spend the cash anyway.

Tapping my fingers against the steering wheel, I take a deep breath and turn into my parking lot. Carefully choosing my favorite spot–one I can see from my kitchen and office–I mentally make note of what needs to be done before I can crawl into my bed, and what can wait until morning. Well, I guess it technically could all wait until morning... and doesn't that sound like a plan.

Tonight I sleep; tomorrow I bust ass.

I shove my files in my go bag and climb out of the car. As I unlock my back office door, I notice lights on in the front room. *Weird.* It's not unusual for me to leave a light or two on in my upstairs apartment, but down here I usually leave it dark. I dislike coming home to a dark space, but I prefer that no one be able to peek in from the street when I'm not in my office. The expensive tint that I paid for on my front windows assures that if the lights are off, the view is totally dark.

Of course, it wouldn't be the first time I mentally switched up my tasks as I rushed out the door in the morning. ADHD is a pain like that. The person I am before my coffee is more than capable of making me question reality–creamer in the cabinet, keys in the fridge. Heck, I once spent a half hour searching for my phone, using its own flashlight app to look in the couch cushions. I forgot to prepare the coffee pot last night, instead grabbing my morning brew from my favorite place on my way. Mixing up which light gets left on isn't out of the realm of possibilities.

I'm just really not looking forward to the darkness that waits for me upstairs.

"Amy, you're late." Kyle's crisp voice cuts across from the lobby. "I thought maybe, just maybe, you were actually out on a so called case. But, just as I thought, not a single file here for you to be working on."

My blood boils, and the edge of my vision tinges red. I broke up with Kyle three months ago. After six years of his degrading remarks, petulant attitude, and horrendous mood swings, I *finally* found the courage to walk away. He has never supported me. Instead, he constantly whittled down everything that makes me *me,* pruning me back until I fit into his neat little box labeled *trophy wife.* Everything is always about him, his dreams, his career goals, his needs. I doubt he knows anything about my business other than where it is–as evidenced by his rude remarks about my files.

Stepping fully into the light of my front office, I can't help but glance at the now destroyed, empty filing cabinet–despite knowing that my files are actually in my bag. My hand clutches the strap, and I force myself to relax, refusing to give Kyle the satisfaction of seeing me second guess myself. I grit my teeth at the sight of the destruction that I can now see, hidden as it was from the dark hallway. I take a long slow breath, forcing myself to relax. The destroyed cabinet was merely a decoy, anyway.

He looks handsome as ever, smugly leaning against my desk, dressed casually in dark jeans and a red button down. The obliteration of my things around him is a striking contrast to his relaxed stance. His

dark eyes glint with malice as he drinks me in. The taut smile on his lips mocks me.

That's right. Judge me, asshole. Just a naive little girl playing detective.

"Don't try to tell me you locked your files away, Amy. I've already opened every drawer in this office. There's so little paperwork. It's no wonder you're failing here. Really now, I think it's time you come home and quit playing *detective*. Your little temper tantrum has gone on long enough."

Every word out of his poisonous mouth ignites the fire in my blood. He knows so little of who I really am, too obsessed with who he wants me to be, but I have to play this carefully. His rage has always been explosive and I'm in no mood for a hospital visit tonight. Because I will no longer cower in fear. We are in my space and I will fight back.

Thankfully, I'm a little paranoid and overly cautious–comes from being a dead cop's kid.

The little vein in his forehead starts to throb as I cross the glass covered floor, shards crunching under my boots. My eyes flit from his reddening face to the busted front windows and glass door. *That's going to be a bitch to replace.*

I grit my teeth at the total annihilation of my space. The floor to ceiling windows aren't just smashed; it looks like he ground his expensive leather shoes into every shard. My printer is in pieces, spanning the entire lobby, as if he threw it in a fit of rage. My precious coffee maker smashed right in the middle of the lobby. He even seems to have taken the term "throw pillow" seriously. He gutted them and threw the stuffing everywhere. Nothing was left on my desk. In fact, it looks like he just swept his arms over it, sending everything crashing to the ground. *Good thing I took my laptop with me.*

It took me years to slowly make my space what I wanted–years of decisions shattered by a man who can't take rejection–who thinks coercion is consent.

Carefully, I make my way to the coat rack and hang my backpack on one of the empty hooks, running my fingers over the hidden panic button–one of many concealed throughout my building. Then, I step over to one of my oversized lounge chairs and sit nonchalantly across it, sideways.

The files he's looking for? Today's are tucked safely away in my go bag–unfortunately, my gun isn't in there. I locked it in my trunk at the courthouse this morning and didn't even think to grab it before leaving. If only I hadn't forgotten to grab the gun case this morning. Then it would have safely been on my front seat, in plain sight, reminding me to reconceal it in my bag.

My other files are locked away upstairs in my storage room–the second bedroom makes a great evidence locker of sorts.

"My name is not Amy." I speak as calmly as I can manage, although my voice still carries some bite. He never called me by my real name. At first I thought it was a cute nickname, but over time, I began to realize it was to disrespect me. A way to demean my value.

"Come off it, Amy. A pretentious name like Armani may make a cute alias for a so-called private investigator, but we both know that no self respecting parent would name their child something so obnoxious." Kyle rolls his eyes at me as he speaks.

"Well mine did."

"Sure, Amy."–My tenuous grip on my temper slips every time that name falls out of his mouth. It was one of the many ways he tried to strip me of my identity.–"A Setting beat cop and kindergarten teacher definitely decided to spice things up by giving their daughter a name that is best suited for the strip clubs. They *clearly* had such high expectations for you."

Five minutes, I remind myself. *It only takes five minutes for an officer to get here from the station. Don't try to attack him; you won't win.*

And, that was on a test call–during lunch time traffic–not during the quiet evening hours. Most of the Setting, Alabama police department worked with my dad. There are a few younger guys, who hadn't, but most of them had my mom as a teacher. Besides, Uncle Ludwig drags each new member of the department here at some point during their first day. Only the newest of the academy recruits don't know who I am, and those aren't even rookies, yet. Not that Setting gets many rookies; most stay in Auburn, down the road.

"Armani means warrior." My voice comes out colder than I intend. A deep breath steadies my racing heart.

Keep his attention, keep him talking. Buy time.

"Probably because Daddy wanted a boy instead." Kyle laughs. *Fucker.* The bastard actually laughs, like a thrice damned movie villain. "Anyway, *Amy,* it's past time for you to come back home. I get that you love this little pet project of yours, but it is hardly worth giving up our life together. Besides, you will never make it without my income to back you up."

"*Seriously?*" He startles a small laugh out of me. "You think I left you for my business? I mean, it certainly doesn't help that you clearly think of it as lesser, but it is not the reason I left you. Your temper is."

"Come on now, *Amy,* this little tantrum of yours has got to end. You've been gone long enough now. Let's go home and talk about this like civilized adults." His voice is unnaturally soft and deceivingly calm. This is the proud, loving, professional Kyle–the public face.

"Civilized adults don't break into each other's work places, Kyle. They don't smash windows, break into locked cabinets or snoop through private files," I snap at him, spinning upright in my seat. I lean forward, elbows on my knees and stare him in his eyes. "I'm not going anywhere."

"They also don't play hooky from their pretend jobs, Amy." His calm demeanor breaks. His eyes harden and venom fills his voice. "They don't spend months sleeping on fake office furniture to avoid having real conversations with their partners either."

"And I have done neither," I snap back. "So, clearly, I am the more civilized person here."

He straightens up, no longer casually leaning against my desk, and stalks across the room. He pins me against my seat with rage flaring in his eyes. Forcing myself to not tense, I pray my back up shows soon.

"Try again, Amy. I've been here since ten this morning. You have not."

"Sounds like you're the one playing hooky." I grin up at him, trying desperately to seem unbothered. "I was testifying in court, you're throwing a tantrum. *My boss* excused my absence. Does *yours* know you're here?" My heart races in my chest, and I hope that my face isn't turning red. He doesn't get to see my fear anymore. Real or pretend.

"So full of lies, Amy. Really now, grow up. First, you claim to work for yourself, but your boss had to authorize your absence. Which is it?" *Oh my god. He really is an idiot. How did I miss that while dating him?* "Second, what decent lawyer would let you testify looking like that?" His eyes roam over me, lingering a little too long on my chest.

A short blast of a police siren startles him into stepping back from me. I glance over his shoulder to see my dad's old partner closing in. There are benefits to living in a small town.

"Step away from the woman." Uncle Ludwig speaks clearly and calmly as he approaches.

Kyle raises his hands in a placating manner. "All good here, officer, just a little misunderstanding. Tell him, Amy."

"Sorry, Uncle Lud." I push my seat back as best I can, allowing room for him to step between Kyle and I. "My ex seems to have gone a little crazy. He keeps telling me I can't leave him, and to come home. Worse yet, he keeps calling me Amy."

Kyle's face reddens rapidly, like he actually expected me to agree with his insanity. He lunges at me, anger written into every line of his handsome face. But, Uncle Ludwig is faster, stepping fully between us, and catching a fist to the face for his effort.

"And that, my friend, is assault on an officer." He slaps cuffs on Kyle's wrists and practically drags him from my office. "Officer Doe will take your statement, Armani." He waves the younger man toward me.

Officer Doe is completely foreign to me. I thought I knew everyone at the station, but apparently they've had at least one transfer that hasn't been forced into my office for an introduction by Uncle Lud. Then again, that could be why he accompanied the Chief. Uncle Ludwig likes trying to set me up with his younger officers.

I'm quick to go over the evening with Officer Doe, giving as much relevant detail as I can. He asks a few questions that I didn't cover, and I answer them patiently. I don't know everything, and I am not trained as a police officer. Just because I'm an investigator, does not mean I'm a detective.

"And he didn't recognize your uncle?" Doe asks, one eyebrow raised.

"He never bothered to meet him." Not once in six years. "Claimed if he was really such good family, he would have kept me from the foster system. Part of why I left him. He was quite controlling. Manipulative." I just wish I had gotten out sooner.

"Understood. Well, Miss Smith, with the level of destruction wrought by your ex, we have no way to secure the upstairs apartment from the street. Do you have somewhere safe to stay tonight?" Officer Doe's voice cuts through the quiet that followed my statement.

"Upstairs has a whole separate set of locks. I'll be fine."

"Those locks have been jammed. If we bust open the door for you, there is no barrier. Waiting for a locksmith is your best bet. I must really insist you find somewhere safer to stay tonight, until you can have a good look at any damage that may have been caused. It's for your safety."

Yeah, sure.

"Are you saying I'm barred from sleeping in my own apartment tonight, because that's what it sounds like." I press my teeth together, lips thinning.

"Ma'am, I'm not saying you *can't* stay here. I'm saying you *shouldn't*–for your own safety."

Seriously, do they train officers in how to sound pretentious and soulless, or is it just this man's natural ineptitude? I don't like this new guy, and I will not hesitate to tell Uncle Ludwig. Later. After I recuperate from dealing with Kyle's bullshit. I have no more energy for presumptuous men today.

"Yeah, I've got everything covered for tonight. You don't have to worry about me, Officer." I smile sweetly as we make our way out of the disaster zone that my office has become. Hopefully my tone doesn't give me away. A hotel is an uncalculated expense. Maybe I should have taken that bonus.

I look around for the cruiser. My uncle left with Kyle already, leaving the new kid here with me. It's not the first time Uncle Lud has not so subtly tried to set me up with one of his officers. I think it's his way of trying to look out for me, but I find it ridiculous. I'm definitely not taking the bait tonight.

"Ludwig left without you. Guess he thought you were taking too long.

"Nah, old man Ludwig knows I rode out here on my motorcycle. Just finished all my paperwork approving me for motor patrol, when your alarm triggered. I just have to turn in tonight's paperwork and I'm out for the night."

"I see." I'm not sure how else to respond. There *is* a nice bike parked on the street, but I feel like any further conversation will give him the impression I'm actually interested, and I am *so* not. "Well then. Have a great night."

I give a small wave over my shoulder but otherwise ignore Officer Doe as he leaves. I walk the opposite direction, ignoring the urge to look over my shoulder and watch him leave.

According to my research the local biker bar, Chris's HandleBar, is only one mile away. By my calculations, that makes it a fifteen minute leisurely walk–or if necessary a seven and a half minute full out sprint, with my go bag weighing me down. Today, a leisurely walk sounds like a great way to unwind the coil of tension inside me.

As I near the parking lot full of gorgeous bikes, I swing my pack off of one shoulder to pull my patch out of the side pocket, before putting it back on properly. Back damage is no joke. I can hear my dad's voice telling me to use both straps. Same as he did the morning... I shake that thought away.

My patch is a little unusual. It's old, but well taken care of.

Bikers wear their patches on vests, called cuts. These patches tell the world who they are–which club they're in, who's under whose protection, and even their rank in the club. Women and children can also be given cuts, telling the world that a club has their back.

My patch is a protection patch, but I have no leathers to put it on. It was given to me when my dad died, by a friend of the force, Big Mike. No one knew where I'd end up, so instead of a cut that would need to be replaced as I grew, he strung it onto a leather cord that I could wear as a necklace.

I slip the cord around my neck and stuff the patch under my shirt as I ready myself to enter the bar. Having never been here, I'm playing it cautiously. The patch can always come out if I need it, but otherwise, I prefer to have an ace in my pocket–a fuck around and find out trump card.

This particular bar may be new to me, but it's not the first biker bar I've been to. Bouncing from foster placement to foster placement, the only constant in my life was biker clubs. Every place I went, I found the closest motorcycle club. I'd research all their businesses, and measure how long it would take me to get to each from both my placement and school. More than one has saved my skin in some form or fashion–a safe haven from abusive fosters, a job, a hot meal or ten. Big Mike's protection patch has served its purpose many times over.

I hesitate just outside the door. Something about this bar feels *different*. It's not as loud as the others I've been to–there's no yelling and screaming. The bikes are parked in groups with huge divides. There's no bouncers at the door. I know Setting hasn't been kind to the biker clubs' liquor licensing. *Are they worried the city will shut down the one place they can gather and drink?*

Entering the bar feels like coming home. *Which is weird, isn't it?* I've always been welcome around the clubs that looked after me growing up, but I never belonged to them. So why does this place feel so *right*?

TWO

The music is low, not so low it can't be heard, but lower than any biker bar I've ever been in before. It is, however, the expected rock mix. 5FDP floods my senses, as I take a seat near the bar, and consequently, the speakers.

With my back against the wall, I look around. The place is full, but not packed. Not everyone here has a patch on their cut, and most of the women are dressed quite tastefully. The members of all four local motorcycle clubs mingle here. They stay mostly separate to drink, but the pool tables and dart boards seem to be a neutral zone. So is the bar itself, of course, where a rather good-looking man is pouring drinks.

Bar food has been a favorite of mine, ever since I first stumbled into one at 14. Mrs Maggie had taken one look at the bruises on my face, the patch around my neck, and the tears on my face, and just melted. She served me the most delicious burger and onion rings, before sending her old man to straighten out my foster parents. That placement didn't last much longer.

Watching the bartender as I look over the menu, I can't

help but notice the muscle definition in his arms as he shakes a drink.

One woman laughs obnoxiously, hurting my ears even from across the bar, but he just grins at her, shaking his head. His silver flecked hair radiates under the fluorescent lighting. Another patron is quick to grab his attention, this time a muscular black man. I force my attention back to the menu; I'm here to eat, not to stare at the staff.

"What can I get'cha?" The waitress is pretty–dark black hair, push up bra, and full red lips. Her shorts are short, really short, but her plump ass is covered–no cheeks hanging out.

Before I can answer, the black man I saw speaking with the bartender slides into the seat across from me. "She'll take the Newcomer's Special, Missy. Thank you." He dismisses her with a flick of his fingers, and she doesn't even pause to glance back at me.

"That's awfully bold," I say. "What if I have allergies?" I poke my lip out in a faux pout, gauging his reaction.

He leans back in his seat, with a wide grin on his face. "Do you?"

"No," I admit, my own small grin tugging at my lips, against my will. "But, I do prefer to make my own order. I was looking forward to a greasy burger."

His cut identifies him as Boss, President of The Cadillac Squad. A small glance toward the pool tables shows the other presidents mingling. None of them are watching out right, but they are clearly aware of my presence, trying to figure out if I might be a threat.

"Do my friends make you nervous?" Boss asks. He crosses his arms over his chest, flexing his biceps.

"Are they really your friends? I was under the impression MCs didn't like to share territory." I snap back.

Boss doesn't know I've done my due diligence before

coming here. I researched every Motorcycle Club in town when I moved home. He doesn't know that I know this place is neutral ground. I know none of the compounds can serve liquor. I know the Setting cops will bust them for too much beer at their parties. He doesn't know that I know *everything*, except which businesses they own. Those records are buried deep, and my caseload has had me a tiny bit too busy to dig.

"Setting is special."

"It is," I agree. "Four motorcycle clubs in one town. Definitely makes it *unique*."

"We may not be *besties* but us presidents at least work together. Not on everything, but when it comes to watching out for this place, all bets are off."

"I'm sure. Not many places to drink in town that would be comfortable with a whole club showing up at once."

"Exactly." Boss grins at me.

The perky waitress comes back with a platter of food and a shot glass full of clear liquid. I don't trust it.

I pull the platter of food toward me and inspect the rations. Lucky for Boss, there's two cheeseburger sliders. There's also a pile of onion rings, fried mushrooms, green tomatoes, and mozzarella sticks. I don't know what I'd've done if I didn't get a burger tonight.

"No jalapeño poppers? I'm disappointed." Not really, but this man doesn't need to know this is a nearly perfect plate. I'd rather have a full size burger, but this works. It *really* works.

"Not everyone can take the heat." Boss's eyes flash in challenge.

I push the clear shot toward him. "You can have this, I don't drink turpentine."

That startles a laugh out of him. He slides it back. "It's a Belvedere 10."

That startles a laugh out of me. “Bull-shit.” I do *not* want to know what that cost.

He flicks the rim of the glass with his finger. “Taste it. A Newcomer’s Special can only be ordered for fresh meat, and only by one of the four presidents. We pay a good price to treat our guests well.”

I pick up the glass, and give it a swirl. At least it's not that obnoxious drink with the gold flakes. This is part of why I don't drink; the good stuff is wasted on me.

I make direct eye contact with Boss, as I lift the vodka to my mouth. I don't drink much, barely enough to wet my tongue, and get a taste, before setting it back in the middle of the table.

“There. I tasted it. You can have the rest. I don't drink.”

He raises one eyebrow. “You don't drink, but you came here? To a biker bar? Come off it, *pig*, we don't take very well to pork trying to sneak in.”

I laugh. “I'm more of a turkey: a decent substitute for bacon. It'll get the job done, but nowhere close to the real thing.”

Boss glowers at me, but I pull my wallet from the front pocket of my bag anyway.

Tossing him my ID and a business card, I tell him, “Go have whoever run that. Any decent MC has at least one hacker or tech guru. There's four of you here.” I pull my patch out from under my shirt. “Then one of you can call Big Mike for a reference.”

Boss looks over my ID, a small grin tugging at his lip. “You've got fire, *Smith,* I'll give you that.”

I'm not sure why he emphasizes my last name that way. Does he think the ID is fake? Too generic? It's my actual name. I have a fake ID, or ten, but those aren't needed here. *Right now, anyway.*

He snaps his fingers and one of the bikers with the same patch as him jumps up and rushes over. Probably a prospect. One with three teardrops tattooed under his eye-three kills.

Boss hands this killer my information, never even glancing at my business card. "Take this to Tank. The Cavalry has the best investigative resources. He can do his part sorting out this Newcomer." Boss turns back to me, effectively dismissing his subordinate. "Now tell me, Armani Smith, why come to a bar, a biker bar at that, if you're not going to drink?"

The shot of Belvedere slides back toward me. Ugh. Are we back on this again?

"I told you, I'm hungry. Was hoping for a burger, but then some jumped up asshole who thinks he knows better than me commandeered my meal. If I wanted someone to order for me and control my food, I'd've stayed with my ex."

Oops. That was a tiny bit more than I intended to reveal. And a lot more sassy. I quickly stuff a fried mushroom in my mouth. Maybe some good fried food will curb my sharp tongue.

But, Boss surprises me. He laughs–a kind laugh, nothing like Kyle's deranged cackle–like he is laughing with me, not at me.

"And not drinking?"

"I don't drink and work," I tell him. "I've got reports to finish tonight, and I can't accurately do them with a fuzzy head." I flick my fingers toward the business card still in his hand. Not entirely true, but not a complete lie. I want a clear head when I decide where to sleep tonight.

He looks down at it–long and hard. His brow furrows.

"Besides," I continue. "I did not see this shot get made, and the waitress who brought it over clearly jumps to your command. Add to that the fact that you won't touch it. I'm not stupid, and I don't feel like getting drugged tonight."

Boss's gaze jumps back up to me, like he never considered such implications. Of course not, he's a man. He stares me right in the eye, as he contemplates his next move.

Then he leans back in his seat, and shouts across the bar. “Hey, Keep! Got a minute?”

The bartender freezes, just for a moment, before dropping the rag he was wiping the counter down with and coming over.

“Boss.” The tone in his voice makes me smile, for just a moment. Someone isn't happy to be interrupted from his work.

Boss grins, clearly amused with the bartender's ire. “Sis, here, is worried I may have had someone spike this very expensive shot of vodka. Would you mind vouching for me? Let her know she's safe. And maybe, letting Missy go halves? To prove it's not poisoned.”

The bartender turns his attention to me. I can feel the weight of his stare as he assesses the situation, his grey-blue eyes swirling like storms are brewing inside him.

“If Boss says you're safe with him, I doubt the devil himself could land a blow against you. He's a force of nature like that. But I get it, stranger-danger.” He winks. Then, looking me in the eye, he takes the shot himself, his throat tightening as he swallows.

Damn. That was hot.

Without another word, he spins on his heels and disappears into the crowd.

Boss's grin grows impossibly larger. “Chris likes you.” There's laughter in his voice.

“Excuse me?”

“Chris doesn't drink during open hours. Bad business for the owner-slash-bartender to be drinking. He did that shot just for you. He has a halves policy for suspected drugged drinks. A server brings a fresh shot and a shaker. They mix the two drinks and pour the new mixture back into the glasses. Then the suspected spiker takes the first shot to prove it's safe. That's what I was suggesting that Missy do. Waitstaff is allowed a certain number of drinks each night, but Chris took it instead."

"And, why won't you just take the shot, Boss?" I ask.

"I'm five years sober." Boss tosses a five year sobriety coin on the table. "I come out here to keep an eye on my guys, mingle with the others, and make sure everyone gets home at night. I'm not afraid to confiscate keys. From anyone."

"That is admirable. Sobriety can be hard."

"Thank you. Now, I'm not usually one to push a drink onto someone, but you actually look like you need one, little sis. If you're not going to drink, can I at least have Missy bring you one of my teas? I keep a small stash here for when I'm really tempted to drink. Chris is a good man like that. Sometimes he even spikes it with fresh minced ginger to give it that extra burn."

"What's the catch?"

"You tell me what has you looking one inconvenience away from drinking an entire shelf."

"Do I really?"

"Not so much now, but you did when you came in, folded in on yourself, trying to look small. What makes a woman with the fire you've shown me try to make herself invisible?"

"A bad encounter with an overbearing ex."

Something about this dark skinned man makes me want to tell him everything. After all these years, have I conditioned myself to spill to the first person in leather to talk to me after a problem? I only ran to the MCs when I couldn't handle a situation on my own, as a kid. I haven't crawled to one looking for help in years. I wasn't actually looking for help when I came here today. *Was I?*

Before Boss has a chance to further question me, an older white man with a scar across his left eye helps himself to a seat at our table. He slides a manila folder across the table to Boss, not even glancing at me.

"Girlie's got a history." His voice is gruff.

"Doesn't everyone?" I snark. "After all, history is just his story." I can't stand when men act like I'm not there. My eyes narrow at the man's audacity. I get that he is a big bad biker, but I am not just some *girlie.*

Grumpy doesn't reply, instead locking eyes with Boss. They seem to have an entire conversation this way. Or maybe it's a battle of wills? Grumpy looks away first, Boss seeming to have won their little standoff.

Maybe I should try to get Grumpy's actual preferred name from his cut, but he's angled away from me. I can see that he is a member of The Calvary, so I could, *probably,* safely assume this is Tank. But, we all know what they say about assuming. Besides, Tank is the President and could have easily sent his Vice, Sergeant-at-Arms, or even the hacker himself with my information.

"Sit here with Tank, while I make that phone call," Boss says to me. "I'll ask Missy to fix us both a tea on my way out. I think we might need it tonight. I know I do."

Ha! Point goes to the investigator!

Tank turns fully in his seat to watch me, as Boss heads toward the door. "I hope you don't think you can weasel your way into our turf on behalf of that boyfriend of yours." His gruff voice full of venomous ire.

Ex-fucking-cuse me?

"I don't have a boyfriend."

"Not according to my information." He crosses his arms over his puffed up chest.

"Then your information is outdated. By at least 3 months." I shove a mushroom in my mouth, chewing to keep my barbed tongue in check.

"Really? Because *my* sources say that Kyle Dutcher spent the whole day at your apartment, today. He even bought a ring last week."

"Did your sources tell you he smashed every piece of glass in my office? That he broke into my filing cabinets? That he completely ransacked the place? That it's going to take a whole business day to clean up that asshole's mess, if not longer?" I notice Boss come back to the table, but I don't hesitate in my rant. "Did anyone tell you I'm going to be living off ramen for the next month, while I save every penny I can, because I have no clue how much it's going to cost me to replace all my floor to ceiling glass windows? My destroyed belongings? That he smashed my things after busting not just my glass front door, but also jamming up the lock to my upstairs apartment. Did your so-called source manage to find a locksmith quote for me? Price the glass? If no one told you that he's an abusive piece of shit, and that I barely managed to crawl out from under his thumb three months ago, then your info is not worth the paper it's printed on." Tears leak from my eyes. I furiously brush them away, keeping my glare on Tank.

Boss gives a slow clap. Tanks eyes narrow. I grip the table so tight my fingertips start going numb.

Missy slips over to our table with two steaming coffee cups, eyeing me warily. I guess someone snapping at a MC president isn't something they see around here very often. *Oh well.*

"Thanks, Missy." Boss is the first to break the awkward silence that followed my little tirade. "Do you take it straight, sis? Or do you need sweetener?" He winks as he retakes his seat, sliding the glass to me.

I sniff the cup, pressing the rim against my lower lip. It smells a little lemony, but not quite like a black tea with lemon. I take a small sip. *Lemongrass.*

"It's delicious," I tell him. Then I turn back to Tank, as what he said fully hits me.

"What, precisely, do you mean about Kyle weaseling into your turf? Last I knew, he dealt in stocks. Brokering or some shit. He has big dreams of Atlanta life."

"Well he ain't buying shit in Atlanta, right now. He's buying in on almost every one of our suppliers, and blacklisting us. Looks like he's trying to starve us out. It's not working, but he's trying. Not just The Cavalry, but all of us." Tank twists his finger, indicating all the bike clubs here.

"And how long has he been doing that?" I question leaning forward in my seat. The coldness in my voice shocks me.

"Six months." Tank locks his eyes on mine, "Before you *supposedly* left him."

"Shit."

That bastard knew I was trying to leave, long before I had the means. If he was blacklisting them that far back, he had to have spent some time researching. I may have had the resources to run everything down in a couple days, but Kyle certainly didn't. He isn't from here, I am. He doesn't believe in my 'little business'. He has no clue what I can do. And all of *my* research has always been locked upstairs–in the apartment Kyle doesn't seem to realize is there.

I wonder what he thought he was breaking into. A storage closet? Attic? Crawl space?

"He's trying to cut me off." I turn to Boss. My heart races and I grasp onto the kindness he's shown me like a life raft.

"The asshole realized I was leaving." My breaths shorten and my pulse races.

"And what, exactly, does that have to do with us?" Tank questions gruffly, eyes full of hatred.

"Bikers have always had my back." Shit, how else could I explain it?

"Even if it's been eight years since she last used Big Mike's protection patch," Boss adds, leveling a heavy look at Tank.

"Seven," I correct. One of his buddies picked me up and brought me home the day I turned 18.

"Eight since he got a call about it, then," Boss concedes with a shrug.

I pinch my eyes shut and force myself to take several deep breaths, before I hyperventilate.

"I'm starting to wish I took that shot."

"You didn't drink the Belvedeer?" Tank shoots a dangerous look at Boss.

"Don't look at me." Boss grins back. "I tried asking for Missy to go halves, but Chris downed it himself."

"I think it's time I go home." I groan as I get to my feet, ignoring their byplay, mind spinning. "Tomorrow is going to be shit after that ass makes bail."

"I'll take you." Boss stands too. "Tank, keep an eye on my guys, would ya? Nobody bikes drunk. I'll come pick them up in a cage if I need to."

"Like hell," Tank growls. "Assign one of your own. I got my own idiots to watch over."

Boss sighs, glancing around the bar. Tank leaves us, staggering back to his dart game. Boss shakes his head, muttering under his breath about neutral ground.

Eventually, he walks over and exchanges a few words with the bartender. He keeps his eyes on me like he thinks I might run. Which, I totally was planning to do. Instead, I take the offered ride. The bartender watching as we pull out the lot.

"So," Boss says, getting off his bike at my place. "What exactly is your plan tonight? What, with the busted glass and locked apartment?" He gestures around at the mess. Someone was actually listening to my tirade.

"I was going to clean the glass, do my paperwork, and crash on the office couch."

"Absolutely not, little sis." Boss's eyes roam over the damage. "I'll help you clean up, if you want, but you are not staying here tonight. There is no security–nothing between you and the street."

"I'm not exactly flush with options," I snap. "Hotels are freaking expensive. And I am not going back, I don't care what shit he pulls." I blink back the tears threatening to fall. *What can I say, I'm an angry crier.*

"Hell to the fuck no!" Boss agrees, venom dripping in his words. He takes a slow deep breath and continues. "I've got a spare room in my apartment at the compound. Shit, the apartment next to mine is empty too, but all it has right now is a mattress on the floor. No little sister of mine is giving in to an abusive ass, not while I'm around for back up."

"Why do you keep calling me that?" I ask, wrapping my arms around myself, fixating on the odd word choice.

"Little sis?" Boss grins at me. "Well, not only am I also one of Big Mike's patch kids, my last name also happens to be Smith. Feels to me like the universe decided to give me the little sister my parents never did."

Holy shit. Big Mike's patch worked its magic once again. For the first time in seven years, if not longer, I don't feel alone. I've been adopted by the president of an ex-felon bike gang. Never mind that he was falsely convicted.

"Come on, little sis. I think it's time for you to call it a night. I'll help you deal with this mess tomorrow." Boss wraps his arm around me, leading me back to his bike. "Everything will look better in the daylight."

THREE

Boss's apartment is gorgeous; steel grey walls pair wonderfully with cream-colored accents. He gives me an extra shirt to sleep in, and shows me to his spare room–taking an extra moment to point out the locks–before going downstairs to make sure all of his guys come in. The bed is soft, and the blanket is warm. I drift easily off to sleep; the years I spent in the foster system taught me to sleep well in unfamiliar territories.

The next morning, Boss offers me another tee shirt to wear, as well as a pair of leggings he borrowed from a house mouse. His black shirt swims on me, but paired with the pink leggings, I feel almost fashionable. Shoot, add a chunky belt, and I would call it high fashion.

Instead of taking me straight back to my office, Boss opts to make a pit stop at my favorite café, Elixars.

"How do you take your coffee?" I ask as I head to the counter to order for my new friend and I.

"I take my coffee like me," Boss says with a grin. He slings his arm over my shoulder and pulls me to his side. "Earthy dark roast with just enough sweet cream to make it match my skin. Not enough to dilute the expertly roasted taste, but enough to sweetly compliment the natural tones."

"Okay, Sommelier." I grin up at him. "Just say you drink it for the taste, and not the caffeine. Let me guess–you're secretly a morning person."

Boss grins. "Guilty. Let me guess–you need caffeine to function, like a true addict."

"It is my drug of choice," I agree easily. "My treat today, as a thank you for letting me crash at yours last night."

"If you insist," Boss agrees–too easily–finding us a table after telling the barista his roast of choice. I can feel his gaze on me as I order.

When our drinks come out, Boss is quick to grab mine and pop the top off. "As I suspected," he grins. "Your coffee is as light as your skin. Some sugary monstrosity, I'm sure."

"Hey! Don't hate on my white mocha! I even added a protein shot to make it a complete breakfast–carbs, protein, and lots of caffeine. It's heavenly perfection in a cup."

Boss laughs again at my loving description of the drink. Either that, or the way I grab my cup and hold it close like it's a precious gem.

"Whatever you say, little sis. It's just another way we're alike. We both make our coffee as a personal avatar of ourselves." Boss pauses to take a long drink of his coffee. "All kidding aside though, you can tell a lot about a person by how they order their coffee."

"Oh really, what does my incredibly white drink tell you about me?" I ask with a grin, genuinely curious what insight he may have gained, and how accurate it is.

Boss lets out a rumbling chuckle that soothes my soul. His laugh is nearly as deep as his voice. "Less the drink itself and more how you ordered it. This place is busy, while I knew instantly I wanted the darkest roast they had, rather decisively

I might add, you held back while you assessed your options. You, very considerately, did not approach the cashier until your order was ready, allowing others who were ready to go first, and showing you value everyone's time. Your eyes first went to the drip coffee options, looking for the easiest drink to make, saving the baristas energy for other orders. You clearly were disappointed with the options..."

He trailed off, clearly for me to fill in what we both know. "Columbian roast is not a light roast, it's medium at best."

Boss grins at me, a little half smirk that makes me smile in turn. "Exactly, but you didn't complain about the less than satisfactory option, you just went to the next easiest drink to make, that still had the flavor and caffeine content you would enjoy, a mocha."

"I mean, Columbian roast may be a medium roast, but it is lighter than the other two options. Complaining would just be rude." I don't know why I feel the need to defend myself, Boss didn't say anything that wasn't true, or that was negative in any way.

"That's exactly what I mean, sis. You're polite, considerate, kind. You shoved a twenty in the tip jar, when the cashier turned to hand off another order. You're generous, but don't want or need recognition for such simple acts. Which is probably why your face is as red as it is, right now. I didn't mean to embarrass you."

"I'm not embarrassed," I mumble, head down and totally contradicting my words. "I'm just not used to being so seen."

Isn't that the truth? I've lived my life in the background. Heck, I made a career out of blending in. I drink my coffee and mull over his words. Maybe, I should start paying a little more attention to people's coffee, and the way they order it.

After our coffee, Boss takes me back to my office...where nothing is as we left it last night. It's absolute chaos in motion.

There are two work trucks parked in front. A couple men are hammering up plywood. I even see Uncle Ludwig arguing with–*is that Tank*?

I swing myself off of Boss's bike in a rush, nearly face planting into the sidewalk. Lucky for me, Boss catches me by the arm just in time, the motion catching my uncle's attention. Tank uses my fiasco as a distraction to slip away from the conversation.

“Armani! Do you know any of these men? I came to let you know Mr. Dutcher posted bail, and found the place crawling with *bikers*.”

“Yeah, Boss here is one of Big Mike's buddies.” Sadly, Big Mike is the only biker that carries any respect with Uncle Ludwig–or most of the Setting Police Department. They can't deny all the good work he has done or the cases he helped close.

“Well, Dutcher made bail this morning. For your safety, Doe is going to hang around and keep an eye on things.” Uncle Ludwig flicks his fingers at the bakery café across the street.

I turn to see Doe sitting at one of the outdoor tables. Blues Brews and Pastries is the local hot spot for cops. It has to be at least half the reason Uncle Ludwig helped me buy this place. The realtor wouldn't take me seriously on my own.

“Coffee over there any good?” Boss asks, no doubt wondering why I didn't mention the place when we decided to get coffee this morning.

“The best,” Ludwig answers before returning his attention to me. “Doe has you covered today, Armani, if Dutcher tries to show back up today. I can't say I can afford to lose him for long, but we've never had a Motorcycle Patrol Officer before, so who knows. I, however, just came off the night shift so I'm going home. You know how it is.” He wraps me in a tight hug.

“Night, Uncle Lud.” I grin as he heads back to his car. I wait until he's out of earshot to tell Boss, "The coffee over there is better than the station's. That is the best that can be said for it. Ludwig boasts because his sister runs it. Her pastries are amazing, the coffee is not."

"Ah, nepotism, coffee at its finest." Boss grins as Tank comes back from wherever he stepped off to while Ludwig had his say.

"You forgot the cost and time to board up your broken glass, last night in your little tirade," Tank says with a grin. "Preacher and I set our prospects to work this morning, fixing the place back up."

"Why?" I honestly didn't think Tank liked me, and I never met Preacher.

"Because, girlie, you got brass balls. And these idiots needed work to do." Tank grins waving his hand, as if to dismiss my concerns. "I'm just here to make their task lists with ya, then they are all yours."

It's too early in the morning to deal with this circus. I need another coffee, and maybe I should make it an Irish one. The pounding in my head matches the pounding of the hammers.

I turn to take in the chaos. If Tank wants a list, I'm sure I can come up with something. *Not.* I freeze when I see Doe come in from the bakery. He has his motorcycle gloves on and helps a prospect pick up shards of glass. He doesn't say anything, doesn't even look my way, so I continue on with my mental assessment.

"Are any of them capable of picking a lock?" I ask, thinking of my apartment door. "It'll be an extra challenge. I have absolutely no clue what he jammed in there."

"I've got that covered," Boss interjects. "One of my guys has decent locksmith, uh, training. We've been talking about having him open a business with it. And if he can't unjam it, he can kick it in, and we'll replace it. He'll be here in a bit; he had to take his gran to chemo this morning."

"Great," Tank says with what I think might be a smile. "After the guys put up this plywood, they're going to paint it white, to reflect off the sun and keep this place from overheating. Then they're going to hit it with a weather proof sealant, in case it rains before the glass comes in. I got guys cleaning up the broken stuff, too."

I'm so overwhelmed. I have no clue what else I could ask these guys to help with. I know I need to go through my desk and cabinets to reorganize what I have down here. I might as well finish the reports in my bag as well.

Boss steers me over to my desk and lightly pushes me into my seat. "Sit," he says, the words a command. "Let the prospects handle what they've got for now, and if you need more help later, well, I have prospects too."

It takes all morning, but my new friends–acquaintances?–get my office fairly weather proofed and safe. I still can't get into my apartment above, but my office looks nearly normal. The biggest casualty, other than the glass, was unfortunately my coffee machine. I guess it's time for a Keurig of some sort. I bet the pods even come in variety packs.

Tank says something about taking everyone to lunch. All the guys race to the trucks. He waits for me.

"I'd rather stay and work on fixing the place up some more." I need to make a list of things to replace, like wall art and lamps.

Doe also declines Tank's offer, citing that he is supposed to be my protection detail for the time being. I don't actually need a bodyguard–Kyle definitely went home to lick his wounds after last night's humiliation.

I opt to ignore Doe's presence as I finish straightening out my desk. He doesn't know that I've noticed, but he's been watching me all day, as if he expects me to break down. I guarantee that's why he thinks I didn't join the other for lunch. Kyle is not going to push me into a spiral. I refuse to let him have any more control over my life.

The only things left to take care of are superficial, except replacing the coffee pot. With the closest place that has decent coffee being blocks away, a coffee machine is high on my list of priorities. I grab a notebook to take notes on different machines and prices, before getting up to get my laptop from my apartment.

Boss's guy is great at what he does. I don't care if he went to juvie for petty theft, my apartment is open, and he didn't have to break the door down to do it. He grumbles the whole time, but his ire and words are aimed at 'the asshole who broke a hairpin off in the key hole'. Apparently, Kyle tried to pick the lock, and broke his flimsy tool of choice. Lucky for me, Spider has tools to pull the metal out. I still need to replace the locks, but I quickly gain access to my things.

Doe gets up to follow me as I head to the stairs, after Spider leaves. Does he actually think I'm incompetent enough to need protection in my own apartment, that's been locked all day and night?

"I'm just grabbing my laptop," I tell him.

"Okay," he responds, crossing his arms over his chest and leaning against the wall at the foot of the steps. "If you wanted to bring down more, I wouldn't mind carrying things for you."

Ugh. Shove the act. What else could I possibly need right now, besides coffee? I glance at the espresso machine in my kitchen. Too bad the thing is humongous, and wired into my water supply. I wouldn't mind asking Doe to bring it down for me.

I've just gotten back to my desk when a blonde bombshell of a woman walks in. Even Doe is eyeing her up from his corner chair. I swear, he's over there flexing his arms in his uniform. I can't blame him too much. She pops her hips as she walks, bringing attention to her curvy shape.

"Excuse me." The woman's voice is tight, impatient. "I'm here to see Mr. Armani."

Lord help me. I made a conscious effort to not roll my eyes as I stood and offered her my hand. "I'm Ms. Armani," I introduce myself.

"Oh! You're his wife! My apologies. I thought you were his assistant." The blond shakes my hand with a dazzling wide smile. "I have a case I'd like to discuss with the detective. My sister is missing. Do I need to wait for a secretary? Fill out some paperwork?"

Don't strangle the blonde.

I force my smile to stay on my face, as I pull a clipboard with my introductory paperwork from the file folder on the wall. How it missed Kyle's destruction streak I will never know, but I am grateful. He took out my only printer.

"Well, yes. There is always paperwork." I hand her the clipboard. "Less for me than a police detective, but still paperwork. I am Armani Smith, the private investigator." I think I hear Doe stifling a laugh. *Ass.*

The woman in front of me deflates. It's slight, but I see it. All of her boldness and bluster leaves. Great. She doesn't think a woman can do this job.

"Oh, thank God!"

What? That is not the reaction I expected at all.

"I was seriously worried about having to explain this to yet another man." She speaks quietly, glancing over at Doe. "The men at the station didn't exactly take me seriously. They've decided my sister ran away with an ex-boyfriend, and that I'm just being paranoid."

"Does your sister have a history of rash decisions?" I ask,

and her smile falls off her face. "I'm not judging; this information helps me find a starting point. Tell me about her, and your relationship with her. If you're uncomfortable talking aloud, there's a few extra pages on the back of the forms you can write on. And be sure to add what you told the police, and their responses."

She glances over at Doe, again. "I'll write everything down, so you have it in your notes. Krista might not always make good decisions, but they are rarely rash. We share an apartment. She went out on a first date with a new guy, and never came back home. I have his license plate number, make and model of his car, a face pic, and his Tinder profile. He claims to have dropped her off, but only walked her to the building, not our apartment."

"So, someone could have been inside waiting. Or, she could have left after him without telling you. Not sisterly or good roommate behavior, but not impossible." I scratch a few notes on my own notepad. "I definitely want all the information you have. Better to cast a wide net, and eliminate theories as I go. I also need your police report number, so I can see what they've done."

She takes several deep breaths, her eyes never leaving the paperwork in her hands, the clipboard shakes slightly as she writes. "Krista and I have only had each other for so long. I can't believe she'd go anywhere without telling me. We've always taken safety seriously. Hence, I have all this guys info."

"I understand, things like this can be quite nerve racking. I mean, look around. Even I have troubles. My ex decided to ruin my night last night. My next question is, is your apartment safe for you to stay in, alone? No judgment."

The question seems to startle her. Her eyes fly up from the paper and she blinks rapidly. "I never thought of it as unsafe, until Krista didn't come home. It's been a week, and now I'm jumping at shadows." Her voice is so low, like she doesn't want to admit she's scared.

"I can assess the place for security threats. Here." I hand her another piece of paper from the file holder on the wall. "This breaks down the threat level assessment into clear categories. And I give options to help lower the threat level as part of the assessment."

I hear Doe scoff. Or maybe it was a laugh? I can't be certain, he covered the noise with his fist. And he's on the other side of the office. Either way, I don't care about his opinion of me and my work.

"I don't think I'm *unsafe,*" she says. "It's just really weird being alone and not knowing what happened to her."

"Okay. My pricing sheet is at the back of your paperwork. It has a spot for you to make notes about your budget, and any specific tasks you would like done as part of my investigation."

She nods and finishes the paperwork. "I just want to know that she's okay."

After she leaves, I'm quick to start my research into her, her sister, the new date, and her apartment complex. I can feel Doe watching me while I work. I try to ignore him, but I can feel his eyes on me as I work.

Krista Trussell lived a very online life. She posted about everything across multiple social platforms. But, she never posted who she was out and about with. Her sister's information says she was out with Anthony Gibson. *Officer Gibson? Well, maybe Uncle Ludwig will stop pushing him at me.*

'Out to dinner with a new guy friend. Loving the new Mexican place.' 'Out bowling with my sister.' 'Girls night at the bar.'

Anyone could have found her through her media posts, but nothing to start a list of suspects. She may not have tagged exact locations, but any local would recognize our little town's iconic locations. Even the places she goes to in the city are well known to people in our area. It was clear she was attempting to be internet safe, but bad guys look at more than just the tagged information. So I have to, too.

I start putting a file together for-double check the paperwork–Kami and Krista Trussel. I'm going to need to eat soon, and like hell will I leave anything here in my unsecured office. I didn't even leave open cases behind when I had lockable doors. I certainly won't now.

On a sheet of lined paper, I create a small to-do list for my investigation. Nothing crazy, just a few ideas that I don't have the time and energy to follow up on at the moment. I definitely need to talk with Officer Gibson. I add several blank sheets of paper to the back of the folder. That's not something I usually do, but I also don't usually need my office to be as fully mobile as I do now.

As I close my new folder, Doe joins me at my desk. "So, what have you found? Anything I can do to help? Chief has me sitting here either way."

"I'm not sure you actually *can* do anything. After all, Kami claims the SPD wrote her off when she filed with them."

"Well, I can start there." Doe grins at me like this is some huge favor. "Give me the report number and I can get everything we have, including private notes for you."

"And, why would you break protocol like that? Trying to prove something?"

"No." The smile slides right off of Doe's face. "My best friend in college disappeared in a similar fashion. We had an off campus apartment together. She never came home from a date. Disappeared off the face of the world. Her date claimed she never showed."

"Is that why you became a cop?" I asked.

"No. But I don't talk about that with acquaintances. Must

be at least a level five friend to unlock my tragic backstory." Doe smiles again, but it looks a little forced now. "I only mention Stacy because her story is similar."

"Well in that case, bring me Stacy's files too, and any notes you have. May be related, may not. Either way, extra data never hurts. Meet me back here in 2 hours. I'm going out for lunch."

"I don't know that Chief Ludwig would be okay with that," Doe argues.

"I don't particularly care." I try not to roll my eyes. "I can handle myself, and Uncle Ludwig knows it. You are here because my property is currently indefensible, and he does not yet know what to do with a motorcycle patrol. I could write a report of a million other things you should be doing, but I have an actual paying case to work. Feel free to make your own arguments with the boss. I'm getting lunch. Not here, no security needed."

"I'll get those reports for you, and join you for lunch. As long as I'm uselessly stationed here, you can use me to your heart's content."

Ugh. Gross. There went any sympathy or kind thoughts I had for his potentially tragic backstory.

"I already have plans to join a friend for lunch," I lie through my teeth as I text Boss to meet me at Chris's Handle-Bar. "If you so desperately want to watch me, you can eat on your own. Maybe you'll make friends. It is a motorcycle bar."

"Want me to drop you off before I go get your files? Plenty of room on my bike."

"No thanks. I'll walk."

FOUR

Chris's HandleBar is still relatively quiet. Early afternoon business has started, but most regulars are still off at their day jobs. The music is even lower than last night, and the vibes are much more chill. The place is still very biker chic, but less party central and more business casual. I get the feeling that lots of private deals get made here in the early hours.

I take a seat at the bar, thankful that Boss is already here.

"There's my favorite sister!" Boss greets me with a grin. "You know Tank is slightly offended you wouldn't come eat with his boys, just to ask me out later."

"No offense was meant for Tank. I had work to get done. Not just fixing my office, but getting my caseload rolling. No work means no money. I've been trying to save up for a nice leather jacket for years now. Every time I'm almost there, life scoops in and steals my savings. I wouldn't even be here now, if I wasn't already tired of my SPD tail."

"And where is your blue shadow?"

"Making himself useful and gathering some police reports for me. Apparently, he has more trust in bikers than Chief

Ludwig does. Or maybe my argument about being able to handle myself despite my office not being secure hit home. Either way, I have a moment to catch my breath."

"Only a moment?" The same bartender as last night, Chris, or Keep–I'm still not actually sure of his name–asks with a grin. He sets two coffee mugs full of steaming tea down for Boss and I.

"He insists on tailing me, but 'believes deeply in my case' so he's grabbing a few files before joining me for lunch." I roll my eyes. "Do the club presidents still honor him with a Newcomer's Special if they already know he's a cop?"

"Yes, technically," the bartender grins.

"But," Boss interjects. "It can't be Tank or I, since we already met this morning. I'll give Preacher a call. He loves interrogating newcomers. They rarely even realize he's doing it. There's so many Bible quotes and way too much small talk."

"Nice." I grin. "Maybe I can slip out to do some work while Preacher distracts my tail. Now, am I allowed to order my own food today? Or is someone going to hijack my meal plans again?" I playfully glare at Boss.

"Are you ever going to let that go?" Boss asks nonchalantly as Chris/Keep chokes on his laughter.

"No."

"Keep, take her order while I call Preacher. I'll take my usual." Boss excuses himself for the moment, laughter filling his voice.

I notice that Keep has a metal name tag pinned to his black HandleBar t-shirt. Turns out his name actually is Chris. The tag also claims he is the owner, not bartender. Didn't the Boss say he was the owner yesterday? The night was so hectic, I can't remember.

That does mean this fine looking man in front of me is none other than Chris Bitters. Born to the Bitters financial legacy. I have to wonder, how did a rich entitled Bitters child end up living in an apartment above a bar in Setting, Alabama. Bitters children run Atlanta and Birmingham, they don't live in the middle of nowhere.

"What can we make for you today?" Chris breaks me out of my musings.

"Mushroom Swiss burger, please." I order. "Why do they call you Keep?"

Chris rolls his eyes so hard I'm worried I offended him. "They think it's a clever play on the term barkeep. Apparently, the fact that I can't *keep* a long term bartender makes it funny."

"You can't keep a bartender? In a biker bar? Surrounded by bikers?" I am beyond shocked. I really hope my tone doesn't come across as condescending.

"Yeah, they keep getting poached," Chris answers with a small shrug. "I have a rule about not hiring club affiliates. Don't want to be seen as biased toward any one club. I like that this place is a completely neutral zone. Employees agree upon being hired that if they join any club, as prospects or otherwise, to terminate their employment here."

"We don't poach," Boss interjects, retaking his seat. "At least, The Cadillac Squad has more respect for Keep than that. However, if someone comes to us to prospect or house mouse, we don't turn them away. But, we always make sure they are aware of the consequences with Chris."

"True," Chris agrees. "The Cadillacs are very courteous that way. Boss always lets me know when someone enters talks with him. The others not so much."

"The others feel it lies with the potential prospect," Boss explains. "However, The Cadillac Squad is completely made up of people who have done real time. Mostly parolees, but a few mistrial releases. Keep is kind enough to hire someone with a history. It's only fair to give a heads up that they might be leaving."

"I have a hard time blaming those that leave for The Cadillacs," Chris claims. "Boss and his people provide a lot more opportunities for those with convictions. Better financial security and many more job options. Those guys deserve a chance."

"The others just ditch you?" I ask.

"Some," Chris admits. "Preacher, Tank, and Boss all usually demand they work out a two week notice before they can begin their prospect time. However, The Road Kings will take anyone, anytime. They actively recruit my staff too. Leaves me in a lurch sometimes."

"I didn't know anyone was actively recruiting staff, Keep." A frown creases Boss's face. It looks unnatural on him. "I'll try talking to the guys. That shit ain't kosher."

"It is what it is, Boss."

The bar slowly fills while we chat. Lots of small quiet groups. It seems to me like the early afternoon vibe is more diner themed, even if it is still biker packed. I wonder what time the music cranks up and things get rowdy. Then again, last night wasn't very rowdy either.

Around the time Chris brings our plates out, I see Doe slip in. He is immediately clocked by a dark skinned biker who plops down across from him at a corner booth.

"That's Preacher," Boss whispers to me, nodding in their direction. "He will keep Blues Clues busy for a while. Eat your burger. Spider will meet you at your office to keep you company while you run your mysterious errands."

"Boss, I do not need a babysitter, no matter what Chief Ludwig claims. Just because he was my dad's old partner does not mean he is my boss."

"No, I'm the Boss." He grins at his own pun. "Spider needs work today. He wants to join our security firm, but has no experience outside his locksmith training. Let him see what you do."

"I *am* checking out an apartment building for security leaks. It's not actually part of my contract, but is the first step in finding out how my client's sister disappeared. I guess I can take notes on what your prospect notices and how he acts. Should count as a job reference, right?"

"Works for me. Who is missing, and how long? In town or out? Tank claims to take community safety very seriously."

"Address I have is in town. Krista Trussell has been missing for a week. Her sister reported her missing and was blown off by the officer who took the report. Doe offered to grab that information for me."

"Kind of him."

"Yeah, well, I think he's a bit bored. Lud has him on babysitting duty because SPD has never had a bike patrol before. Either type of bike. Doe put in his papers yesterday for motorcycle patrol, and Ludwig's dragging feet. Probably creating extra hoops to jump through. He hates bikers."

"Not many of us like him either."

"Help Preacher keep Doe busy. Please? I need a break and a chance to do my work in peace."

"Sure thing, little sis." Boss grins.

Chris clears my plate when I finish. "Slip out the employee exit, through the kitchens. There's a door down the hall with the bathroom. Officer Nosey's plate is gonna take awhile." My knees damn near go weak when he winks at me. Kind, courteous, and hot are a deadly combination.

The sizzling of friers and the smell of hot grease lead me to the kitchen door. Weary eyes track my every movement, as I slip through the employee only space. Missy holds the back door open for me, cigarette dangling from her lips.

"Smoke break," she says with a grin. "I'm trying to quit, but the patches make me sick. Boss and boss man said we're keeping someone busy for you. Need a cab? Chris takes patron safety seriously here."

"No, nothing like that," I assure her. "Had some trouble last night at my business, so the police chief decided I needed extra protection. I disagree and am making a break for it."

She laughs. "Good luck."

I laugh too and take a jog back to my office, hoping my new friends can keep Doe distracted and disoriented–at least long enough for me to get some work done.

The apartment the Trussell sisters live in isn't the worst in our community, but it's definitely not the best either. There's a key code to get in, but nothing to keep people from propping the door open for long lengths of time. A large rock holds it open when we get there. A smoking tenant ignores us as Spider and I walk right in.

No buzzer, no key code, no identification.

The lobby is nice. There's a classy looking waiting area, a front lobby desk where someone could, and probably should, be running security. However, I only spot one single camera. The damned thing is pointing at the security desk–as if employee watching is the most important job, not that there's an employee to watch. There is nothing watching the halls, elevator, or even the doors. There is no way to verify that Krista really entered the building after her date.

"The keypad is too old," Spider mutters under his breath. When he sees me watching him, he straightens up and speaks more clearly. "Newer models of keypads can track timestamps for entry codes. They also set off alarms if the door is left open for too long. There's still ways to trick them, but they are way more secure than what's here right now."

Smart kid. Boss wants an evaluation of this kid, he's going to get one. This teenager–adult technically–is smart. A little confidence will go a long way.

"Okay, with this current setup and its limitations; you want to slip away with a young woman unnoticed, how do you do it? Let's assume Krista actually came in here. How did our unsub get in and her out without notice?"

"Unsub?" Spider's brows pull together in the middle in what seems to be confusion.

"Do you not watch crime shows? Unsub: unknown subject." I try really hard not to roll my eyes. This kid is young, and has had to have served time, to be in The Cadillac Squad. That doesn't mean he is an expert in crime.

"Not much time for television in solitary," Spider grumbles.

"Plenty of time now." I smile gently. "Hang around my place long enough, and I'll introduce you to the classics. Now, let's roll play. I'm the victim; you're the big bad unsub. How do you get in without notice?"

"Easiest would be to slip in while the door is propped open." Spider waves his hand toward the unsecured door. "But, that risks being seen. If I were being sneaky, I'd slip a magnet over the lock hole, while it was busy. Then I'd slip in later when no one was around."

I look over the door frame. "A small magnet, like businesses use as cards, would be easy to use. I doubt anyone would notice it."

"Exactly," Spider agrees. "But getting back out, unnoticed, with your victim wouldn't be as easy."

"So, did she trust this person enough to go with them?"

"Or, did they have another way to keep her quiet?" Spider's eyes never leave the door as he walks over to the sitting area. "Chloroform would leave no trace behind. If the unsub,"-he stumbles over the word- "is strong enough, they could pretend to be helping a drunk friend."

"Good points," I agree. "But they have to avoid suspicion while waiting."

"The bushes outside." Spider paces as he talks through his train of thought. "Or these couches. He could sit here with a book, and if anyone asked, he's just waiting on a friend to finish getting ready for a night out. Or, he could leave the magnet in the door and slip in behind after the date left. He'd know the outside was clear, but he'd have to move quick."

"Both are plausible," I agree. "But you keep saying 'he'. We have no proof that the unsub is male."

"We have no proof there is an unsub," Spider shoots back at me. He immediately bites his lips, as if trying to take the words back.

"True, but right now we are operating on the assumption she didn't leave willingly. There is nothing here to check that could tell us she chose to leave her sister in the lurch. I'm not discounting the idea, it's just not relevant, here."

Spider releases a huge sigh. "Thank you Miss Armani. I don't want you to think I'm sassing you."

"Not at all, kid. Now, give me a ride back to my office so I can do more research into our potential victim."

The ride back is smooth. I wonder why Spider has a sidecar on his bike. There isn't any pet hair to indicate he rides with a dog.

The Setting sunset burns orange across the sky. It's easy to see where our town gets its name. *Red skies at night, sailors delight.*

Spider walks me into my office, already on the phone with

Boss. “I know your upstairs locks now, but I'm not so sure it's safe for you to stay here tonight, Miss Armani.”

“It’s not.” Doe's voice cuts across from his corner–not his corner, the corner he has been using.

Spider pushes me behind him, startled at the sound. Some deep rooted motherly instinct snaps in me as I see the genuine fear in this kid's eyes as he registers the fact that there is an unknown man here.

“Chill, Spy, it's just my SPD appointed guard dog.” I take a deep breath. “Hasn't Ludwig released you from duty yet?”

“No, and I didn’t feel like telling him that I lost you earlier. So, I decided to do my own research into Krista Trussell.”

“Tell him I sent you home. I'm packing an overnight bag, and meeting a friend for dinner. Spider can drop me off. If Ludwig gives you a hard time, tell him I threatened to sue him for misuse of police resources. It wouldn't even be the first time.” For the threat anyway.

With that, I spin on my heel and headed up to my apartment to pack a bag. Boss had already insisted I stay at his compound until the office is secure. Which, Tank is working on, apparently. I don't want to know how much this is going to cost me, but I am thankful that my new friends are helping me out. Maybe Tank will accept a payment plan.

FIVE

The next morning, I'm back at my office, bright and early with a brand new coffee machine. Once again, I am surprised by the plethora of bikers milling around. I'm not sure what anyone is actually doing. I assumed everything was done, at least until new supplies arrive to replace the windows and door.

Officer Doe is inside, sitting in the same corner as yesterday. Tank is at the table with him, flipping through police files. Ludwig would have a fit if he knew his newest cop was sharing information with 'the seedy underbelly of the motor gang world.' I'm not going to tell, though. I want that information too–more than I want Doe out of my space.

My apartment door is open, too. None of the men milling around my office seem to worry about it, so I can only assume they are the reason. I have no idea why they decided to break into my apartment, but until I have at least three cups of coffee, I'm not going to question things. Worry? Yes. Question? No.

I head to the counter along the back wall of my waiting area. Placing the new machine down, I notice the bikers setting up a row of folding tables and chairs. A couple are moving my furniture to the sides of the room to make space for their impromptu dining area.

I'm still not nearly caffeinated enough to deal with this insanity.

I opted for a nice Kuriug, leagues above the flimsy but expensive pot I used to have down here, but not quite as fancy as my in-home espresso bar upstairs. I spent the night unable to sleep, so I focused my energy on researching the best coffee machines. This one has a large water reservoir that I will eventually hardline to my tap. It also came with a small variety of pods. Tonight, I'll order a bunch more online for delivery.

I barely have the machine out of the box when a biker with a Prospect patch takes over, elbowing me out of the way. He gestures toward the new section of table, and I take the hint.

Have a seat.

I do. I sit close to where Doe and Tank are chatting over files. Before I can text Boss an SOS for coffee, a steaming hot mug is placed in front of me by a busty redhead with a gorgeous tattoo sleeve. The black coffee smells heavenly. Before I can ask, another biker comes by with a tray full of different flavor creamers. I add some to my cup and watch him take them all over to the coffee pot.

"Breakfast will be ready shortly," the redheaded beauty says to me. "One of The Cadillac Squad opened up your apartment so the guys could use your kitchen. I tried telling them to wait and ask. Unfortunately, these guys aren't used to common courtesy. Most of the time I consider the food to be a halfway decent trade. They set the coffee urn up first. None of us function without it. It's a staple at almost every job site."

"I've only seen Calvary here since I arrived. Which members of The Cadillac Squad are here? They may have asked

Boss. He seems to think as my honorary brother he's allowed to make those kinds of calls."

She sits gracefully in the seat across from me. "I didn't get the kid's name. He was the only one here. I didn't see him leave, but that doesn't mean he's still here. As far as I know, it's only The Cavalry here this morning. Tank decided that today's breakfast was going to be here. He started rallying the troops last night. I'm his wife, Ember."

"Miss Armani?" The biker who took over my coffee installation speaks up before I have a chance to reply to Ember. "Are you planning on keeping water on hand for this machine? Or can I tap it?"

"Can you?"

"Absolutely, Miss Armani. Tapping a waterline is really easy."

"Please do," I agree and turn back to Ember. "I have no idea how much Tank is going to charge for all of this, but his help has been over the top."

"I doubt my man will charge more than cost," Ember answers with a smile. "It really bothered him, your tirade about the cost of fixing what your ex did. He kept muttering about ramen, the whole night."

"It wasn't my proudest moment," I admit. I feel really bad about unloading on the man. He was just trying to do his job and protect his people.

"Nonsense," Ember disagrees with a grin. "He was an ass. Let him bask in it."

I choke on my coffee. "Ma'am!"

"His words." She winks at me. "Apparently, the fact that Boss claimed you as kin almost immediately got to him. As laid back as he seems, Boss does not take to people lightly. Tank is convinced he missed out on something. Let him grovel."

“I'm not groveling.” Tank's gruff voice sounds from his seat, not far behind me.

“What do you call it then, dear?” Ember ask with a mischievous twinkle in her eye.

“Tactical accountability,” Tank responds. “And it was Spider who let us in, upstairs. I spoke with Boss last night, and the kid met us here on his way to his gran's this morning.”

“I hope his gran's okay,” I respond. “I know she had chemo yesterday.”

“Text Boss to double check, but I was under the impression he's just hovering a bit,” Ember says, flagging down a passing biker. “ETA on the grub?”

“Any moment, ma'am. Coffee is on, bacon is done, sausages are coming off the grill outside. I was on my way up to check on the eggs, pancakes and potato lines.”

Ember pats his shoulder and he heads up the stairs to my apartment.

Having this many strangers in my space makes my skin crawl. I don't mind them milling about my office, my public space. I get that this is supposed to be a kind gesture, but do they *really* need to be in my apartment–in my personal space. My blood boils at the idea that they have free range of my home. I just don't know how to say anything without sounding ungrateful.

And I am grateful. These men have done quite a bit to help secure my office against the elements. They are cooking a giant breakfast, and my coffee machine is already tapped into the waterline–at least it will be by the time I'm done eating.

Something must show on my face. Or maybe, Ember just gets it–because she leans forward in her seat like she has some big secret to share.

“They're *only* in your kitchen, except for our Sargent-at-Arms. He's sitting in your living room, in direct line of sight of the kitchen. His whole job is to disrupt anyone trying to snoop, or explore. The boys brought their own dishes, and will clean up after themselves. Tank would be up there, too, but he heard about this missing girl. He's real proud of the club's civilian safety initiatives."

As she says that, an army of bikers descends upon the room. Several guys are carrying dishes down from my apartment. Others are bringing platters in from outside–I assume the grilled sausages. A couple more carry in three large coolers. Everything gets set up, buffet style on a couple of the folding tables. Coolers are set next to the coffee pot and propped open; inside they have an assortment of juices, soda, and water.

The bikers congregate at the buffet table, forming a nice clean line that makes me think of a military mess hall. I smile to myself at the comparison; of course they do. These men are all former military. Some habits must be hard to break.

I stand, fully prepared to take my place, waiting in line, when a hand presses against the small of my back. I freeze as a voice growls, "Sit down, Missy."

A breath of relief escapes as I recognize Tank's gruff voice. Letting the familiarity sooth my rattled nerves, I smirk up at him. "That's not my name. Missy works for Chris."

He lightly cuffs the back of my head as I sit back down. "Brat." He laughs as he walks away.

"The Cavalry doesn't let women fix their own plates," Ember whispers conspiratorially. "It takes some getting used to, admittedly. It's an honor thing, and quite possibly in their bylaws. Men fix for their old ladies, sisters, and daughters. Patched brothers usually share responsibility for the Sweet Butts, and Prospect fixes for the house mouses–mice? That term is weird when pluralized."

"So, who is fixing my plate? I'm not a relation of any type, a sweet butt or house mouse." I'm genuinely curious, but I worry my tone is condescending. I am not used to this amount of socializing. Especially this early.

I'm an introvert at heart. I can usually handle client meetings easily, most of them are short and sweet, to the point. They want something I can deliver—for a price. Anything more than a normal meeting and I have to hype myself up, mentally prepare to be a character, play a part. Whichever one that gets the job done. Always. Today? I have no clue what part I'm supposed to play. House Mouse? Sister? Daughter? Who do these men–these complete strangers–think I am? I'm no Sweet Butt, that's for sure.

"If Tank isn't fixing it himself, then he's assigned the privilege to a ranked member. You're his distinguished visitor."

"And here I thought I was the hostess." I wave my hand to indicate our surroundings. *Damn.* I can't seem to stop the sass from spewing out.

"Well then, consider it a coup, Sugar." An older black man sets a plate down in front of me, taking the seat to my right. His cut identifies him as the Sergeant-at-Arms, road name: Sarge.

"Oh, please." Ember laughs, her eyes crinkling with mirth. "This is less a hostile takeover, and more of a Peaceful Transition of Power."

I laugh at their comfortable banter. Maybe my sass will fit in. I look down at my new plate and coffee mug. *I wonder who I need to bat my eyes at for a refill.*

Look at me. Fitting right in. I can fix my own coffee. But, will they let me? Ugh. I am not caffeinated nearly enough for all of these social interactions. Maybe, if I eat some, I can dramatically bemoan my empty cup, without it being too weird.

The oval plate Sarge fixed for me is over-flowing. One half is packed with protein choices: eggs, bacon, sausage patties and links. The other side boasts two of the fluffiest pancakes I have ever seen, next to a pile of mixed berries. *With whip cream on top.* There's no syrup, which I'm thankful for. I've always found it to be messy. There is a pat of butter on the side, but I doubt I'll use it. The serving of fried potatoes is more than generous, but I'm more than a little happy to see a variety of vegetables sautéed in.

I can't help myself; I do a little happy wiggle in my seat. There may be more food than I could normally conceive of eating before noon, but every single bite looks delicious. It will be more than worth the overstuffed bloated feeling, if I manage it all.

A low chuckle breaks me out of my food vision tunnel. I look up to see Tank and Doe have joined us. No clue who is laughing at me, but I do not care. Have you seen this plate? It is absolute perfection.

Doe takes the seat to my left; Tank sits next to his wife, giving her a plate as well. Doe also set a decanter of syrup on our table, in easy reach of us all. All of their plates are less top heavy than mine, but a quick glance assures me that Sarge's plate holds even more. Fair enough. I'm a total stranger to him. I probably would have done the same.

I take a bite of the potato medley and cannot stop the noise that comes out of me. I can't tell if it's a moan of satisfaction or a groan that I have never had breakfast potatoes this good before. I'm almost embarrassed at the sound, but it tastes so good I absolutely cannot find the ability to care. *At all.*

Another chuckle. This time from my right.

"Way better than MREs." Sarge grins.

I nod in agreement and stuff my face. Screw being polite. Screw small talk. And screw social interactions. Nothing exists outside me and my new love affair–this plate full of scrumptious food.

I glance back at my empty coffee cup. Oh well. I'll fix more after I eat. It's not like I'm dying of thirst. All that coffee would be good for is my social skills. I don't care about social skills right now. I care about carbs and protein.

Tank and Doe pull Sarge into their conversation about the missing girls. They speculate openly on what may have happened to them. My stomach twists at their careless words. These men are edging in on my case. Doe has ideas for avenues of investigation, complete with color coded notes. Tank and Sarge are less involved, more concerned with public safety than investigation.

I itch to snatch the files away from Doe. This is my case. My job. My *livelihood*. But they *are* police files, and he *is* a police officer. Not a detective, but still an actual member of the SPD. He has more right to the police files than I do.

I guess I need to play nice until I can take pictures of the files with my phone. I'd run copies, but my douchebag of an ex smashed my printer. Yet another uncalculated expense. One that can wait, for now.

The prospect comes by with a coffee carafe, topping off everyone's empty cups. "Does anyone need creamer or juice?" He asks.

"I'll take an apple juice," Ember replies.

"I'll take the fanciest looking creamer you have." I smile at the slight look of panic on his face. This guy faced down drill sergeants and potentially enemy fire, but the idea of judging 'fancy' creamer crosses the line. "I'm kidding, mostly. I like most any type of creamer."

"Yes, ma'am," he answers, almost robotically, heading for the drink area.

"I think I broke him." I joke to Tank.

"Nah, civilian life is doing that all on its own. The kid is barely out of service. He spent the last four years having every action, breath, and thought dictated to him. Choices are overwhelming at this point. Keep throwing them at him. He needs it, even if it scares him," Tank answers back.

"Especially if it scares him," Sarge adds. "You did perfect by walking back the intensity of your request, but leaving the core of it there. He has to pick your creamer now. A choice with little to no consequences, but someone else depending on it. Choices are scary. My MFLC calls it exposure therapy."

His stance tightens when he admits that. The grip on his fork strains and his hand trembles slightly. His shoulders stiffen and his eyes drop, if only momentarily. His jaw tightens, muscles throbbing beneath.

I'm not going to say anything. I don't remember which case I worked that led me to the knowledge of what military personnel call short term counselors. It doesn't really matter. What matters is this man just admitted to seeing a Military and Family Life Counselor–in front of strangers–and does not want attention drawn to it. Distraction I can do.

Before I get a chance, the prospect returns to our table with three different bottles of creamer. *Decision paralysis.* S'mores, vanilla bean, and plain. All very good choices, but he circumvented the need to choose. I notice Tank shaking his head slightly.

"S'mores creamer for the lady who asked for fancy. Vanilla bean for me to try, and plain for those who didn't speak up." He looks proud of himself as he sets each bottle down pointedly. Heck, I'm proud. What looked like decision paralysis is actually three proud decisions.

I wonder what Boss would deduce from the prospects' choices. What does it say that he thinks s'mores creamer is fancy? Or that Doe not so subtly pours a healthy dose of the plain creamer into his cup?

Brrrrring! Brrrrrring!

I nearly drop my cup in my haste to pull my phone out of my pocket. I don't immediately recognize the number, but given my line of work, that never stops me. Cases come in all sorts of ways.

I excuse myself from the table to take the call.

Sobbing echoes in my ears the moment I answer, bordering on hysterics.

"M-miss Armami?" I recognize the feminine voice but can't quite place it. "I think I should h-have gotten the safety add-on yes-yesterday." Her voice shakes and it takes me a moment longer than I'd like for me to connect who it is.

"Kami? Are you okay?" I ask.

Doe snaps his head in my direction. His nostrils flare as he sticks out his hand, reaching to take my phone. I slap his hand away and turn my back to him.

"Y-yes? Maybe." Kami's response is hesitant. "I'm physically alright, but someone's been in my apartment. I think it was whoever took Krista."

"Most likely a safe assumption, but what makes you say that?" I'm gathering my things as I ask. She is clearly upset, and her apartment is not a safe place to be right now.

"It's–I think you just need to see this."

"On my way."

SIX

Of course, leaving wasn't as easy as saying 'I have to go' and walking out. Every pair of eyes snaps to me when I say I need to go. Doe jumps to his feet, citing his job description as reason he should come with. Tank and Sarge rise, offering protection for 'that poor girl.' Tank is quick to mention what he has found about disappearances in the area. All women, all alone, all leaving no trace. Sarge watches with guarded eyes, reminding us Setting isn't the only place girls are disappearing from. Even the prospect opens his mouth to volunteer, snapping it shut at Ember's dark look.

"Fine. Doe can come with. If necessary, he can make a police report. Kami sounded extremely upset."

"Ride my bike?" Doe asks with a grin.

I am more than aware of the connotations of riding on the back of a man's bike. Not every biker holds to the standard that it's only for their old lady, but a lot do.

Riding with Boss was different, at least in my mind. He'd all but sworn me protection, backed by Chris that day. Since then, he has claimed me as a sister. Family. Allowed.

"You can." I smile as sweetly as I can manage. "But I believe Kami will be coming back with us, and three's a crowd."

I step over to my desk to grab my hand gun from the bottom drawer. The empty busted drawer. *Sigh*. The gun is still in my trunk, I'll grab it before we leave the lot. Or risk forgetting it *again*.

The drive to Kami's apartment is short, and quiet. Doe did opt to take his bike, citing that he would need a separate ride if he does need to file a report. I almost hope he does. Almost. Not because I want something bad enough to warrant his presence, but because I already need a break from him.

The first thing I notice when I get to Kami's apartment is that the door is propped wide open. There's no one on the stoop, or anywhere near the door. I want to think Kami opened it for us, but I sincerely doubt it.

I enter the apartment while Doe is still parking his bike. The lobby looks normal. Or at least, it looks the same as it did yesterday when I was here with Spider.

Kami is sitting in the lounge area. Her arms are wrapped around her body, and she's shaking ever so slightly. Her breath comes out in short little puffs. Then there's her eyes–glassy, wide, unseeing. She looks right through me as I approach.

I quicken my pace to her side, wishing I had a blanket or jacket to offer her. An adrenaline drop is almost always chilling, even in the summer heat. And that's what this looks like to me. Something scared her, and now she is dropping.

"Kami." I'm next to her now. Even though I've been in her direct line of sight since I entered the building, she jumps. Her eyes go wide, before recognition kicks in. Then she spots Doe coming in behind me and she tenses even further.

"I couldn't stay up there." Kami's voice is nearly emotionless as she hands me her key. "You'll see. It's probably good you brought the cop. It might actually be a crime scene."

"Which unit?" I ask, taking the key.

"307, third floor. I couldn't stay up there. The elevator is rickety and slow. I'd still rather take it than go back in. I couldn't stay up there. I couldn't."

"That's fine," I reassure her. "I can act as your agent in this. It was part of the paperwork. I'm not a lawyer, but I am a recognized advocate. Sit here. Officer Doe and I will take a look. I have your number now–the phone you called from. I'll call if I need any information from you before I come down. Just wait here."

Doe gives her a reassuring smile and head nod. I pat her shoulder before I turn toward the stairs. I'm not scared of elevators, but that description was a little sketchy. I'm not taking any chances.

Doe follows behind me. "Let me take point on entering the apartment, please. I'd like to clear it properly. She's really shaken up down there. I'd rather take extra precautions and not need them, than miss something being sloppy."

I freeze in the stairwell. "Are you calling me sloppy?" I nearly snarl the words at his presumptuousness. *How fucking dare he*!

"Not at all. Everything I've seen about you points to meticulous work, but I have no clue about your training. There has got to be a reason you're in the private sector, not the force. I meant me being sloppy. That's why I left my last force. I trusted my partner to do more than he actually was. Sloppy work that cost me collars."

You can't control your partners. Not everyone is as lucky as my dad was, to have gotten a best friend from his partnership.

"I get it." That's all I say, heading up the last flight of stairs.

All of the apartment doors are a dark green color, with golden fixtures-handles, numbers. Apartment 307 is near directly across from the stairwell. I see no signs of automatic locking mechanisms, but I am not an expert. I'm starting to wish I had called Spider.

"I'll unlock, you breach," I tell Doe. "My gun is in my bag. You clear the entryway, and I'll close the door behind us. We can clear the apartment together, and I'll leave my purse at the door."

"Do you know how to properly clear a room?"

No. I'm just taking your comment about an untrustworthy partner as a sign to mess with you.

"Yes." I've actually taken courses on it. "My dad was a cop. Ludwig was his partner. When I started this business he taught me some basics for my safety. Like properly clearing a fucking room."

"Okay." He doesn't try to placate me this time. Instead he just slips his gun from its holster.

I turn the key in the knob, and grab the handle. "We aren't announcing ourselves. We have the renter's permission to enter this space. On three."

Doe nods, eyes glued to the door.

"One, two, three."

I slam the door open wide, as Doe barrels past me, his gun steady in his hands. "Entry is clear." His voice carries absolute authority.

I slip in, and gently close the door. Checking the knob, I note it definitely doesn't lock itself. I set my pack up against the door, and pull my Sig.

"I've got your six," I tell him as I come up behind him.

We clear each room, slowly and cautiously. It was hard not to stop when we saw the living room was trashed. Even harder to not stop after I saw the first bedroom. I may have let out an audible gasp. I know for sure my voice wavered as I called out 'clear.' I could feel the tension in Doe from across the apartment, like he expected me to abandon the task before it was complete.

Once everything had been properly cleared, I came back to that first bedroom. Everything else was trashed completely. But this room...This room is what put Kami on alert. This is the reason she is shaking downstairs.

Her bed is splattered with what I can only hope is red paint. My mini blue light is in my bag, by the door, but I don't want to know that badly, just yet. A collection of perfume bottles are smashed next to the vanity, the smell making my eyes water. Every stuffed animal in the room has been gutted, the stuffing strewn everywhere. But the worst part was the red writing dripping down the wall.

Your next.

A deep-seated part of me wants to correct the grammar. It's a completely irrelevant thought, but it's an insistent one. Whoever did this needs English lessons.

Doe enters the room, already on the phone with the precinct. His eyes widen momentarily, but otherwise he shows no reaction to the state of the place.

"Yes, I am absolutely certain we need a crime lab here. Not only does the tenant deserve to have her breaking and entering complaint documented, and the crime looked into, but there is a visible threat on the wall. It's written in a sticky looking red substance. I don't have any way of verifying the material. Can't even smell if its wet paint over the scent of broken perfume bottles."

I use my phone to take pictures while he argues. I'll need documentation for my own files. Active cases are harder to get information on than complaint reports.

He pauses to listen to whoever is on the other side of that call. "Neither of us are wearing gloves, did you touch *anything*?" His eyes connect with mine, waiting for an answer.

"Just what was needed to clear each room," I tell him. "Doorknobs and bathroom curtains." The cabinets in the bathroom were too small, and Doe cleared the kitchen.

He repeats that information to whomever, before hanging up.

"It's not technically an official crime scene," He says, not making eye contact. "Dispatch says until a crime unit arrives, it's under my jurisdiction. Go ahead and look around, but *do not* touch anything."

"Any chance I can get a copy of this report?"

"That will be up to Ludwig. Apparently, I have to report to him once the crime lab is here."

"Fair enough," I respond, stepping back out toward the living room. "Is the kitchen in as bad of shape as this is?"

"Oh yeah. Plates smashed and knives stabbed into the pictures on the wall." Doe answers.

I step carefully around the damage, taking more pictures as I go. Every single breakable possession is smashed. Whoever did this has a lot of rage. Most of it seems aimed at Kami, not Krista. Krista's room was destroyed, but not as thoroughly as Kami's. Her stuffed animals survived the attack. Then again, they may not be spending the energy on Krista's things because they already have her.

The knives stabbed into the kitchen pictures seem to have no recognizable pattern. Kami in one. Krista the next. An unknown man standing between them in another.

Snap. Snap. Snap.

I take the last few pictures before gathering myself together. "I'm taking Kami back to my office until you're done here."

Doe's eyes widen, just slightly before he rearranges his face into a carefully neutral mask of indifference. "Not going to stay and watch the crime lab?"

"Nah, I got what I can use from this place. I'm not actually a police officer, or detective. I have a different set of parameters to work by. I'm going to go get everything into my files for this case, and I'm going to feed her. With all that adrenaline leaving her body, her sugar is going to crash soon." I smile sweetly at him. "Have fun talking with Ludwig."

I laugh at his groan as I slip out of the apartment.

Downstairs, I greet Kami again. "Officer Doe will stay here and meet with the crime lab. I'm taking you back to my office, away from here. There is nothing more you or I can do. Let the police do their jobs." I hold my hand out to help her off the couch.

Kami doesn't say anything, but she takes my hand. After getting up, she doesn't let go. I hold her hand all the way to the car.

Returning to my apartment, I am genuinely surprised that the place is empty. Other than the coffee machine and a cooler full of juices, I see no sign that my place was full of bikers a mere hour ago.

I guide Kami over to the rearranged seating area, near the coffee pot. She settles easily onto the couch. Her hands strumming the blue seams.

"Apple or orange?" I offer, holding up two of the juices.

"Apple." Her voice is scratchy. Did she scream herself hoarse when she saw what was done to her apartment? To the place that should be her sanctuary.

I hand her the juice, and begin a casual sweep of my property, looking for not just signs that breakfast wasn't an elaborate hallucination, but for what damage may have been missed from Kyle's antics the other night.

I mention neither to my guest. She needs to feel safe right now. Hearing that this place has been broken into, multiple times this week, is not exactly a safe feeling. Let her think when I told her my ex caused me problems, that he came in during business hours.

Upstairs, my door is locked. *Good.* I have no clue what kind of meltdown I would have had if they left my place completely unsecured. I step into my living room to grab a blanket for Kami. I also grab my box fan from my bedroom. Out of the corner of my eye, I see a note on my fridge.

Grabbing and reading it brings a smile to my face. It's from Tank and Ember.

We cleaned up after ourselves and locked up. I hope your client is okay. The third Wednesday each month is family night at Chris's. You better be there tonight.

The leftover potatoes are in your fridge, and we left the juices for you, too. There wasn't enough of anything else to save.

Stay safe

Tank & Ember

What was I thinking, of course the gang of military men locked up after themselves. I'll definitely be going to Chris's tonight. Not only do I want to see family night at a biker bar, I think Kami could use some biker magic.

Nothing to do with the hot bartender who runs the place. *Not at all.*

I take the blanket back downstairs to find her passed out on the couch, clutching the empty bottle of apple juice. I gently take it from her and cover her with the light-weight throw blanket and plug the fan up to get air moving. The Alabama heat settles heavily in the air. The A/C down here is next to useless. I could use it, but I can't afford to cool the outside. The fan will have to do, for now.

Watching Kami sleep, I start to put my notes on paper. While I'm at it, I make a note to research printers so I can add my new collection of pictures to the file. *Fucking Kyle.*

SEVEN

I don't know what I expected family night to look like, but it certainly didn't include a bright red bouncy house. Children's laughter rings from inside. The entire parking lot is stuffed with activities. There's horseshoes and volleyball set up on the grassy side of the building; the volleyball pit sitting empty and unused. Opposite that area, several pop up tents spread across the lot. The divide between them is expansive and jarring.

Kami, by my side, takes a deep breath in what I can only assume is awe. Her eyes light up, and the weight of the day falls off her shoulders. I can't undo what happened today, but we can have fun in spite of it.

Almost every person here has a cut on. Some say 'family', a few say 'protected by', and others say 'associate'. Even the girls I suspect to be club bunnies are wearing leather. It makes me even more bitter that I can't afford that leather jacket this month. Probably not next month either.

Kami holds my hand tightly, as we approach the lot. The sections seem to be separated by clubs. The entertainment looks to be a neutral zone, but in the lot, tensions run high.

The Calvary tent is set up at the front. Ember sits at one of those white tables from this morning. Her amber hair, now pulled back in an intricate braid, gold clips giving her a viking-eske glow, catches my attention immediately. Following her sight line, I laugh at Tank, flipping something massive on the grill, tongs held awkwardly as flames shoot into the air.

"Just the fat!" He laughs, winking at his wife.

No wonder they were able to throw together an amazing breakfast this morning, with such short notice. I bet most of their supplies were already packed up for this. I love it.

Sarge startles me, creeping up behind me on silent feet and whispering in my ear.

"Tank and Ember want to make sure you visit, even if Boss has claimed you as his sister. These get-togethers are supposed to be an extension of the bar vibes." He never even acknowledges Kami.

I can see the attempt being made here. The children freely mingle in the side yard and activities, but the adults aren't venturing very far from their respective areas, unless it's to check on the children. Each tent has its own complete meal. This is not what I was led to believe it would be. Where's the camaraderie?

I honestly expected charity ride vibes, not this emotionless distance.

Ember spots us next, nearly barreling me over in a hug. "You must be Kami," she says kindly, lifting her head from my shoulder. "I was visiting Armani, when you called. I hope everything is okay?"

Why are people touching me so much today? Is this normal friend activity? Or something else?

Kami smiles, the expression not quite reaching her eyes. "My apartment was ransacked," she admits. "Armani got the police to take it seriously."

"The police don't take your apartment safety seriously?" Tank questions, abandoning the grill for his wife's affection.

The kid from earlier takes over, eyeing the meat like it might bite him instead of the other way around. His eyes constantly dart around the space, muscles tense. He only relaxes when Sarge sets his chair to the side of the grill, dragging the boy into conversation.

"Not usually." Kami shuffles her feet a bit. "Our building doesn't normally have problems, but when it does the police write it off completely. The sheriff's brother owns the place."

"County sheriff?" I ask, seeking clarification. "Which county?"

Setting lies on the county line, between Macon and Lee. Jurisdiction lines blur here, all the time. I may be able to use this to Kami's benefit, if my suspicions are correct.

"Lee," she answers, brows furrowing. "Why?"

I grin, feeling almost feral in my excitement. I was right! "You live on the Macon side of the line. I'm not going to do anything, *yet*, but that is handy information. If you continue to have problems after this case, let me know. I know people." I wink mischievously at her.

"I think I might be just the tiniest bit scared right now," Ember says. "And I'm married to him." She jabs her thumb into Tank's chest.

"Don't worry," I tell her, with a laugh. "I only use my powers for good."

Tank's rumbling chuckle catches the attention of those around us.

"Little sis!" I hear Boss exclaim from across the lot. "You made it!" The man acts like *he* invited me, jogging across the open space.

"Who's your friend?" He asks, tripping over his feet as he

nears us. He lands, sprawled out across the gravel, eyes never leaving Kami.

"This is Kami," I introduce them. "Kami, this big bad biker at your feet is Boss. He's the president of The Cadillac Squad."

She looks down at him, still laying in the gravel. "Someone put him in charge?"

I stifle my laugh. Boss's look of playful outrage makes it really hard.

"Hey, it's not my fault I fell for your beauty." Boss grins up at her. "I'm normally a little more dignified."

Kami's cheeks turn a light pink color, and she glances quickly over at me.

"I've known Boss a whole two full days now," I tell her. "He decided I would make a good little sister almost instantly. I met Tank around the same time. They've been a big help with the construction work at the office."

"Speaking of," Boss interjects as he gets up off the ground. "We voted you into your own suite at the compound. Free to use any time." He tosses me a key ring with his colors on it. "Flash this to whoever is at the gate, and they'll let you in. Your rooms are right next to mine. One of the guys is going to make you a plate for your door. Fix it up however."

"Hey now!" Tank tosses his arm over my shoulders with a faux glare. "Who said she's staying with you? Ember is already planning her rooms at our place."

Ember shakes her head, before giving us a subtle nod to follow her. We do, eagerly, laughing at the grown men and their little show.

"Where do you think she's been staying?" I hear Boss exclaim as we make our way to The Calvary tables.

Sarge keeps careful watch over the members, while Tank socializes. Where is the Vice? Wouldn't that be his job–to step up when Tank is busy? Members fix plates, feeding all the women chilling out in the tent before themselves.

I worry for just a moment that Ember is going to expect me to remember a whole bunch of names. Instead, she leads us to a quiet unoccupied stretch of table.

"I'm so happy to have *real* women to talk to." Ember glances at the other women sitting around. "That's rude. They're women. I just..." She blows out a raucous breath. "I am so tired of the club bunnies! I'm the only old lady right now, and none of them like that I have a patched brother, a ranked officer, the president! At least the house mice leave me alone." Her voice never gets louder than a harsh whisper, but the aggravation she feels is palpable in the air.

"Club bunnies? House mice? Am I supposed to know what that means?" Kami looks at me with wide, panicked eyes.

"Oh. I forget not everyone knows the terms. I grew up in a motorcycle club." Ember clears her throat. "Anyway, club bunny and sweet butt are interchangeable terms–club bunny evolved as a show of respect for the girls. The roll of a club bunny or house mouse is essentially the same, on paper. Our club pays them to perform certain tasks, primarily housework. The difference is who is willing to screw the brothers indiscriminately. A house mouse does her job and disappears, quiet as a mouse. A club bunny hangs around in hopes of, well, to put it rudely, fucking like rabbits."

"So, it's a jealousy thing?" Kami clarifies. "They want what you have–status or whatever. Girl, you need to protect your peace, even if you don't have to fight for your relationship. I've left relationships because I fought when my partner didn't." Kami glances at Tank and Boss still bickering. "You don't have that problem. Tell me about these club bunnies. We can fix this."

I am amazed at the transformation in her. She is so full of

life now. If finding her home in shambles drained her, having something to fight for has completely reanimated her. This is the beautiful young woman who blew through my office yesterday. It's good to see her again.

I let their chatter flow over me. Years in the foster system, followed by years under Kyle's thumb taught me not to fight back. That's a challenge I'm overcoming, slowly, on my own. I can't do this for Ember; I don't even have advice for her. I never had an opportunity to openly fight back against my bullies.

But, I *can* gather information. And I will. Here, at the office, maybe even in their own compound. Research is my bitch, and I wield it with absolute proficiency. Ember is my friend, or at least I hope she will be. These *bunnies* won't be her problem for long if I have my way.

As their words wash over me, I take my time to really observe the event. The hard lines. The way at least three members of each club are watching Tank and Boss bicker. How each club holds to their own-no others crossing the divides.

Conversely, the children mingle as only kids can. The only divides I can spot are age and gender. Teenagers play horse-shoes. Adolescent boys play cops and robbers, or some form of it. Tiny children jump in the bouncy house under careful watch of slightly older girls–sisters, most likely.

I see Chris–and his staff–under a tent at the door. The smile on his face looks fixed. His eyes are a little *too* crinkled. The crew passes out drinks to people wearing wristbands. Missy sits to the side with an ID scanner.

I find myself wanting to ask questions. How does this event actually work? And how was it intended? Because this...this could be amazing, if only given a chance.

I excuse myself from Kami and Ember with a tight smile. I hate that I have nothing to contribute to their conversation. My lifelong habit of running to the nearest biker business isn't exactly going to help here. Biker business is the root of her situation.

Instead, I make my way through the lot, watching closely. When I stop in front of Missy, she glances at Chris.

"Which club are you drinking with tonight?" She asks with a perfect smile.

"I'm not. I'm researching. Or at least, I'm learning."

She laughs. "Well, I can't tell you much, but ask away. I'll answer whatever I can."

"Let's start easy," I say. "What do all of the different color wristbands mean?"

"Each club gets assigned a color. We change it up too. They tell me who they're with, if they're not wearing colors, and I give them the band, after scanning their ID. Everyone has to have a band to drink. Giving out drinks, Chris has a system. It's basically a tally system. No hard liquor tonight, all beers are the same price. At the end of the night, he charges each club's account."

"And the kids? Too young to drink?"

"Well most bring juices and sodas to their cookout tents, but Chris also gives sodas for free."

The system is pretty genius. No need for extra technology to track drinks. Everyone is treated equally. I see a few ways it can be taken advantage of, but not on Chris's part.

"My other question is how is it *supposed* to work. I was told it was supposed to be an extension of the bar's vibes out here, but everyone is even more segregated than normal."

Missy takes a deep breath, glancing over at Chris again. "I wasn't here when he started these, so you'll have to ask Chris for more in-depth answers. But, it was explained to me just like that, too. Every month, Chris goes all out with entertainment–he spends ages looking for the next best thing. Things that will make them intermingle. Like the volleyball court. Multiple clubs could be over there trash talking and laughing. They wouldn't even have to co-mingle to make teams. But every month, when nobody crosses the divide, his eyes look a little more dead. In fact, I saw the most life in him in a while when he spotted Boss and Tank talking."

"He's trying to build a community." The words are out of my mouth faster than I can blink.

"Exactly." I don't jump, it's like my body knew Chris was there, even if I didn't. "This is supposed to be neutral territory. Colors don't matter here. Every month, they mingle more and more inside, but come family night, the walls go back up."

"Do you want sympathy, a place to vent, or solutions?" I ask.

"What?"

"It's something Mrs. Maggie used to tell me when I had a problem. There's three reasons to share a problem with a friend. You either need sympathy, a place to vent, or a solution. Clarifying which helps the friend best help you. So, what do you need? Sympathy? A place to vent? Or solutions?"

Silence falls over our little corner, as Chris contemplates my words. "I don't think I could stomach any overt signs of sympathy, but maybe words of encouragement instead. That rant sums up anything I could vent. And I am definitely not in the head space for solutions right now. But if you have any to share, I will take them."

"If you're not in the head space, I'll hold on to them for now," I tell him. "This is an amazing concept. I can see the vision you had for it, and look, even if the adults aren't ready, the kids blur lines."

"Thank you." His voice is weary. "Encouragement wasn't one of your offerings, but you gave it to me anyway."

"Yes, it was." I grin. "Encouragement is born of sympathy and understanding."

Boss and Tank have moved their conversation by the time I've finished with Chris. Tank has his arm draped protectively around his wife, while Boss has taken a seat suspiciously close to Kami.

I skim over the other tents. Should I attempt making acquaintances there? Or has my association with Boss and Tank already branded me in their eyes? Only one way to find out–in person research.

Wait, was that really? Officer Doe? What is he doing *here*?

He's sitting with the members of On the Lamb. He isn't in uniform, but surely they are aware he is a cop? Didn't Preacher interrogate him yesterday? Was he in uniform yesterday? I can't remember. But Boss told Preacher he's a cop, right?

I don't want to be caught staring, so I decide, doubling down. Yes, I do need to chat with each club. I need to at least try opening communication with them. Especially if I want to convince Chris to let me run one or two of these family nights for him, to try new things. He wants a community, and I know bikers. It can be done, but it will take work.

I start with The Road Kings. No one here has an old lady's patch, but then some clubs just use the standard protection patches. No judgment here. All of the women seated in this area are dolled up to the nines, a lot trashier than the event calls for–shorts so short I would rather call them thongs, and shirts so skimpy and tight they are one deep breath from a nip slip. Their makeup is flawless. None of them would look out of place on a stage.

No judgment, Armani. Open minds only.

As soon as I enter the tent, someone grabs my ass. *Oh hell no!* Faster than a blink of an eye, I grab the hand, twist and flip. The *gentleman* attached comes up out of his chair, over my shoulder, and onto the ground, where I pin him.

Everyone's eyes are on me now–not just the members of

The Road Kings, but all four clubs. I just put a grown man on his ass. A King.

Straightening up, knee still pressing into the chest below me, I dust myself off, keeping my expression neutral. “Anyone else want to touch me without my consent?” I speak loud and clear, letting my voice travel across the lot.

A slow clap draws my attention away from the watching crowd. King, the President of The Road Kings, approaches, still clapping.

The other clubs go back to what they were doing, but a few people stalk closer. Tank's hand sits loose at his hip. Boss flips a switchblade open and starts cleaning his nails. Their eyes on me bolster my fading confidence.

“What a little lady,” King says. “That was quite the impressive feat. Maybe you'd be interested in joining our fight nights? Rash here usually headlines.” He gestures at the man pinned beneath me.

“No thanks,” I reply, keeping my smile soft and lady-like as I stand. “The only reason that worked was the element of surprise. He wasn't expecting me to fight back. No one does. But in a fight ring, I have no advantage. And I don't do *anything* without an advantage.”

“And what advantage do you have coming in here?” Rash snarls, pulling himself up off the ground.

“I have friends and this is supposed to be a family event.” I take a seat, looking up at King.

I can tell I've unseated him, just a little, by the slight flare of his eyes. Normally, one tries to take the high ground in these discussions by towering over the other to assert dominance. Instead, I've lowered myself —literally—after dropping one of his men in front of him. We both know I hold the power now, still smiling sweetly as if King's towering over me means nothing.

"And to what pleasure do we have to welcome you today?" He sits as well, lounging in his camp chair, as if to prove he's more at ease than I am.

"Community relations." I lean forward, elbows on my knees, with a slight grin. "Boss and Tank introduced themselves. I've seen the way the four of you Presidents confer with each other over the neutrality of the bar. I'd like to be an extension of that neutrality."

"Are you denying Boss's claim on you? As kin?"

"No." I let my smile slip a little more feral, eyes flashing. "That's my brother." *He chose me. No take backs.*

"Then there is no neutrality," King answers, like the royalty he thinks he is.

"Shame. I can be a real asset."

"Yes, you can." Rash licks his lips, eyes gliding eagerly over me. "I'll keep things neutral for you. As long as you keep my dick warm."

I laugh. "No thanks. I have my eyes set on higher prizes."

"Like what? President cock?"

"No. You may be a president named King-lord over your Road King kingdom. But I'm a Princess of this town. And one day, I'll be Queen. You Presidents will bow down before me." With that, I stand, walking away, their eyes burning into my back. I pop my hips just a little. Their glares roll off me.

Honestly, I have no intention of interfering with the club structure here. It was King's pretentious tone that bothered me, reminding me too much of Kyle. I may have painted a target on my back with that little stunt, but at least I have more information. King and Rash gave away more about why these events fail than they realize. *No neutrality, indeed.*

Without looking back, I make my way over to the On the Lamb tent. Doe sees me coming first and jumps to his feet. He pulls a chair for me with flair, as I enter. After my little show with King, I don't want to be seen as rude, so I just take it. Even if I'd rather sit anywhere else.

"Nice show," he says, with a lopsided grin. He gestures to the man he's been talking with. "This is Preacher. His guys are helping me look for more cases of missing girls. They've noticed a decline of young women at the food pantries. We're hopeful that they just found help, but the reality is that odds are not in their favor."

"Hello, Preacher."

"Hello, Miss Smith. You sure are making a name for yourself."

"Thank you, I think." I'm not certain that was a compliment, but I'm going to pretend it is.

"It's been a while since someone talked down to King like that. The fact you're a lady is going to really piss him off. Instead of him tearing down religion every chance he gets, he'll be griping about you. Though, I am sorry that my breath of fresh air comes at your expense."

"Let him be pissed." I shrug one shoulder. "I'm a paranoid daughter of a dead cop, with my own investigation business. I was raised in the foster system, in some of the worst homes. I can hold my own."

It's true. That little flip move isn't all that I'm capable of. One of the clubs that watched over me as a blossoming teenager owned a gym. There, I was taught to handle my own, under the guise of cleaning. The fosters I was with took the paycheck, and had no clue I was learning to fight back. Until I did. *Good times.*

"How'd your talk with Ludwig go?" I ask Doe, changing the conversation. I don't like the attention on my past.

"Well, I've been told to leave things alone. The Trussell apartment was staged, and 'the poor girl's sister left for bluer waters.' Also, they found a patrol car to pair me with in case of, well that part wasn't clear. Apparently, I need both a bike partner and patrol car companion to get on the streets. Luckily, the car just has to stay in the same sector as me and my partner."

"Staged?"

"Yeah, sorry. I tried to deliver that the way the Chief did. Breeze over the important stuff and yak on about bike patrol. I was there. I saw her reaction. That wasn't staged. So, I'm snooping."

"I'll talk to Uncle Ludwig," I tell him. "Not about you and your motorcycle. I want to know why he thinks it was staged. I'm missing information, and I need it."

"Well, this is yours." He gives me the briefcase. I open for a peek, and see that it's actually an accordion file. *Fancy.* "It has everything I've found on missing people in the last 30 years. Weed out whatever you don't need, but please don't toss it. I doubt they'll let me pull everything again."

"Why did you pull so much?"

"My mom was a Jane Doe, 23 years ago. She still doesn't remember who she was before her accident. Unfortunately, her lack of identity made her easy prey for some nasty groups. She's out, but still looking for family. I'm hoping if I can find out who she was, find out who my dad is."

"Is that why you became a cop?"

"No."

He doesn't elaborate. We just sit in silence for a few moments. The noises of the day whispering around us.

"If you get me a list of Krista's exes, I might be able to sneak through some background checks. If that helps any."

"I appreciate the offer." I stand, files in hand. "But, I have my own access to the database. I'll get this back to you when I'm done with it."

"I'm still on protection duty," he says, morosely. "Until I have a partner. I'll get it from you in the morning."

"I'll make some calls. Sitting at my place is a waste of your *talents*." I suppose he has some, or Uncle Lud would never have hired him.

With that, I head toward The Cadillac Squad festivities. Boss has managed to coax Kami to his tent, and he's showing her how to throw darts. Spider has a bunch of books spread out over a small picnic blanket, flipping furiously through them. Others are dancing, or playing cards. Poker by the looks of it.

I take a careful seat on the ground next to Spider. "What are you working on kid?"

He startles slightly. "Oh, hi, Miss Armani. Boss got me a date to take my GED. But, I have no clue what to study, so I'm going over it all."

"When's the test?"

"Eight weeks from Friday. I spent high school in juvie. I don't know what I need to know! Miss Armani, I don't know what I'll do if I fail this."

"Eight weeks is a lot of time for revision," I tell him. "I'll talk with Boss about a schedule, you can study at my office. Burnout and exam anxiety are real things. I'll get you ready."

The kid looks close to the verge of tears. Barely eighteen, lived a hard life, and he is scared of a test. A high school equivalency test. I don't know the exact reason Boss set it up for him, but I assume it can only be for his benefit.

"Now, pack this all away. You are at a social event. Socialize." I pat him on his shoulder and stand.

Everyone else here seems to get the party vibes, even if they aren't intermingling with the other clubs. That's okay, it'll get there.

Lastly, I make my way back to The Calvary area. It's fairly subdued. Everyone is hanging out here with a summer cookout vibe. The bunnies have their feet in a kiddie pool. They've taken off their tank tops to reveal skimpy bikini tops. Sarge and Tank are settled at the other end of the tent, next to the grilling prospect, drinking beers and watching. Ember has left the area. I glance around and find her playing horseshoes with some teenagers. *Good.*

"Mind if I sit?" I ask Tank, gesturing to an empty chair next to him and Sarge.

"Please do. The bunnies keep batting their eyes at me," Sarge grumbles. "After your little display, I'm hoping you sitting here will deter them."

"I am but a humble shield."

I didn't bring any of my work with me, unless you count Kami. I wasn't planning on going through anything more tonight, and instead starting fresh in the morning. Unfortunately, that means I don't even have a notepad on me. Which sucks, because I am bursting full of ideas for Chris.

Ember joins us around the same time a group starts whooping and hollering. I look around to see Boss dipping Kami in a deep kiss. When they pull apart, Kami has stars in her eyes. I guess I know where we should crash tonight.

One more night at The Cadillac Squad compound. Then I will purchase extra chains and locks, if that's what it takes to be back in my own bed. The guys have been good to me, but the bunnies are starting to get antsy, wondering if I'm there to steal Boss's attention. Maybe I should have paid more attention to the girls' conversation earlier. Kami might need help too.

I relax in my seat, taking in the red and orange sunset. The old wives' tale fills my mind. *Red skies at night, sailors delight. Red skies at morning, sailors heed warning.*

EIGHT

The next morning, I am at the office before the sun is even up, leaving Kami with Boss. I barely slept the night before, my mind stuck on the files from Doe–there's more than I expected. The coffee helps some, but still I flit from task to task, buzzing with unfocused energy, accomplishing nothing.

The files from Doe are spread out across the floor in carefully curated piles. I have a notebook where I'm taking down notes for Chris and for Spider. There's a mess of hardware on my stairs where a new security chain is halfway installed on my door. Somewhere, I've stacked a handful of flashcards I made for Spider to use during his mom's chemo treatments. I abandoned *that* task when I cut my knee on some leftover glass.

Did I finish making those flashcards? Yes. It was the worksheets for him to practice that need to wait. I *still* need a new printer.

I glance at the clock on my phone; the one behind my desk was collateral in Kyle's rampage. I should add that to the ever growing replacement list. Almost time for Ludwig to get his early morning coffee at Blue's Brews and Pastries; I want to talk to him about Kami's case.

Which means I need to order something. Better go pick out a pastry because there is no way I am drinking the slop they call coffee.

I make it halfway across the street and suddenly I'm soaking wet. So much for a 10% chance of rain today. Oh well. It's summer in the south; that 10% can strike anywhere, anytime.

Opening the door to Blue's, the smell of blueberries washes over me. Hot, damp, most likely muffins. My favorite.

Leah, Ludwig's niece, is behind the counter, furiously scribbling in one of her notebooks. Good. I prefer her over dealing with her overbearing mother.

"Oh! Miss Armani! I don't have anything blueberry in the case yet!" Leah looks genuinely upset to tell me this. Then she notices my state. "You're wet. I mean, the rain caught you! Do you need to borrow an umbrella to head back?" She is so sweet.

"No, Leah, I'm already wet. I'll just change when I get back. Best benefit of living above work." I wink at her and she giggles.

"I have blueberry muffins cooling now. I literally just pulled them out of the oven. I also played with the recipe a bit for a second batch. I'm trying blueberry and lemon, like the coffee cake bars. They'll be another five minutes before they come out of the oven, if you want to wait."

"Does your mom know you're playing with recipes today?" Linda has thrown more than one fit about Leah 'wasting ingredients with her experiments.' Never mind that the girl is president of the school culinary club. Somehow, I seem to always come in when Linda is in a mood.

"I got approval this time." She bounces in excitement.

“Mostly because the coffee cake bars sell so well. And I agreed to pay for the ingredients myself.”

“Well then, I'll take one of each to compare.” I wink at her little squeal of joy.

“They'll be ready soon. Can I get you a drink while you wait?”

“No thanks.” It takes everything in me not to give a full body shudder at the thought.

The bell above the door rings, echoing over the pounding of the rain outside. I turn, wondering who else is out in this mess? Uncle Ludwig stands in the doorway, shaking out his SPD blue umbrella, coming for his daily swill. I mean coffee.

“Good morning, Angel.” He greets me with an one armed hug. We're both soaked, so it doesn't matter, and I pull him into a full hug.

Ludwig wasn't just my dad's old partner; they were best friends. If my parents had been Catholic, he would've been my godfather. He stood as the best man for my dad, who returned the favor.

He didn't get to raise me, though. The courts didn't care how close he was to my dad. He wasn't family, and not foster certified. I bounced across the state until I turned eighteen, when I showed up to the Setting Police Department with nothing more than the clothes on my back, and my bug out bag.

Charlie Ludwig took me home that night for dinner, and by dessert time, his wife, Mindy, had me staying in the guest room. She swore the room was always mine, just waiting on me to find my way home. I cried that night, on her shoulder.

Three months later, Aunt Mindy had a stroke. She left me her life insurance. Not her husband. She left everything else to him. Her will only asked that I make myself happy and be free. Ludwig helped me pick my office and move the next month.

"Morning, Uncle Charlie." Leah grins with a wave. "Let me pull the muffins from the back, and then I'll come get my own hug." She is probably the only person who uses his first name.

"Lee-Ah!" I love the way he draws out her name. "I'm wet, child!"

"Don't care!" Her sing-song voice carries from the back. He and I have our own little chuckle.

"Uncle Lud, can I bug you about a case?" I ask. "I know you can't give open case details, but something about my case isn't lining up."

"Which case?" Ludwig steers me to a table. His niece knows his order, there's no reason to take up time standing at the register.

"Kami Trussell came to me to find her sister. The missing person report is a waste of paper, and then the apartment was broken into. I was told, well, that it was a case of hysterics."

As much as I don't like him, I'm not going to throw my inside source away. Ludwig has always been very clear that police business is police business, and mine is not. It's an unspoken rule that he doesn't bend rules and share inside information with me. He can't, if anything is going to be clean in court.

"There was no evidence that anyone was in her apartment other than her," Ludwig tells me. "No damage to the door, that she relocked while supposedly leaving in a panic. Only fingerprints in the suite were hers, her sister's, and yours and Doe's from clearing the place. I can't work your case for you, or give you anything else. As far as my office is concerned, her sister left her and she is having a mental breakdown because of it. Be careful with her." He takes a deep breath and leans forward into my space. "I really shouldn't tell you this. The sister's date that night was with Anthony. He walked her to the door where she politely but firmly said goodbye. I.A. has already spoken with him. Apparently, she spent the whole night texting someone else."

He has good points, but he didn't see Kami that day. He doesn't *say* it was staged, but heavily implies it. Maybe I need to dig deeper into Kami's history, not Krista's. I don't think she is anything other than sincere, but maybe the sister was taken to get in her head.

"Armani, I helped James pull the missing person cases to look for his mom," Ludwig continues.

"James?" Confusion fills my voice.

"Officer Doe." He gives me a firm look, like I should know my guard dog's name.

Huh. I thought for sure his name would be John.

"Anyway, just to put things into perspective, Setting has only had twelve reports of missing persons in the last thirty years. I told the boy to check with the local sheriff stations for more. Most of our cases are resolved quickly."

Twelve? Then why are there twenty in my office, waiting for me to find relevant information. And Uncle Lud says that is total cases, not open ones.

Leah comes out with Uncle Ludwig's coffee and my muffins. "I marked both muffins," she says, grinning wide. "Let me know what you think, please."

One more hug from them both, and I run through the rain back to my piles of paperwork and confusion.

Hours later, I'm still sitting on my office floor in the middle of a paperwork nightmare. No matter how I try to rearrange the files, nothing is coming to me. I don't see any patterns.

Twenty files, five men, three red heads, youngest is 12; oldest is 72.

I have stared at these faces all morning, drilling every detail into my brain. The only common thread is that they are all missing from Setting. Which, that makes sense. Doe pulled the files from the SPD database. County files would have more open cases. But, would that be *too* many data points?

I start sliding the folders around again. I haven't tried putting them in alphabetical order yet. Not that I think the names mean anything. It's just another way to view the information.

There has got to be a reason Doe brought me all of these supposed cases. I guess I should look into each name individually. Which means getting my laptop. I was trying to avoid electronic devices. I get distracted too easily. With the shopping I need for my office, that may be a dangerous combination for my wallet.

Focus Armani.

First, I rearrange the files again, chronologically this time, then I start a cup of coffee. This is going to take me a while. While my cup is percolating, I run up to my apartment and grab my laptop. I spread my stuff out in the conference room at the back of my bottom floor.

Supplies. I need supplies if I'm going to do this right. Multicolor markers, sticky notes and magnets. *Have I created a conference room kit yet?* No.

I keep little kits for different activities or areas everywhere. Like housecleaning supplies, or the box of bookmarks on my bookshelf. Then again, I haven't actually used the conference room yet–not once in the seven years I've been here. Which is disappointing, it was one of the biggest sales features when I bought the place.

It takes me forever to get everything together, but eventually I am ready to take a deep dive into twenty people's lives. Time to filter out the unnecessary data. This is where I thrive.

So why am I suddenly anxious?

I grab my coffee and begin my giant chart. On my whiteboard, I create three huge sections. Open, closed, not missing. If Setting only ever had twelve missing people, then at least eight of these never were.

Then I put a sticky note on the front of each file with name, age, and report date. Once I have filtered my files, I can add more to the notes I need. Maybe even replace them with whole sheets of paper and magnets.

Now, I begin actually digging for information, starting with the oldest file: Forest Greughn, age 45.

By the time I finish, my back hurts, my neck aches, and my board is a flurry of notes. Out of the five males, only one was ever missing. Twelve-year-old Tucker Grant was found in the woods one week after his disappearance. The girls still missing are all between 20 and 30 years old when they disappeared. Five girls are still missing, and four who have been found. Luckily, none of the missing girls have turned up dead.

Looking over my data, I take a drink of my abandoned coffee. It's cold and gross, but I suck it down anyway.

Five missing girls, four found girls, one found boy. Ludwig said twelve and Doe bought me twenty. I have both not enough data, and too much.

I focus on the missing women. Pulling their pictures from the corresponding folder, I create a line up wall.

Smash.

My coffee cup falls to the floor.

I've seen these faces before–playing around with one of those AI apps, where you can change small features to see what you look like... Each one of these women look like me. Not exactly alike, or I would have noticed the pattern sooner.

But with only them, all lined up, I can see it clearly. Our eye colors all differ, but are the same shape. Hairstyles are vastly different, but all compliment our round faces. Noses are all different, but everyone has full cheeks. These women could be my sisters.

I sit roughly back into my seat. I want to cry. I want to throw up. I want to scream, throw things, smash things. I want to hit something, to fight.

The room spins around me. I place my head gently on the table, even though I want to bash it, repeatedly. The urge to hit and smash is hard to fight. At this point, I don't really care if all I damage is myself. I need to clear my head. I've never missed having unlimited access to a biker gym as much as I do now.

A biker gym. My head snaps up at the thought. There are four motorcycle clubs in this town. At least one must have a public gym. I bet Chris knows which is best, too.

I wish I had taken the time at some point over the last seven years to deep dive into club records. I could head straight to one. But, I didn't; having the bar nearby was enough to soothe my nerves.

A plan in place, I pack myself up to go. I'll take my car today, no telling where the closest gym is. Besides, I can lock my files in the trunk while I beat the shit out of a punching bag.

Chris's HandleBar is full this evening. That's okay. I don't need a booth, just a few minutes at the bartop with the handsome bartender. I take a seat at the end.

That's not Chris.

Some younger guy is tending bar today.

“Want to test out the new hire?” Boss's rough voice tickles my ear. “Order the most obnoxious drink you can think of. Chris left him on his own for the next two hours. Told us to give the kid hell.”

"I wasn't planning on hanging out long." I tell him. "Just wanted to know which MCs have good gyms. I need a good workout."

"The Cadillac Squad has a good one, DeVille, on 2nd street. But The Cavalry also runs The Barracks, on 32nd. As my little sister, they'll set you up well at DeVille."

"I'm not looking for an easy workout, big brother. I need a real challenge. Your guys don't want to chance rocking the boat. There is no way they will really spar with me. Tank's guys on the other hand, they won't pull their punches."

I hate to hurt Boss's feelings, but the truth is as his unofficial baby sister, I have princess status with his guys. And I am not looking for *Princess Treatment* right now. I am looking for a no holds barred, full out, knock down, drag out fight.

"Well, when you're ready for a lighter workout, you'll be set at DeVille. But you are absolutely right, there isn't a single one of my men who would willingly put you through your paces. Not because you're a girl, but because they are terrified of pissing me off."

"Exactly," I answer. "That is not the vibes today. But don't feel too bad, I'll still visit your gym sometime too. Just not today. Speaking of bad vibes, keep a close eye on Kami for me?"

Boss's laugh echoes through the bar. "I'd love to. If I had a choice, I would never take my eyes off her. Just, uh, test the kid before you go. For Keep."

I shake my head lightly, as the new guy approaches for my order. "Can I get a virgin mojito, please?"

"Sure thing, ma'am." The kid grabs his mixer, mint, muddler, and sugar cubes. "Would you like that made traditionally, with soda water? Or would you like to try my personal twist, with cucumber-mint sparkling water?"

"I'll take the twist." Doesn't it sound refreshing and perfect for a pre-workout drink? "What's your name, anyway, kid?"

"I'm Mikey."

Mikey mixes my drink with showmanship and flair. He flexes his muscles while muddling the mint and sugar. He pours the sparkling water from higher than the cup, making it look like a longer pour. Not a big deal for a virgin drink, but would be a great trick for pouring a shot. Lastly, he garnished with a fresh sprig of mint and a slice of cucumber.

"Didn't realize Keep kept cucumber behind the bar." Boss speaks up, startling me out of thought.

"He doesn't." Mikey grins. "I got permission to try a couple of my own drink ideas and twists. Didn't want the bossman to foot the bill for my experiments, so I brought my own supplies. If they do well, Chris said he'll add everything to the inventory sheet."

Boss grunts in response. "Is it any good?"

I slide him my cup. He looks at it warily. "It's a virgin mojito."

"No rum?"

"Nope, sparkling water. Which is a twist. I like this way better."

Boss takes a hesitant sip. His eyes widen slightly. "You got any other fancy mocktails kid?"

I grin and slip away, letting Boss take over hazing the new guy.

The Barracks is a small industrial building on the rougher side of town. Its fresh grey paint contrasts heavily with the faded houses with 'for sale' signs surrounding it.

There is a perky receptionist behind the front desk. "Hey!

Welcome to The Barracks! How can we assist your fitness goals today!"

"I'm here to hit something or somebody." I answer, handing over my ID and debit card.

"Ma'am! We cannot condone violence! Or allow you to put your hands on staff or other patrons!"

I don't even bother attempting to stop my eyes from rolling. I wave my hand toward the boxing ring in the back corner. "I mean, I'm here to spar."

Her cheeks tinge pink. "Oh, sorry. We've had a lot of handsy patrons lately." Her nails clack on the keyboard. "Fang has openings tomorrow morning. Twitch is here after dinner. And, Radar and Venom have the weekend covered. Do you have a trainer preference?"

"No," I answer. "But I was hoping to get in a ring, or set up with a bag today. Now."

"Oh. Uhm." She leans forward like she has a big secret. "Sarge is running that area right now. He's kind of ruthless with his training sessions. I've been instructed not to sign up first timers with him."

"First timers to the gym? Or first timers in the ring?" I ask. "That's quite the distinction. I've sparred at other gyms before, but it's been a couple of years. I may not be a seasoned boxer, but I certainly ain't a beginner either."

"Well." She glances around and wrings her hands. "I can ask Sarge. He might be willing, since you *claim* to have experience. But don't feel bad, if he says to schedule with the others first. Its policy."

"Policy, I can respect," I tell her. "But, If I can't spar, I need to get set up with a sandbag somewhere. It's been a rough day."

"Put her in the ring, Belle." Tank emerges from what I suspect is an office behind the receptionist. "If Sarge complains, tell him it's on my orders. Miss Armani can handle herself." He gives her a hard look. "She's the one who put Rash on his ass, yesterday just before you got there."

"Yes, sir." Belle bats her long fake lashes at him. "Can I do anything else for you, sir?" She pushes her chest impossibly higher.

"Yes, actually. Order my wife a bouquet of lavender, forget-me-nots, and purple roses."

"In the doghouse with Emily, sir?" Belle leans forward in her seat, nearly shoving her tits out of her shirt.

"Who's Emily?" Tank growls. "I want to get my wife, *Ember*, a beautiful bouquet of flowers that symbolise love and loyalty, all in her favorite color. I spent all morning looking up flower language. If you can't be bothered to get the Club Queen's name correct, you may find yourself in need of new employment."

"Sorry, sir." She deflates faster than a punctured silicone tit. She brushes her blond hair back from her face and hands me a clipboard. "Our safety disclaimers and contract paperwork, ma'am."

"And, Belle," Tank raises his voice ever so slightly. "Miss Armani gets the family rate." He raps his knuckles on the counter and taps my shoulder before meandering into the gym.

Belle's glare at me could cut glass. "How are *you* related to the club?"

"Is that an official admin question?" I retort. "Because, if it was, I'm sure Tank would have told you."

"Tank's side piece, then," she grumbles under her breath. "He never goes for the actually pretty ones."

It takes a conscious effort not to slug her in her painted face. I came here because I need to hit something, and she is not helping my temper. Only respect for Tank and Ember keeps me from bloodying her nose.

I fill out the paperwork in a flurry, refusing to further acknowledge her attitude and rude remarks. As soon as she starts her gym policy spiel, I snatch my debit card and ID off the counter. The look on her face as I storm through the gym to Sarge and the boxing ring almost makes me smile. Almost.

"How're we doing this?" I ask, immediately, leaving no room for pleasantries. "Bare knuckles? Wrapped hands? Or gloves?"

"Dealer's choice," Sarge answers. "No holds barred, full out. Only way I can properly gauge where you are."

"Wrapped then." I grab the tape and start wrapping my left hand. "I want to feel the hits, but would like to avoid unnecessary damage. A broken finger would be a bitch to deal with."

I almost miss the huff of air masquerading as a laugh.

"Oh the horror," Sarge deadpans. "Get in the ring."

Hands wrapped, I climb in. Ducking under the ropes, it hits me. I didn't bother changing clothes before I left my office. I showed up to the gym without workout clothes and wearing a baggy tee and jeans. At least my hair is pulled back.

"I know I said no holds barred, but we need some basic rules. No crotch shots, no hair pulling. No open hand hits. Preferably no drawing blood. Hard hits happen, but blood is not the goal. Match goes until someone taps out. Knockouts are not the goal, a workout is. Any questions?" Sarge rolls his shoulders and shakes his arms loose, bouncing from foot to foot.

"Yeah, can we start?" I know I have a bit of an attitude. That's why I'm here, to blow off the steam threatening to make my head explode. If I don't leave here exhausted, arms and legs jellied, Sarge isn't doing his job. "Let's go."

I lose myself to the rhythm of the fight. Jab, hit, block,

dodge. Hit, hit, block, jab. Jab, jab, dodge. Hit, block, jab. My body flows from move to move, hitting and countering. Forward step, jab, jab. Back step, dodge, pivot. Time is meaningless. Stress flows away. All that matters is me, Sarge, and the red boundary ropes. Jab, dodge, block, jab, jab.

Bam!

Sarge swings. I drop. One swipe and his feet come out from under him. He lands on his ass, hard.

I surge back to my feet, hands held in a defensive position. He double taps his left shoulder with his right hand.

“That's time, kid. Hell of a drop.”

I sag in on myself. As the adrenaline of the fight leaves me, fatigue settles into my muscles. “One hell of a workout,” I respond, gasping down huge gulps of air. “Kept me on my toes and wore me out.”

“But did you die?” Sarge asks, flagging down the prospect for fresh bottles of water.

I grin. “Nope. I guess that means we need to go again.” The water is icy cold. I pour half the bottle over my hair.

“Screw that.” Sarge huffs out a laugh. “I'm about ready to cancel the rest of my lessons. I knew you were good, but I was thinking intermediate, not advanced.”

“Really? You think I'm advanced? Neat. I've never had any official training, just self defense lessons with various MCs growing up.”

“I'd offer to put you in the running for fight night, but I think some of my guys would cry after you whooped their asses.”

“All the more reason to do it.” Tank's rumbling voice makes Sarge jump–a barely noticeable hitch of his shoulders. I wouldn't have noticed, if I wasn't watching closely.

“Don't do that, bossman.” Sarge glares at his president. “That's how people get black eyes around here.”

"I know. I came prepared to block." The smirk on Tank's face is infectious.

"You're the second club to suggest I get in the ring with their guys." I shake my arms out. "Maybe I should."

They exchange glances, both shaking their heads, grins stretching wide.

"Yes, you should," Tank agrees.

"Did Barbie upfront get your flowers ordered?" I ask, changing topic.

"Barbie? Flowers?" I adore the momentary look of confusion on Sarge's face.

"Belle," Tank corrects. "And she better have. I wonder how long it will take for the bunnies to notice that every time they disrespect my wife, I'm going to send them on a kiss up errand."

I laugh. "I wonder how long until your wife realizes why she's getting so many romantic gestures."

"Alright, get out of my corner if you're going to gossip," Sarge interjects. "My next client is going to be here any minute. The man hasn't had a decent spar in weeks."

"That's because I haven't had a decent bartender in weeks." Chris's gravelly voice sends shivers down my spine. "Hard to find time to spar when I'm doing the job of three people."

Sarge indicates that Chris should get in the ring. "Well, quit yapping then."

Tank throws his arm over my shoulder and steers me toward his office. "Come on, Sassypants. Help me come up with clever ways to punish the bunnies. Then, you can tell me what's bugging you bad enough to ask for a second round with Sarge."

NINE

"So, bunnies?" I would much rather help solve Tank's problems than deal with my own right now.

"I'll let you deflect for now, because I really need to figure out how to deal with this problem, and I said I'd give you a short reprieve before we get into your mess. But we *will* be discussing whatever has you tied up in knots."

"Sir, yes sir," I snap, not mockingly, but not exactly respectfully either. "Why don't you just fire the lot?"

"We only have one prospect." Tank shrugs his shoulders. "The bunnies may be willing to *service* my brothers, but that isn't what we actually pay them for."

"Well then, what *do* you pay them for?" *And is it worth grating on my new friend's nerves? Don't worry, Ember, I'm doing my research.*

"Housekeeping, mainly. A few take on extra duties like shopping and cooking. If they work at any of our businesses, they get paid for that too. If we let them go, our prospect won't have time to sleep."

"You could hire out housekeeping. I understand wanting to

keep work in-house, but bunnies don't have the same permanence as a patched brother." I shrug, continuing, "You could hire family of members. Surely, someone has a sister or something that could use the work."

"No one would go for their sisters or cousins being club bunnies. That's down right disrespectful."

"Not bunnies, hired help. House mouse at worst." Typical man, automatically assuming sex would be on the table. "If no one has family that could use the work, advertise it as an on location housekeeping position. Shoot, describe it like that when asking the brothers if they have any family that might be willing-younger siblings, bored mommas. Cut the troublemakers loose."

The solution is so simple, but men thinking with their dicks can't even begin to see it. He might be married, but even Tank thinks of the help as loose.

"Cut our entire bunny crew?" Tank gasps. "They are part of biker culture. Can we really call ourselves a Motorcycle Club without bunnies?"

"Does On The Lamb have bunnies?" I ask, glaring across the table. *I bet not.*

"No, but we ain't exactly God fearing church men, either." *Point to me.*

"So, rehire the bunnies who respect the club wives and old ladies–oh wait, you only have one old lady. They're used to having the rule of the roost. Take the high road with who you have, introduce them to the other club presidents. Maybe make an offer to 'trade them out.' Or whatever."

"And that's not sexist and offensive?" Tank raises his eyebrows.

"Of course it is," I answer, my face heating up. "I'm just trying to give solutions. I don't necessarily agree with all of them. But they do fix your problems."

"Speaking of fixing problems," Tank leans forward in his seat. "Tell me yours." His tone leaves no room for argument.

But I try anyway. "*I* don't have a problem. My case might be problematic. There may be coincidences a little too close for comfort. But *I* don't have a problem."

"Smith!" He cuts in, his gruff voice stern.

"Getting bogus reports from Doe isn't a problem. I fact check all source materials anyway. Missing a couple reports isn't a problem. It's Ludwig's problem if one of his officers is giving out case files, and definitely his problem if said officer is hiding things. Not my problem at all." My voice climbs higher as I talk. My hands shake, so I shove them under my legs, forcing them to be still.

Dropping my head, I continue, my fierce tone wavering. "It's definitely not my problem if the five confirmed missing girls all look like me. An unsub having a type is perfectly normal. Me being that type isn't *my* problem. It might be *theirs*, but it's not mine."

"You what?" Tank's voice is deceptively calm.

"What?" I blink up at him, clearing tears away, aiming for the picture of innocence. "Which part of that do you need clearing up on?"

"The missing girls look like you?" A sharp line forms where his jaw tightens, nostrils flaring.

"Kind of. Mostly they all look like we could be sisters. Similar shaped faces. It wasn't until I had them all lined up in a row that I even noticed. It could *totally* be a coincidence."

"Do you really believe that?"

"No, but if I try hard enough, I can pretend to be unaffected." But, even thinking about it makes my heart race and my throat close up.

He levels a look at me. "So, how can we help?"

"I don't know. This one is harder to solve. I can't fire

everyone and hire new missing people." I fake a grin, cheeks aching from the force of it. *If only.*

"Don't quit your day job," Tank deadpans. "A comedian you are not."

I shrug my shoulders and sassily add, "That's not my problem either."

"You realize we have a personal security business, right? I can assign a couple guys to keep an eye on you. Well, less on you, and more on your surroundings and people around you."

"I don't need security, Tank." I don't mean to be rude, but I definitely can't afford private security. "I can handle myself."

"I know you can. My guys would be less there for protection, and more for recovery. You are this guy's exact type. If he comes for you, my guys can follow."

"I'd rather have a panic button," I mumble. I hate having strangers in my space. "Something innocuous like a necklace."

"If you agree to keep *one* of my guys around until we can get you one, I'll consider a tracking device to be a fair trade."

I release a slow breath of air through my clenched teeth. "I won't stop your guy from following me, but I'm not going to help a stranger learn my routine and safety measures."

"Great. I'll send Sarge with you when he's done sparing with Keep. No strangers needed."

Why do I feel like I set myself up for that?

I stand from my seat. "Great." It takes great effort to not roll my eyes. "Can we go watch two grown men wrestle now?"

Tank laughs and stands. "I dare you to call it wrestling in front of Sarge."

"No thanks. I choose life." I graciously accept Tank's arm. Noticing Belle's icy look, I laugh obnoxiously and pat Tank's arm. "Oh my God! You're so funny." I let my sentence turn into more ridiculous giggles, and bat my eyes.

Belle glares, furiously restacking the papers at the front desk.

"Problem?" Tank asks.

"Yeah, she called me a side piece. Which, rude. I am clearly an entrée."

Tank leads me toward Sarge's ring of destruction. "Isn't that what people say when someone calls them a snack?"

"No, old timer. Someone calls themselves a snack, and the snarky reply is 'I'm a whole damn meal'. Snacks are usually stick thin, and meals are curvy. *Usually.*"

"You young people and your slang. It's always changing."

I shake my head, he's not *that* old. Older, yes, but not old.

Chris and Sarge are just climbing out of the ring when we approach. Sweat drips down their faces, and Chris's shirt clings to his sculpted chest–not that I am looking. Sarge has forgone his shirt already, using it to wipe down his neck.

Tank immediately pulls Sarge to the side, leaving Chris standing awkwardly with me.

"So." I shuffle my feet. "I saw you got a new bartender. Letting him play with recipes already?"

"Kid has good ideas. He went over them with me, and I offered a limited supply of ingredients for a trial run. He doubled down and said he wanted to get his own to start. How could I say no to that?"

"Well, his virgin mojito was amazing. I left him going over other mocktails with Boss."

"I hope he does well." Chris scratches the back of his neck. "I really need the help. My social life is dead right now. I know I live above the bar, but I'm practically living *in* it."

"And what exactly does a fancy motorcycle bar owner do when he has real free time?" I tease.

"Hopefully, I'll get a chance to ask out a pretty new patron. Just got to find a chance to not make it awkward."

"Smooth." Tank claps him on the back, rejoining us. Chris glares, and I have to stifle my laugh. "Hope you don't mind Sarge tagging along. Armani officially has a babysitter."

"Rude," I grumble. "You don't even know he was talking about me."

"*Everyone* knows he was talking about you." Sarge grins. "Everyone except you that is. It's an open secret that he has been crushing on you since you turned down the Belvedere."

"Sarge," Chris hisses at the trainer. "Shut up."

"Why?" He crosses his thick arms over his sweaty chest. "Anyway, Tank, I think Chris is proficient enough in the ring that Angel-face here won't need extra babysitting with him around."

Now it's my turn to glare at Sarge.

"Ah, but Keep doesn't have your keen eye for surroundings. The deal is one permanent babysitter until we can get her a hidden tracking device to carry. Something that won't get stripped or noticed. We need something that can find her quickly."

"Wait. Why does Armani need security?" Chris interjects. "What happened?" He looks at me with concern written all over his face.

"The missing girls all look like me," I answer with a shrug. "The case I'm working on–it started with Kami's sister, but I found a few more. When you line the pictures up, we all look like sisters. I asked Boss to put extra security on Kami too."

"I think we've drifted from the point," Tank redirects. "Does Armani even want to go out with Keep?"

I glare. If looks could kill...

"I haven't actually been asked." Deflect, deflect, deflect. "Besides, he said he didn't want it to be awkward. So thank you for that. Topic change! If I give you a full list of the missing girls, can your tech guy do a deep deep dive on them? I've got basics, but I have too much going on. If I deep dive, I will never see the patterns."

"I can ask Ghost," Tank answers. "What exactly are you looking for?"

"Two degrees of separation," I say. "The six degrees theory is that anyone can be connected to anyone through six people. What I'm looking for is closer to home. It's less likely to be the grocery store clerk's sister than it is the sister's grocery store clerk. I need someone to filter for me, because this is *too* interesting, and I know myself well enough to know I will get hyperfixated. And that is the last thing I need."

"Okay. Give me the names, and I'll pass the request on," Tank agrees. "Better yet, since Sarge is babysitting, give him the names and he can pass it on."

"Wait here, while I get changed," Sarge instructs. "I'm going to hand everything here over to Tank, and then we will head back to yours for a security run."

Like I'm going to share all my tricks. My panic buttons stay my secret.

Chris shakes his head as they walk off. "That was not how I expected that conversation to go."

"I bet."

"So, now that it is indeed sufficiently awkward. Would you be willing to take pity on a poor downtrodden overworked bartender and show him a fun afternoon?"

"Depends on how you define fun." I bite back a grin.

"I have options. First dates are for getting to know people. So, coffee and pastries? Picnic in the park? Or hiking trails outside of town? I'm also open to suggestions."

"Oooh, a nice balance of properly planned and open endedness. Me likey." I pause to really think through the options. "As fun as a hike would be, it's a little Last 48 for a first date." He laughs, good. I didn't offend him. "A picnic in the park is a tiny bit *too* public. This is a small town, I don't need everyone in our date. But, I am very picky about coffee. So the successfulness of our date may depend on where we go."

"Not Blue's Brews." The words come out of his mouth so fast, I think he even shocked himself. "Sorry, their pastries are good, but coffee is not."

"Oh, I know," I agree. "I live across the street. I go a couple blocks over to Elixars. That is, if I don't just make my own."

"That sounds tempting." Chris smiles. "Maybe for a second date, if I am so lucky. I can buy the treats and you can do the brew. But, this time, an afternoon at Elixars sounds perfect."

"Great!" Sarge startles me, now in khaki cargo pants and a black tee. "I'll even be nice enough to sit at a different booth. When is this long awaited date?"

"Tomorrow?" Chris asks. "Three?"

"It's a date," I agree.

TEN

Sarge may be a security badass, but he's a pain in mine. Apparently 24/7 protection includes from myself and my own destructive habits.

Like, not eating.

As soon as we got back to my place, Sarge started going over dinner options. "You'll need a lot of protein after a workout like today's. But something light, maybe. What did you have for lunch today?"

"Uhmm." I don't think I ate lunch. "A virgin mojito?"

He glares. "And, breakfast?"

"A couple muffins." I grimace, sitting at my table. Saying it out loud sounds way worse than I feel. "They were blueberry. I kind of hyper focused on the files. They were a total mess."

"So, not too light for dinner. You definitely need the calories." He then starts browsing through my cabinets, muttering under his breath.

After what feels like forever, he starts typing vigorously on his phone. "Now, while I have this thing out, what names am I sending Ghost?"

I drop my head to the table with a thud. “I left everything locked in my trunk. Have I mentioned that today has been a mess?”

“Put your keys on the counter, and go take a bath. When Prospect gets here with the groceries, I'll send him to get the files from your car.”

“Invoice me,” I grumble into the table.

“Nope. Tank is covering it. Go. Shower. Bathe. Something to unwind. Do you drink? I can have Prospect pick up some wine or beer.”

“I don't drink alone. So if you aren't joining me, don't bother.” I pick my head up from the table, barely. “Is Prospect a road name or a title? Most use an article of speech with the word: the, an.”

“We use it kind of as both,” Sarge says. “We only keep one or two prospects at a time, so we use it until they earn a road name. Some come with one and have to earn the right to use it. Prospect and Senior Prospect we keep as place holders. Now, go.”

I heave myself out of my seat and give him a one finger salute. “Going, going. I didn't realize you took the title 'babysitter' so literally.”

Sarge just grins, waving his hand toward the door. “Do I need to order bubbles?”

Ass.

I *do* add bubbles to my bath, though. A lovely hibiscus blend I got at a farmer's market quite some time ago, completely forgotten, until Sarge's sass reminded me. The scent curls through the steam, making the bathroom smell like a spa.

I settle into the tub with a sigh. As much as I hate being bossed around, Sarge is right. The bath is exactly what I need. I slip down further into the water, closing my eyes.

Meditation isn't easy for me. My ADHD makes it hard to let stray thoughts go, but I do have a system.

Deep breath in. Count to four.

Deep breath out. Count to eight.

Something good from the day: Chris's smile.

In. Count.

Out. Count.

Something good for tomorrow: a date.

In. Count.

Out. Count.

Something good for right now: free dinner.

In. Count.

Out. Count.

My muscles slowly release. Between the controlled breaths and aromatherapy, I actually relax. I'm warm, content, *safe.*

I sit in that steaming hot tub until the water starts to turn cold. Even then, I don't want to leave its freezing embrace. I contemplate refreshing the water, but my stomach rumbles.

I dress quickly, chasing that cozy feeling. An oversized shirt and a pair of workout shorts. I toss my hair into a messy bun.

The scent of chicken and garlic fill the apartment, making my stomach growl. The sight of Sarge cooking makes my ovaries explode. A man as fit as Sarge doing domestic tasks, is easily a woman's wet dream. *I wonder if Chris cooks?*

"Sit. Dinner will be ready in a few. Just reducing the sauce."

"It smells good."

He winks at me over his shoulder. "It tastes even better. Prospect brought up your files. And your handgun."

Oops. I forgot I put it in the trunk at the gym.

"At least you have one," Sarge continues. "Tomorrow we'll head out to the range. Shooting practice. Evaluation. Whatever you want to call it."

"A distraction," I mutter.

"Something to do while Ghost runs down information on your victims," he counters.

"To-may-toe, ta-ma-toe."

The plate of food this man sets in front of me immediately makes my mouth water. Pan seared chicken with a golden brown sauce that smells garlicy. Brown rice with sautéed vegetables. And a bowl of diced fruit: strawberries, grapes, pineapple, watermelon.

Sarge takes the seat across from me. "While I was waiting on our food delivery, I took a moment to go through apartment security. I did not enter your room, though, so I still need to check it out. Given the general layout of this place, I don't foresee a security risk there."

"No fire escape." I agree.

"I will sleep out here on the couch, with direct line of sight to your room and the front door. Same as I sat while supervising breakfast the other morning. Keep your gun within reach of your bed."

"Yes, sir."

"Next order of business, do you want Ghost running down information on all twenty of these names?"

"No, just the top five. The others have either been found, or were never missing in the first place. What I was given doesn't match my information. I was told Setting has only had twelve missing persons in the last thirty years, but Doe brought me twenty cases. On top of that, after going through them, I only have ten missing person cases. Five found. Five still missing."

"Ghost can look into that too."

"I can't outsource *all* my work. I'd go bankrupt in a week. I'll start with what I have, and run a search algorithm for missing people. It may be irrelevant, but it is suspicious."

This food tastes even better than it smells. Silence falls as we enjoy every delicious bite. Afterward, Sarge insists on washing the dishes, as it was 'his mess.' I scowl when he shoves me off to bed like an errant toddler. He's lucky I'm tired and don't feel like fighting anymore. Before my bath, I could have easily gone another round. *Clever bastard.*

The next morning, I wake to the smell of bacon. I dress quickly–shorts and a tank–perfect for the Alabama heat. To complete my ensemble, I holster my gun in a concealed carry waistband, tucked under my tank.

A small buffet of food is spread across my kitchen counter. Bacon, potatoes, eggs, more fruit. Sarge stands in front of my espresso machine, a look of confusion on his face.

"How do you work this damned thing?" He growls at me.

"Carefully and with experience," I answer. "What would you like me to make?"

"I just want a simple black coffee," Sarge groans, glaring at the machine.

"Well, I could make an Americano with that." I gesture to the machine. "Or there's a Kuriug downstairs. I might have a normal coffee pot in a cabinet somewhere, but any coffee grounds would be in the cabinet downstairs where my office pot was."

Sarge turns his glare at me. "What the hell is an Americano?"

"Watered down espresso. Basically a very strong black coffee."

"And you use this contraption before being caffeinated?"

"Not usually. I'm messing with you. Just a tiny bit. There's a coffee pot in the cabinet next to the microwave. I usually set it up the night before if I have to go somewhere early. Otherwise, I just make coffee downstairs in the office."

He pulls the pot from the aforementioned cabinet. "And are the grounds really down stairs?" He whines.

"No. Coffee and espresso grounds are kept in the back of

the fridge. Since I don't grind them fresh, they keep better there. Nothing worse than stale coffee."

"I didn't know coffee could go stale," Sarge mutters.

"Only if neglected long enough. I drink so much coffee in my office, I often forget I have stuff up here, unless I absolutely need it."

Sarge meticulously sets up the coffee drip. Every movement is methodical and precise. He moves as if the process is a ritual–one as important as the caffeine itself. Once the brew percolates, breakfast moves quickly.

Before I know it, Sarge has hustled me out of the building and to the gun range, Sniper Shot. The building is an old five story warehouse, and I find myself excited to see the inside.

Sarge checks us in at the front desk, while I look around the front. The place is very industrial themed, with crisp lines and grey furniture. The artwork on the wall is all of guns-mostly close ups, but a picture or two show a pile of weapons. Everything about the front room screams 'professional'.

"Target range covers the entire first floor," Sarge tells me, taking the lead. "Second floor is weaponry. Third is basically a ballistics room. Well, a cluster of them. Knife and axe throwing goes on up there. Fourth and fifth are empty for now."

His phone beeps just as we reach our stalls. A quick glance at it, and he silences it. "Tank has the guys putting in a new glass storefront. I'm surprised it came in this quick. Your ex has been stonewalling us through our suppliers."

"Yeah, he's an inconvenience like that."

I pull my gun from my waist band. Disassemble and reassemble it with deft hands. Sarge watches my mechanical movements with an eagle's eye, clocking every movement like the professional gunman I'm sure he is.

We soon lose ourselves to the rhythm of the action. Load, shoot, assess, repeat. Sarge never comments on my targets. I never comment on his. We just shoot. At some point, someone brings us more ammo. We just keep shooting.

Something about the defensive activity soothes me more than my bath and meditation did. Much like sparring with Sarge yesterday, these actions I can control. Practiced movements give desired results. Aim. Shoot. Adjust. Aim again.

Hours fly past my eyes. I could live here, with unlimited ammo and unbridled rage. Eventually, Sarge stops shooting and just watches. Another refill of ammo, and he stops me.

"As fun as watching you destroy paper target after paper target is, I believe you have a date to get ready for."

I check my watch. It's just barely noon, and I question his timing.

"Not only have I heard it takes awhile for a woman to get ready, you aren't leaving without a small lunch. Coffee and pastries are not a nutritious meal. Though, they are a wonderful snack, and a great date idea." He grins.

I glare at Sarge. "Okay, *dad*."

Sarge laughs. "That's Uncle Sarge to you. I'm pretty sure Tank has claimed the role of surrogate father." He checks us out of the range and leads me back to the car.

Three o'clock comes faster than I expected. Sarge was right–don't tell him–I take forever to decide what to wear. Eventually, I settle on a nice blue sundress, one I have never worn. Something I bought on a whim and lost to the depths of my closet, forgotten until today. My hair falls in natural curls, pinned back from my face. No make up, no polish. Shit. Should I have put in more effort? I dress up the look a little by grabbing my one pair of strappy heels. The silver compliments the blue perfectly.

There's a hesitant knock at my door, and I can hear the baritone of Sarge's response through the door, though I can't quite make out what is being said.

Deep breath. Close my eyes. Slow deep breaths. I like Chris. He likes me. It's just coffee. Deep breath. I look good. *Right?* Deep breath. Yes. I look fabulous.

I step into my living room, where Chris and Sarge are exchanging pleasantries. When he sees me, Chris's breath hitches. Sarge turns and gives me an approving once over.

Chris's navy shirt button up, with the sleeves rolled and cuffed, shows off his strong forearms and makes his stormy eyes even more vibrant. And those jeans...yum. I love a man in a pair of well-fit Levi's.

“I'd say have her back by ten, but one: I know you have to be back to your bar long before then. And two: I'm following you anyway.” Sarge grins at Chris, eyes full of mischief.

“Three: I'm a grown ass woman, and you're not my dad.” I add with a mock glare.

“We already had this conversation,” Sarge says. “*Uncle* Sarge.”

I roll my eyes and take Chris by the arm. “Can we go now?”

“As my lady wishes.” Chris takes my arm and leads me down the stairs.

I pause to take in the commotion. The guys haven't started the real work yet, but The Cavalry is setting up to put in the new glass front. Crowbars are strategically placed down the panelled front. Groups are assembling to quickly transition from one task to another. It's as if an assembly line is being created before my eyes.

“If you thought Sarge was embarrassing,” Chris whispers in my ear, “be glad you weren't down here for Tank's lecture.”

"Please tell me you are joking," I grumble as we make our way through the construction.

I wobble a bit stepping over some tools. Maybe I shouldn't have worn heels. Chris catches me by the arm and steadies me. He glances down at my feet and his eyebrows furrow together.

"I didn't think about footwear," he admits. "I came on my bike. I thought you might enjoy it, since you rode with Boss the other day."

I look down at my feet, then back toward my apartment. There is no way I'm going back that way. Not while Sarge is attempting to give us an illusion of privacy.

"I can ride, if you pinky promise not to crash. *Or* Elixars is just a few blocks away, we could walk. Third option, we walk around back and take my car."

He stares at his bike for a moment, indecision warring on his face. "Can you walk that far comfortably? My sister always complained about walking in heels. I'm worried your feet will slip off the pegs of my bike, and I do not want to know what kind of damage that would do to your feet."

I take note that he doesn't mention my car. Not surprising. I've been around enough bikers in my life to know they take extreme pride in providing.

I rarely wear heels, but this pair was a break up gift to myself. Kyle hated when I dressed up. He would accuse me of trying to 'look good for someone.' The first thing I did when I left him was buy myself some sexy shoes. That I've never actually worn. Until today.

"Let's walk then." It is unbearably hot, but Chris's company is totally worth walking in the sunshine.

I offer him my arm, but he steps around me to the other side, placing himself between me and the road. Chivalry isn't dead.

Elixars isn't packed this afternoon, only a few booths are

occupied. I accompany Chris to the register. Boss's coffee analysis springs to the front of my mind. What will Chris's coffee order say about him?

He smiles at the barista, a quick glance to her name tag, but not an improper stare at her chest. "Good afternoon, Becca." He greets her by name. Plus one point.

"Good afternoon!" She is very bubbly. "Can I interest you or your friend with today's special? It's a cherry white mocha with a homemade syrup."

"That sounds great. Are any other syrups homemade?" Point two, listening to the barista and engaging in related content.

"No sir, but the owner has plans to try a few more."

"Then I'll take a cherry special. Armani, what would you like?"

"I'll also take a cherry special."

"Two cherry danishes too," Chris adds.

"Two specials and danishes! I will have those right out. Please take a seat anywhere you like."

Chris pays and we take a seat in a corner booth. I sit with my back to the wall, so I can see the whole room. He indulges me, sitting sideways on his seat, so the room isn't at his back, either.

We grin at each other when Sarge comes in. He has his cut on, which means he either walked or borrowed a buddy's bike.

"So." Chris drums his fingers on the table. "It's been a while since I have been on a date. What do people talk about these days?" He stops drumming, only to run his hand through his silver flecked hair.

"Well, my last boyfriend was a narcissist who only ever took me out to show me off, so, I don't exactly know either." I shrug my shoulders. At least we are equally clueless.

"First dates are for getting to know each other, right? Can

we skip the awkward small talk and dive into real conversation?"

I lean forward in my seat. "Like what?"

"Inflation," He deadpans. We lock eyes for barely a moment before we burst out laughing.

Sarge looks up at the sudden noise and shakes his head. He points at me and then a booth at the other side of the building, before giving me a thumbs up. I guess that's where he's going to station himself.

The bell above the door chimes. Doe walks in, him and his female companion dressed in uniform. Both have motorcycle helmets tucked under their arms. She must be his new partner. I wonder which officers got stuck with babysitting duty.

"Wow, it looks like Setting officially has a motorcycle patrol."

"Yea, Doe mentioned Chief Ludwig wouldn't let him bike patrol without a partner or a backup car." I study her for a moment. She looks familiar, but I can't place her.

"Do you know *all* of the Setting police?" Chris asks jokingly. "Or just him?"

"Actually, yes. My dad was a patrol cop here, and Chief Ludwig was his partner. He and the other old timers find an excuse to drag each new hire into my office sometime during their first week."

"How did they introduce Doe to you? You don't seem to like him much. Personally, I thought trying to be a motor cop in this town was pretty ambitious of him. Maybe even a little cool."

"Oh, it's cool. But I'm more impressed that Ludwig let a female officer be a motorman."

"Sexist?" Chris asks.

"More chivalrously old school, I think. As for how we met,

Uncle Ludwig brought Doe to a B and E at my place. My ex was causing trouble."

Doe and his partner approach our table, stalling our conversation.

"This is the P.I. Ludwig was telling you about this morning," Doe tells her. "Armani is a bit of a legacy around here. Armani, this is my new partner, Officer Wynonah Lovelady."

I smile politely. "Hey." *Awkward.*

"Anyway," Doe continues. "I don't mean to interrupt, just wanted you to know I'm finally off babysitting duty."

I laugh, and hope it doesn't sound fake. I look over at Sarge, realising I've traded one babysitter for another. He starts taking pictures of Doe and Officer Lovelady, probably sending them to Ghost.

Becca brings us our order, and Officer Lovelady's eyes light up. "Cherry danishes!" She grabs Doe by the arm and drags him to the counter to order.

"She seems...nice," Chris says, watching her bounce at the counter like an overexcited chihuahua. "Are you related?"

Related?

"No, why?"

"Well." He clears his throat. "You look a bit alike. Since you're a P.I. and you mentioned your dad was a cop, I thought it might be a family thing."

I look back over Office Lovelady. I don't see the resemblance, she is much more beautiful than me. But, I take Chris's comment as a compliment. He sees *me* like *that.*

ELEVEN

Bang. Bang. Bang.

My eyes fly open as I quickly roll off my bed and drop to the floor. Snatching my gun off the nightstand, I curl tightly towards my bed, making myself small. The muzzle of my gun points at the door. From here I could shoot feet, or spring up for a headshot.

I pause, listening. The Cavalry finished construction yesterday, so I don't think the noise came from my office downstairs. It sounded much closer. My eyes widden–Sarge is between me and the apartment door. I listen for any sign he might be in trouble.

Creak.

My door slowly opens. Barely an inch. I take a slow deep breath, waiting.

"Miss Armani," Sarge calls softly, settling me. "I hate to intrude, ma'am, but that police officer from yesterday is at the door. The one who's been following you all week."

Doe? How did he get to my apartment door? My office is locked up. *Right*? Any nerves settled by Sarge are now back in full swing. A quick glance at the clock. Six a.m. Shouldn't Doe be on patrol right now?

I stand, my gun pointed at the floor. I edge around the bed, heart hammering in my chest. I grab the door, and slowly inch it open. Sarge is standing so that even as the door opens, he blocks me from Doe's line of sight.

“I don't like this,” He grumbles, gun still in hand.

“Me either,” I admit. But, I inch around him.

“Officer Doe.” My voice is steady, unwavering. “I'd ask how I can be of assistance, but I mostly just want to know how you got up here.”

Doe pauses, glances over his shoulder at the open door. “The stairs?”

My gun raises at the smart ass remark. I'm not pointing it at him, but I'm not pointing it at the floor anymore, either. Out of the corner of my eye, I see Sarge has taken no such half measures. His gun is aimed solidly at Doe's chest.

“Woah!” Hands raise, next to his head. A silver key ring dangles around his left middle finger.

“The office was locked.” Sarge's glare could cut diamonds. “I locked it up, myself.”

The hand with the key ring shakes just a smidgen. “Ludwig sent me. I'm back on babysitting duty. Wynonah didn't show up to work this morning. Chief sent me here to keep out from under foot while he investigates. I would have just waited at Blue's, but I gave you all the missing person files. Maybe she fits a pattern, or something.”

Shit. Shit. Shit.

I turn to Sarge. “Chris asked if we were related.” That's all I need to say.

His eyes widen slightly. He marches around me, grabs Doe by the arm and slams the door shut behind him. He steers the panicked man to my living room and pushes him into a chair.

"Sit." That's it. One word. He then turns to me. "Kitchen."

I go. Obediently.

"If I wasn't here, would you still be?" The words come out barely a whisper. "Bad information, missing girls who look like you. Telling you about Officer Wynonah could have been a trap. A pity play. He has a key, no one would suspect anything."

"I know," I answer. "But you are here. And we have information that could help Uncle Ludwig. Besides, you're only here until I get my hands on a subtle tracking device. The goal is to actually get taken, so there can be a directed rescue."

"I really don't like that plan." His voice is low and soft, barely a growl. He drums his fingers on my counter and glares toward my living room.

"No one does. But it's the best we have right now." I lead us back to the living room. "There is a pattern. A group of girls in their twenties that all look similar, Kami's sister included. I don't have a picture of Officer Lovelady to add to the lineup, but she looks close enough."

"Those are police files." Sarge states it plain as day. *Doe gave me these files. He could get in trouble for it.*

"I'll take the hit." Doe doesn't hesitate to volunteer.

"No need." I haven't figured out why he brought me so many files, and not all of the missing person ones. "I can tell Ludwig I ran a search for local missing persons. Pictures with notes only. The top sheet in each file." The last line I say directly to Sarge, who is pulling the relevant papers.

"What about the other files?" Doe asks. "You ran a search and only got a handful of collaborating data?"

"No. I just left all the extra here. I've known Chief Ludwig my whole life. Relevant information only is a building block of our relationship. It's how we keep any conflict of interest out of our personal lives. I'd be surprised if he even asked about the other files."

Extremely surprised, since they are bogus reports.

“We have a plan then.” Sarge's voice carries a final weight. “Go back downstairs while Miss Armani gets ready for the day. She has no need for a second babysitter.”

“And you are?”

“Her uncle.” Sarge's tone leaves no room for questions. I trust him to handle the situation while I get dressed.

Mechanically, I throw on a basic outfit. Jeans, tee, boots. Right now I wish I had a leather jacket. Something to boost my confidence.

An hour later, my boots clack on the precinct floor. Doe follows behind me, glowering at everyone. Sarge chose to wait outside on his bike.

“Chief is busy right now, sweetie.” The receptionist uses her sugary ‘go away’ voice. Marley has been screening his appointments for years. She is awesome at keeping him on task, but a pain to deal with.

“I know.” I jab my thumb at Doe over my shoulder. “He sent a watchdog. A retired watchdog, who was supposed to finally be out of my space. Luckily, for Uncle Charlie, I have relevant information.”

I only ever call the chief ‘Uncle Charlie’ when I need to get my way here. It's a subtle reminder that I can and will tell him what I want. The only deterrent is how long it will be, and how much said person is annoying me.

Her fake smile turns icy, but she does buzz Uncle Ludwig.

“Chief. Your niece is here to see you. Claims to have information regarding Officer Wynonah.”

That's not exactly what I said, but it will do.

“Send her in.” Lud's voice answers back, but I'm already around the desk and heading to his door with Doe following behind. At the last moment, I snap the door shut in his face.

"Armani." Ludwig's voice sounds disappointed. "That was rude."

"Yeah, well so is giving him the key to my office. And putting him back as *my* responsibility just because his partner didn't show up to work."

He pops his top drawer open, and searches. "I didn't give him the key." His face is grim. "I sent him home this morning."

"How would he know where to get the key? I just gave you the new key last night." After The Cavalry finished putting in the new glass front, the first thing I did was bring Uncle Lud a new set of keys.

He furrows his eyebrows. "I didn't label it either, but it was the only set without a label. Marley should be the only one who knew I had it."

"A mystery we can solve another time," I concede. "The reason I'm here is that I found a pattern in the missing persons."

He sits back in his chair. "And how do you know who's missing?" An eyebrow raises.

"Puh-lease. You know very well I have my own search engines. I ran an algorithm looking for missing persons in Setting. I only got ten, including Miss Trussell. I then dug a little further and discounted all the closed cases. That left me with these five." I lay all five profile sheets out in a row. "I don't know how much it helps, but they all look like they could be sisters." I do not mention that I fit in that category as well.

Ludwig adds a flyer with Officer Wynonah's picture to the line up. "Wynnie, too." His voice sounds defeated. He drops his head into his hands. "I need you to share this with the force. I don't know how it helps, but all information is a tool. If it were all blonds, or something easily defined, we could put out a warning. While this looks concrete, it's speculative at best." He groans into his hands. "I'm too tired for this. I've been leading the night shift a lot this month. I'm only here now because Officer Lovelady didn't show up."

"Vigilant eyes are the best deterrent for kidnapping. Hold a series of self defense lessons with emphasis on not being an easy target. I know running defense lessons is usually assigned to the lower ranked officers, but put your best on it. Let them look for girls who fit the target profile. Pull them aside, warn them, and make a list. Addresses and areas to increase patrol."

Ludwig lifts his head, tears in the corners of his eyes. "Your daddy would be so proud of you. He would spend every Sunday dinner trying to convince you to join the force with that sharp eye of yours, Little Detective."

The old familiar title settles heavy over us both. Dad always called me his Little Detective at the station. Mom, too, was impressed with my pattern recognition skills.

"But he would be proud of you as you are. I am." Lud continues. "I'll pull everyone in for a debrief and get Marley to start scheduling classes. Every night this week, and next."

"Get flyers made, and I'll help get them put up in the best places. The other commonalities are their age range and socio-economic status." I don't mention that I fall here either. I do not need a force issued guard dog. I have a military one of my own right now. Besides, no one on the force would let me pull the little stunt I have planned.

A small smile graces his face, if only for a moment. "Thank you. You really are the Angel your daddy wanted."

Tears fall down my cheeks. Trust Ludwig to make things emotional. I take a moment to gather my thoughts while he pages Marley to get things scheduled.

I always mention that Armani means warrior when people try to make fun of my name. It is an unusual and unique name, especially around here. But the part I rarely mention is that my middle name is Celeste. Of the heavens.

My parents had a hard time conceiving, I was told. Mom had many miscarriages before they were blessed with me. There were two scares with me, and mom was put on bed rest. Dad said only a heavenly warrior could fight that hard to be a perfect blessing, so they named me such. But only Uncle Ludwig has called me dad's angel since they died.

"Marley says she can have everyone back and ready to be briefed in thirty minutes. Go get something for breakfast. I won't make you take Officer Doe with you."

"Good." I don't mention the biker waiting for me outside. I slip out of the office, leaving him to the whirlwind of schedules and mayhem.

The entirety of the Setting Police Department sits in front of me. Waiting for profound words of wisdom. Words that I failed to come up with in the thirty minutes it took to gather everyone. Several officers are in plain clothes, mostly off duty. Half of them look at me with weary, sleep crusted eyes.

"I'll keep this as brief as I can," I start. "You all know me. You know what I do, I'm not going to waste my time going over my credentials, or process."

A few half hearted claps. Lots of head nods.

"Krista Trussell." I put her picture up on the board. "Reported missing two weeks ago, by her frantic sister. When police found no sign of foul play, Kami came to me. I ran a database search, and found four other missing women." Their pictures join the Krista's. "I noticed yesterday that these women could all pass as sisters, and encouraged Kami to seek extra security." A small twist of the truth. I told Boss who upped security on his new girlfriend.

“I met Officer Lovelady yesterday, and thought nothing of it. But this morning when I was told she didn't show up to work, I realized she, too, could be a sister.” I add Officer Wynonah's picture to the line up. “I'm not a detective, or even a police officer.” I remind them to light chuckles. “So, I don't know the protocol here. I have, however, given Chief Ludwig a few ideas on how to help protect the public. Or more accurately how to get the local women to help protect themselves. Some of you will be receiving info on that shortly. As for everyone else, keep an eye out for more pseudo sisters. If you see any, invite them to defense lessons directly. Get follow up information.”

Ludwig takes over here. “Everyone stop by and see Marley on your way out. She has extra assignments for each of you. Some are running defense lessons, others may be making fliers or running tip lines. No shifts have changed, but everyone has at least one extra duty.”

Smart. Now the higher ranked officers won't feel demoted to defense lessons. They'll feel special, that they got the best end of a short stick.

I watch as everyone files out. Some grumble about the added work, but most seem relieved to have even this smidgen of a hint, a direction to go in. Officer Wynonah is one of them, no matter how new. They take that personally.

Ludwig throws his arm over my shoulder, leading me towards the station door. “Thank you, Armani. We have it from here. Krista Trussell's case is officially police business. Tie things up with the sister, and take a much deserved break. Go on a date, and think about giving me grandkids.” He waves pointedly toward Gibson, who smiles and waves back. I think he takes the idea of family business a little too seriously, sometimes.

“I'll see what I can do, Uncle Ludwig. I may have met someone worth a second date.”

“Remember, third date means background checks.” He ruffles my hair.

“Rude,” I faux gasp. “How dare you assume I haven't already run one of my own?”

He laughs. “That's my girl.”

I give him a long hug, then skip out the door. He never fails to make me feel like a little girl, and not always in a bad way.

Sarge raises his eyebrows at my exit. “Went well then?”

I drop the little girl persona. “No. I did my bit, but I've been warned off the rest. Told to tie things up and leave it to the professionals.”

“And?”

The question holds so much subtext. I think for a moment. Do I back off? Or do I double down?

“Leadership meeting. My office.”

I thought Sarge would call Tank. I messaged Boss. I expected maybe twelve bikers to join me in my conference room. Not twenty. The complete leadership of The Cadillac Squad, The Calvary, and On the Lamb. Six each; eighteen. Then both King and Rash arrive, surprisingly, to represent The Road Kings.

“I hear women are going missing,” King snarls as he enters. “How can we stop them from being taken in *our* territory?”

“That's what we are here to discuss.” Boss's calm voice settles any feathers that King may have ruffled.

“I don't have solutions,” I tell them. “I just noticed a bit of commonality. The more eyes out for trouble, the safer Setting is. The police department is watching me for direct involvement. I have a history with them.”

Boss and Tank laugh. They glance at each other's smug expressions and fist bump over the table, making me shake my head. My relationship with SPD isn't exactly secret, but it is irrelevant.

I put all six pictures on the board, including Officer Wynonah in uniform. The men before me need to know the police are taking this extra seriously.

"As you can see, all six women could pass as sisters. They all live in the lower class neighborhoods. Yes, even Officer Lovelady. She moved here in a hurry, snagging a chance at motor patrol."

"Boss has an informal claim on one of the victim's sister," Lockdown, the Vice President of The Cadillac Squad, tells the room. "She is being guarded tightly, as she fits the profile as well. We have also checked out her apartment complex and identified two more possible victims. We have brothers with eyes on the place."

"Have all the victim's residences been checked out?" Rash asks, cleaning his fingernails with a pocket knife.

"No," Boss answers. "Kami came to us through Armani. We have no connection to the others. I was going to suggest getting them checked out."

"We can do that," King says. "A lot of our guys live in those communities. Not all of us can afford huge compounds."

I'm not sure if that's a dig at Tank and Boss, or just a statement of fact. An explanation for being in the areas we need eyes.

"Especially on the government's dime." Rash grumbles under his breath.

That is clearly a dig. Boss started The Cadillac Squad with reparation money, from ten years in prison, falsely convicted of killing his girlfriend's other lover.

And The Calvary? Well, soldiers on the front line have little use for their paychecks. The men came home with a tidy little sum of cash between them. According to my research, they pooled their resources to start their club around the same time Boss did. But their compound is still just a large expanse of land fenced in behind the gun range.

"Regardless of where we stay," Preacher interrupts, making Rash huff and glare, "we can all keep an eye out. What are the police doing?"

"Obviously, I don't know *everything,* but I do know there is going to be an increase of station run self defense classes. It's part of an awareness initiative."

"We can run some at DeVille," Boss volunteers. "May catch some who aren't comfortable with police presence."

Sarge and Tank hold a short silent conversation with their hands, using some sort of military sign language, other Calvarymen adding in, as needed.

Eventually, Sarge speaks. "I'll personally run some defense classes in the public parks. Tank and the others will run a few at The Barracks as well."

"I'll have coupons made for everyone to give out," Tank adds. "Free handgun safety lessons and a one hour target session at Sniper Shot."

"Well, not all of us have resources we can so easily throw away." Rash rolls his eyes and crosses his arms over his chest with a glare. I'm starting to get really tired of his attitude.

"True," Preacher agrees, "but, we can all give a little time. Spread the word about defense classes and pass out coupons."

Mantis, On the Lamb's Treasurer, types on his phone for a moment. He quickly receives whatever he was looking for. "If any women find themselves feeling uncomfortable in their homes, a friend of mine just shut down a hotel. The one near HandleBar. He just agreed to let us use it, temporarily."

I see another snarky remark forming on Rash's tongue, but

I speak up before he can spew anymore venom. "Thank you. This is exactly why I asked you all here. To share information and network resources for the safety of our local women."

"What information do we have access to?" King asks. "Other than these pictures, do we know anything?"

Sarge and Tank exchange another series of hand gestures.

"Nothing definitive," Tank admits. "Just some suspicious activities. Could be unrelated. Might not be."

Sarge takes over the conversation. "Officer Doe's actions don't quite line up. He supposedly pulled all the open missing person cases from the last thirty years for Armani. Which, one, is against the rules. And, two, was inaccurate. He brought twenty files, only five of which were open cases. Several were never cases at all."

"That's true. I started digging into each person when Chief Ludwig mentioned that Setting has only had twelve cases total in the last thirty years."

"Why would he bring useless documents?" Preacher asks. "I spoke with him about that. He's hoping to find information about his mom. He seemed so sincere."

"The best villains do," King says. "So there is a *potentially* dirty cop."

"More reason for classes not run by the station," Sarge agrees.

"Anything else?" Mantis asks, still clicking away on his phone.

"That's all I have for now," I admit. "I just wanted this information out there as fast as possible. I honestly didn't expect this many of you to show up. Thank you."

"Thank you." King stands. "Get me those coupons and class details. My guys will do what we can." He and Rash leave without another word. They don't even look back.

"Get us the info, too," Preacher adds. "We will pass it

through our congregations. It's a dangerous world for women these days." He and his club shake hands with everyone, making their way out.

Tank makes a round up gesture with his finger. "If you don't know Miss Armani personally, it's time to leave."

The Cadillac Squad looks to Boss. "You heard the man. One of you relieve Spider from the front desk and send him back here."

They all quickly comply and I find myself with a much smaller inner circle. Spider looks surprised to be included, but I know he has earned this. His attention to detail has been a boon. Besides, he is among the bikers I know personally.

"We left out one detail." Sarge looks to me for permission. I nod. "Doe managed to get a hold of a key to this office. He claims the Chief gave it to him and sent him back to 'babysitting duty.' However, the Chief claims he sent Doe home. There is no indication of how Doe not only found the brand new key, but knew what it's for. No other keys seem to be missing."

"I know Armani is in charge of her own life, but I do not want her staying here until this is figured out. There is no telling if he had a copy of that key made while it was in his hands either." Boss, well, bosses.

"I agree, mostly. There's a trap in the works that we will need her to set, but until that's ready, she really shouldn't be here. It's too open." Tank crosses his arms and stares down the rival president.

I roll my eyes. "Look. I've listened to a lot of safety lectures. I've taken a bunch of self defense lessons. I have conceded to a temporary watchdog. I will not have this stopping my life." I glare around the room. "Now, Boss. I have been ordered to tie up my case with Kami. And I will. I've done what I can, and now the police are taking Krista's case seriously. The rest of this is community responsibility. These are our people."

"And you are part of our community, Miss Armani." Spider lays the guilt trip on thick. "Your safety is important, too."

"I agree. I just refuse to be treated like a child who can't think for or defend themself. I am a grown woman." My jaw clenches in irritation. I've handled myself just fine before these guys burst into my life, demanding control.

"I'll stay here with my favorite niece, until Ghost has our tracker ready," Sarge announces. "If we change too much then switch things back suddenly, our kidnappers may suspect a trap."

"Are you seriously suggesting we use my sister as bait?" Danger echoes through Boss's words. His knuckles whitening as he grips the edge of the table.

"No." Sarge chuckles, then deadpans, "She did."

Silence falls. All eyes turn to me. I step purposefully next to the photo array, highlighting the similarities.

"The Calvary is getting me a hidden tracking device, something inconspicuous nobody would think twice about. I can be tracked to wherever these girls are being taken."

"I don't like it." Boss's jaw locks, a faint tremor running along the muscle.

"You don't have to. This isn't just my choice, it's my plan."

Spider raises his hands like a kid in school. "Miss Armani, what if they have a way to block the signal?"

"Well, I won't be sitting around waiting for a rescue, either way. If I can get others out I will, but my primary goal is to be taken, escape, and note the location. The tracker is to speed up the process after. So someone can be nearby with fresh clothes, food, and water."

"Once we have a location, Ghost can pull schematics and we can plan a full ambush and rescue." Tank adds. "It's risky, but we are mitigating as much risk as we can."

Boss and Spider still don't look too happy. Both cross their arms across their chests, glaring. Spider bites his lip, while Boss takes deep breaths, nostrils flaring.

"What's risky?" Chris stands in the doorway. "Sniper said all the fun was back here. Sorry I'm late, Missy didn't show up for work. I had Mikey serving until I could get another waitress in."

Tank and Boss exchange heavy looks.

"Does anyone have a picture of Missy? To compare?" I wave my hand at the line up, heart dropping in my chest. The timeline is definitely speeding up. The other disappearances were spaced out months, years even. Now, Krista and Officer Wynonah in a week, and potentially Missy too."

Chris stares at the board of women. "I missed something big, didn't I?"

"It's been an informative morning." Boss grits out, teeth clenched. "And it's testing the limits of my sobriety."

He fills Chris in, while Tank and I go through Spider's phone for a good picture of Missy. Luckily, the kid takes photos of everything. A few minutes later, I am, again, foaming at the mouth about the destruction of my printer.

Chris looks nearly as happy as Boss about my plan. "I'm not going to add my opinion to the stack. I just ask that you be careful. I want that second date."

Boss turns his icy glare to Chris. "You're dating my sister?"

Chris grins. "For as long as she'll keep me."

TWELVE

"Miss Armani." Spider's voice carries under the door, splitting my head in two. "Gran wants to know if you prefer waffles, pancakes, or French toast?"

"Wha'?" I groan, face smashed into the pillow.

How much did I drink last night? I vaguely remember spending yesterday afternoon with two shadows, Sarge and Spider. I remember going to Chris's for drinks. I only planned on two, but my drink never emptied. I remember boldly telling Chris that my plan wouldn't risk his second date, if we had that date while I still had babysitters following me everywhere. I even remember suggesting he take over those 'watch Armani' duties. *Ugh.* Did I actually suggest a private show?

"Miss Armani, are you okay?" I almost feel bad for the worry in the kid's voice. "Gran left you some acetaminophen and water. Do you need anything else? I've never had the pleasure of being hung over."

Bless this kid. I make a silent vow to myself that for his 21st birthday, I am getting him completely wasted.

Pulling myself to a seated position, I take a long drink. The water is cool and refreshing, perking me up just a bit. Spider was at the meeting yesterday, which means...

"Tell your gran not to fuss about breakfast. Sarge will take me to Elixars on our way to my office. You gran doesn't need to be trying to fix me something, she should be worrying about herself."

"It's how she copes, ma'am," Spider whispers through the door. "Controlling what she can. She insists on making a big breakfast every morning, even if she can't eat it."

My heart breaks. Spider's grandmother–"call me Gran"–struggles so much on chemo, but she insists on taking care of everyone around her before herself. That's part of how I ended up here last night, instead of my own bed.

Halfway through the night, Gran called Spider to ask if he was staying at her house or The Cadillac Squad compound. He had the brilliant idea that nobody would think to look for me here, and spilled the situation to her. Next thing I know, I'm on the phone with a very demanding lady, and agreeing to everything. Both Boss and Chris were pleased with Spider's initiative.

"What's easiest for her to make?" I ask as I gather myself. I climbed into bed–or was poured into it–fully clothed, so I just need to find my bag–leaning safely against the nightstand–and make the bed.

He sighs a breath of relief. "Waffles. The machine has a timer and she can sit while it works."

"Then I would love to have one of Gran's amazing waffles. And so would Sarge."

The old grump isn't getting a choice. I should call him. He needs to be here before Spider and Gran have to leave for chemo.

"Yes ma'am. He's folding up his blanket now. Gran got mad when he offered to cook instead."

I open the door, blinking away the confusion. “His blanket?”

“Well, yeah.” Spider scratches the back of his neck. “He stayed here last night, too. Took him awhile to get Gran to agree to him sleeping on the couch and not in a guest room. Can I take your bag down, Miss Armani?”

I tug the strap even tighter. “No.”

Deep breath. The kid isn't trying to take it away, he just wants to carry it for me, like the gentleman his grandmother is raising.

“You can tell me how we got here last night, though. I don't think Sarge and I could both fit on your bike, even with the sidecar. I don't think I was even sober enough to hold on.”

His face pinks, just a little. “Well, Boss, Keep, and I gathered up everyone's cuts and called a bunch of Ubers last night. But, Chris drove Sarge on his bike, and you rode in my side car. I might have been able to bring Sarge on the back of my bike too, but Boss was worried you wouldn't have transportation this morning, so he brought Sarge's bike.”

“Chris drove Boss back?”

“Yes ma'am.”

“Did you get pictures?”

“All night long.”

“Good. I want copies.”

I think I'm gonna take up scrapbooking. That sounds like an entirely safe, responsible, ADHD friendly hobby.

When we enter the kitchen, Gran immediately hands me a glass of amber liquid. “Best cure for a hangover is hair of the dog that bit ya–watered down a bit.”

I don't want a shot of whiskey water, but I can't bring myself to say no to Gran and her twinkling eyes. I throw it back and cough, choking on the taste. That was not whiskey. It was apple juice.

“I said it was the best cure. Not that I had any.” She giggles, patting my hand. “Second best cure I can do though. A belly full of warm food.”

Gran already has a stack of waffles in the center of the table. I raise an eyebrow at Spider, who mouths ‘texted Sarge’ back at me. *Smart kid.*

“Thank you, Gran.” I kiss her cheek with a grin. I love this old lady.

We fill our plates and eat in silence. Sarge clears our plates after, and holds his ground against Granny in the fight for washing up. Even when she called him ‘a washed up excuse for a twice used condom’ while waving her wooden spoon at him. I would have given in at that. Mostly, because I was laughing so hard.

Eventually we pull out on two bikes. Me on the back of Sarge's; Gran in a sidecar riding with Spider. Her head scarf blows in the breeze. I wave when we split and go separate directions.

The ride from Gran's to the office is quiet. Daylight just breaks the horizon, casting the clouds in an amber glow.

The hairs stand up on my neck and arms when we park. The windows are dark, but the door is cracked open. Not enough to be seen from the street, but open all the same.

Sarge pulls his gun faster than I can swing my bag off my back.

“Stay here.”

“Like hell.” I grit out

I load my gun and follow at his six. I nearly freeze at the sight inside, but I force my feet to move, clearing the building one room at a time. My apartment door is still locked, but I don't trust it, neither does Sarge. We clear it and lock back up.

I was expecting another of Kyle's tantrums–another trashed office, having to replace all my appliances, again.

Instead, the only thing out of place is my conference room

mobile crime board. It's sitting front and center in front of a graffiti message. *You're Right. Not a Detective. Pseudo Sister.* And on the board, Missy's picture has been replaced with another. A sticky note stuck to the bottom. *Thanks for the shopping list.*

"Pseudo sister?" Sarge asks, snapping pictures with his phone.

"Yeah, it's what I called the missing girls during the police brief. I also said I wasn't a detective and didn't know what protocol was. Whoever did this was in that room." I pause to get my holster from my bag. Putting it on, and disarming my gun. I bite the inside of my cheek, wondering. *How were they in that room?*

"They took Missy's picture. We still don't know where she is. Do you know this other girl?"

"No, but I suspect she's one of the missing case files." I snap a picture of my own, and reverse image search. "Alivia Bennett, missing 6 years, age 21 when she disappeared. Mother claims she was on a date with her college boyfriend, and never came home. Unnamed boyfriend was never questioned or came forward."

"That's suspicious," Sarge mutters. "I'm sending the name to Ghost. Let him work his magic and dig up more information."

"Sure," I grumble. "Make my job obsolete."

Sarge flashes me a glare. "No longer your case, remember?"

"Yes, but what happens when I no longer have Ghost on speed dial, and I can't remember how to search for something on my own? Research is my bitch. It's my one defining trait. I can't lose that."

"You are being hyperbolic," Sarge says. "You're ours now. We'll butt out once you're safe again, but we will always be here as resources for you. The Cadillac Squad, too."

He says it with such certainty that I can almost believe I

have found people who will always be there. I've never had that. The closest I've ever had to family is the promise behind Big Mike's patch. Ludwig tried, but the system kept me on the move and he couldn't be there the way he wanted.

Tears prickle my eyes. "The way everyone is here for Chris," I whisper. "The way you claim his place is neutral territory, but nobody crosses the invisible lines on family night? The way only the kids intermingle? As parents watch with eagle sharp eyes, waiting for an offense that never comes? The way you all claim Chris is a friend, but not one of you has put a protection patch on him. There may be an unspoken rule that he's off limits, but nobody breathes word of it."

Tears are streaming down my face now, the tracks sting my cheeks. My chest heaves woth ragged breath. How can I trust that they will show up for me, when they haven't for him? Even with everything, he's always shown up for them.

"Armani. Doll." Sarge's voice breaks and he reaches for me.

I turn and flee up the stairs, sobs racking my body. My hands shake as I unlock the door. I slam the door shut and lock it behind me. Sliding to the floor, I cry. Openly and wholly. I cry for everything I never had, and for everything I ever dreamed of having. I cry for the angel my dad wanted me to be, and the devil I became instead, with no one to catch me when I fell from grace. I cry until I can't cry anymore.

At some point, Sarge sits at the top of the stairs, leaning against the door. He doesn't speak. He just sits sentry, guarding me from the outside world.

We sit like that, back to back, for hours. He never moves. I do. First to wash my face, then for my laptop. After staring at it blankly for who knows how long, I get up again and make myself a mocha. After another soul searching stare into space, I decide to make an Americano for Sarge.

I open the door and he just tips his head back to look at me.

"Still here," he says. Then, in a shaky quiet voice, "You're right. We owe Chris better."

I hand him the hot drink, careful not to spill it on him. And without a word, I retreat to my living room, snagging my laptop on the way. I sit in silence, staring at the open door but he doesn't come in. He sits, drinks his coffee and keeps silent watch, all from the top step.

It's nearing lunchtime now, and I half expect him to insert himself back into my space, the way he has for days now. To take over my kitchen, demand I eat, but he just sits.

A new wave of tears threaten my eyes as I sit there. Broken. In a way I haven't been since my parents died. I fall asleep still holding them back.

I wake with a throw blanket tucked around me. I glance at my door, but it's shut. I can feel the dampness of tears staining my cheeks. I wipe at them in frustration as more fall; I must have resumed crying in my sleep.

I tug the blanket tight around me and stalk to the door. I throw it open ready to...make amends? Demand forgiveness for my fit? Apologize? Invite Sarge in? But instead, I find an empty stairwell; my stomach drops.

I hear voices coming from the front lobby, too faint to identify. I pull my gun and check the chamber. Loaded, good. I creep down the stairs on silent feet. Flashes of foster homes fly through my brain. Sneaking down stairs to steal a drink of water. Creeping around corners to avoid drunks. Alone. Always.

I step into the lobby, gun level, hands steady, and I freeze at the sight in front of me.

Sarge, Tank, Boss, and Kami.

There's a small buffet set on the counter, and plates on the table. They're talking, quietly, gesturing at the information on the crime board. A bucket of dirty water on the floor behind it.

My gun lowers. “I thought you left.” My voice is gruff, thick with emotion.

“I told you I wouldn't.” Sarge's voice is quiet, cutting. He doesn't even look at me.

Kami stands, circling the table and pulling me into a tight hug. “It's gonna be okay,” she whispers into my hair. “You're safe.” I cling back. Barely holding on, but grasping with all I have.

She pulls back first, brushing loose hair away from my face. “You're an angel, you know? That's the only way you could have gotten the Setting Police to take my sister's disappearance seriously. Thank you.”

I pull her back into a hug, squeezing tightly.

That word keeps coming up, over and over. Angel. I don't feel like an angel. Well, maybe a fallen one. I feel like a plague, like an omen of bad fortune–a horseman of the apocalypse rather than an angel of the lord.

“Come, eat. You'll feel better.” She drags me to the table, an empty chair between her and Tank.

Tank fills a plate and hands it to me with a wink. Chinese, all my favorites.

Brrrring!

Tank pulls his phone from his pocket and answers. “You're on speaker Ghost. What'cha got for me?”

“Who all is there?” The voice is mechanical, like a computer reading a prompter, not the least bit human.

“Me, Sarge, Boss, his woman, Kami, and Armani,” Tank answers.

There's a crackle on the other end. “I need Kami's last name for a background check,” the same mechanical voice says.

"You should already have her information." I don't look at Kami as I answer. "She's the sister of a victim. Krista Trussell." With a slight squeeze, Kami rests her hand on my leg.

Another crackle. Longer this time. "Trussell sisters background still running. Started with the oldest cases." The voice isn't mechanical this time. "TTrustworthiness probability: high. Miss Kami engaged in external sources to find sister."

"It's good to hear your real voice, Ghost," Tank answers, like this is a normal conversation. "Thank you for trusting us with it."

"I owe Miss Armani an apology. She deserves to hear it in my real voice. My information on her was faulty. Built on false leads. She may have left her ex, but he was still posting their perfect status all over multiple social media accounts. There was a ring purchase, days before she walked into Chris's HandleBar. I failed to verify what seemed like hard evidence. False evidence that led to a less than ideal first conversation with my president."

"You're forgiven. I am all too aware of the pitfalls social media has on research. It's hard to verify, but harder to disprove."

"I don't think that's why you called though, Ghost," Sarge interjects.

"No. I found information on Officer James Doe. After some deep digging, Officer Wynonah isn't the first woman to go missing around him."

"I know about the college roommate " I answer. "She disappeared from Auburn. Did you get a picture of her? Does she fit the profile?"

"She does," Ghost confirms. "I sent a picture to Sarge for the crime board. Did you know about the girlfriend?"

"What girlfriend?" I tilt my head, brows furrowing.

"Alivia Bennett."

“The woman that the unsub added to my crime board?”

“The very same. She went out with him. Confirmed to have been at the restaurant together, that day. She never came home. No records of him ever trying to contact her again. Or the police.”

Sarge pins two pictures to the board, labeled in military precise handwriting. I look around the table for answers, and Kami points. A brand new printer is set up behind my desk.

Tears burn the corners of my eyes. Dehydration is becoming a concern at this point. The thought barely crosses my mind and an open bottle of water appears in front of me–the cap still in Sarge's hand.

He doesn't speak, but I hear him loud and clear. *Still here.*

“Thank you, Uncle.” It's the best apology that I'm capable of right now. The only words that I know means something between us.

His lip twitches, and all is well. For now. I have no doubts that he will revisit our conversation later, but he gets it. I've known them for barely a week. Time will prove one of us right. I hope it's him, even if history tells me it isn't.

THIRTEEN

As soon as Ghost ends the call, Kami bounces out of her seat and grabs me.

"We need to get you ready! Chris will be here soon enough." She starts dragging me toward the stairs.

"What?" Confusion laces my tone.

"You *do* remember demanding a second date from him last night, right?" Tank is laughing at me. He isn't making a sound, but his shoulders shake, just a bit, and his eyes twinkle with mischief.

"Yes. But I don't remember him agreeing."

"Well, he did," Kami states plainly. "And he texted me his plans so that I could have you dressed appropriately. Something about a shoe fiasco on your first date?"

"It wasn't a fiasco! I wore my favorite heels not knowing he wanted to take me on his bike. We walked instead; it was only a couple blocks, not miles."

The room falls eerily silent.

"He was going to take you *on his bike*?" Boss questions.

"Yes? Why?"

"Because Chris subscribes to older biker rules. Like the one that the only women who should ride on the back of your bike are close family: mom, sisters, daughters." Boss explains.

But Tank interrupts, "Old Ladies. The only woman who doesn't share blood allowed on the back of his bike is his Old Lady, whoever he decides that to be. By biker customs, he's declaring his intentions for forever."

"I've ridden on Boss and Sarge's bike though."

"Neither of our clubs hold to that tradition, even if certain individuals do. My understanding is that The Lambs do, and no one ever knows with the Kings." Tank answers.

"I do," Boss admits. "But you're my sister. Plain and simple. Blood or not. I spoke with Kami about it when we met. She understands."

A knot forms in my throat. I have no clue what to say in response, so I just nod and follow Kami upstairs.

"To the closet!" She squeals.

"I was under the impression he and I had agreed for a second date, I'd make coffee and he'd bring pastries." I open my closet anyway.

"He mentioned that." Kami's bubbly attitude and grin lightens the whole room. "Two things, he said. One: he wants to save that date as a reward for keeping yourself safe during whatever secret mission you have planned with the guys."

A soft smile graces my lips. Honestly, I would too.

"And, two: he said I need to be distracted until then. So he planned a nice date and put me in charge of getting you ready. Got any boots?"

I point her toward the back of the closet where I keep my small shoe collection.

"Cowboy boots? Really? This ain't Texas."

"No, but, the high school regularly hosts line dances as fund raisers. I go all out for them. There's a red plaid shirt and a denim skirt back there too. Oh and a pettiskirt, to make it fluffy."

I'm not entirely sure what the look she levels at me means, but I can tell she isn't impressed. "You're wearing them tonight–the boots, not the *costume*."

She pulls out a pair of old jeans, a pair I forgot I had, with bedazzled skulls on the back pockets, pairing the jeans with a black tank top.

"There should be black boots in there, too." I may not know much about fashion but I know you don't mix brown and black unless there isn't another practical option. At least, I think that's the rule.

She levels another look at me. "I saw them." She's still rifling through my clothes. Shirt, shoes, jeans. What else does she need to pick?

She comes out with a red cardigan and a clunky gold belt. "It's a little early 2000's but put these on over the tank top. Use the belt to pull in the cardigan and define your waist."

I dress as directed, picking out my own undergarments. This new friendship only goes so far. The jeans are a little tight, but overall the outfit is amazing.

"Do some squats," Kami demands.

"Excuse me?"

"The jeans are stiff. Do some squats to loosen the material. Better they rip now, and we put together a new outfit than they rip while riding on the back of Chris's bike."

I do as ordered, squatting as low and wide as I can. Our first date was awkward with Doe interrupting. I do not want to make this one awkward too. No ripping.

Kami riffles through my bathroom drawers. "You have pretty curls, but I don't think they will hold up to a helmet. I'm still new to this world, but my research into biker fashion says that braids and/or headscarves are recommended. I ordered headscarves, but those will have to wait. Would you prefer a French or a waterfall braid?" She stands triumphantly with her find: my hair brush and a sleeve of hair ties.

"If you're doing it, waterfall."

"Of course I'm doing it. This is girl bonding one-oh-one. Getting ready for dates. Doing each other's hair. Gossiping." She bounces on her heels, a mischievous grin spreading across her face.

We sit on my bed, her on a stack of pillows to make herself just a smidge taller. I relax into the feel of her brushing my hair, and listen as she mutters under her breath, "only hair product is mousse. Guess who's getting a self care gift basket."

"I've never had girlfriends," I admit softly. "I've never really had any friends. I was the weird girl who moved all the time. I had a protection patch, a backpack full of trauma, and a firm belief that everyone leaves."

"Do you still believe that?" She whispers.

"Nobody has proved it wrong yet," I whisper back.

Her fingers tighten in my hair for a quick second before smoothing it back into place. "Give it time; you're stuck with us. You could move across the country, and Boss and I would send care packages, call daily, and schedule surprise visits. I can't speak for Tank and Sarge, but Chris...that man would follow you to the end of the earth."

Those pesky tears make their threats again.

She tips my chin up, to make eye contact. "I've only ever had my sister. I get it. But you are stuck with us now. Speaking of, what do I owe you? None of this 'you didn't complete the job' business; you put in the hard work before the police pulled their heads out their asses."

"Uhm. I haven't made the invoice yet. It's been an emotional couple of days. But, Boss insists I send the invoice to The Cadillac Squad. Something about a finders fee."

“Oh, I'll be having words with him. I pay the bill, he can tip you whatever he wants.”

I laugh. “Can you tell me where Chris is taking me?”

“Nothing fancy.” She grins. “I think he just really wanted to distract me, and make sure you were in bike appropriate shoes.”

We laugh. It’s soft floaty laughter, the kind that bonds not mocks.

“Now, makeup. Do you have any?” She looks at me like she cannot believe my lack of supplies.

“Uhm. Two tubes of lipstick and one eyeshadow pallet.” I get up and grab them for her.

The pallet is all basic neutrals, so she checks the colors of the lipsticks. The mocha shade is no surprise to her, but her eyes widen comically when she opens the other. Fire engine red is not a color anyone expects me to wear. Not even myself. It was another of my post break up ‘screw Kyle’ purchases.

“Hand,” she demands, practically snatching it when I don't move fast enough.

She swatches the lipstick to the back of my hand. After waving it air dry, she inspects it like a bomb technician expecting detonation any moment. Then she opens the eyeshadow and swatches a few right up against the red. She eyes her artwork critically for a moment, then marches to the apartment door.

She calls down the stairwell for someone to bring up her purse. Boss practically flies up the stairs to deliver the requested item.

“Get back to your RPS tournament.”

“Already lost.” Boss grumbles. “Who knew anyone could be that good at rock, paper, scissors. I didn’t win a single round.” But he leaves as directed.

“Here.” She tosses a wet wipe at me. “Use this to remove

the makeup on your hand, then wash thoroughly with soap and water."

I feel like Mulan in that scene of the first movie, when the aunties dump her in the tub. *With good fortune, and a great hair-do.* But Kami is both the auntie getting me ready and the terrifying matchmaker deciding my fate. *Bring honor to us all.*

Her phone dings. "He's here, and he brought flowers. Boss wants to know if you have a vase?"

"I don't think so. No one has ever brought me flowers, before. I *used* to have a vase with fake ones in my office, but it was lost to the same disturbance as the front windows."

"The ex." Kami nods. "That's okay. It will give Boss something to do while you're away. I'm going to stay and man the office with Spider."

"Spider is a good kid, but you need a grown man here while Boss is gone. We are both picture perfect targets. Someone could come here looking for me and–pardon the phrasing–settle for you."

She lets out a large sigh. "I know. Don't worry about me though, go enjoy your date. Boss and Sarge have teamed up on this over protection thing. I'm assigning Sarge to the conference room. He and Ghost are going through something. I don't know what–probably my background check, if I had to guess. Spider will stay up front with me. I'll help him study unless someone comes in."

"Do I need to show you around the paperwork?"

"No. For someone with ADHD, your office is very well organized. I'll just let anyone know you are out of office, and will get back to them as soon as you can after returning. I've worked a few receptionist jobs."

"Thank you." Pesky tears.

"Now, now, don't cry. You'll ruin the look. Have fun. Stick

with Chris. And remember Tank is there if things go south." Kami pushed me toward the door with a firm steady hand.

"Is that a possibility?" I ask. Where in the world is Chris taking me?

"You'll be in public. Anything is possible. Girl code one-oh-two, make sure the other has an exit plan."

"Speaking of exit plans, can I still carry my backpack or do I need an actual purse?"

"That bag is clearly part of who you are. It goes, but I need to hear more about how it relates to an exit strategy later. For now, let's get you downstairs and off on your date."

Chris looks sharp. Black leather jacket and black jeans. Helmet tucked under his arm, spare hanging off his fingertips. Heat rushes up my neck as I look him over.

Someone, probably Boss, has taken the flowers and put them in one of my taller coffee cups. They are nearly as breath-taking as Chris is. It's a huge bouquet, threatening to fall over. Red roses, carnations, and chrysanthemums steal center stage. Baby's breath, white daisies, and forget-me-nots bulk it out and bring it all together. Absolutely stunning.

"Beautiful." The word is barely a breath across his lips, like he doesn't even realize he is saying.

Tank and Boss exchange looks. Sarge rolls his eyes.

"Leave the bag," Tank demands, when I reach for it. "You don't need it."

My hand tightens on the strap.

"Trust it to one of the others. It's a date, not a stake out. Leave it." His voice leaves no room for argument.

I'm not happy about it, but I give the bag to Sarge, and an apartment key. "Put it in my room?"

"On the bed," Sarge agrees. "Tank is on chaperone duty today. Kami and I will be here when you get back. Have fun."

"Oh, we will." Chris grins. "I have a wonderful afternoon

planned." He offers me his arm and escorts me to his bike. "Kami did a great job. No heels, and perfect for today's activity." The wink he gives me nearly makes my knees buckle. Who is this girl I turn into around him?

Tank revs his bike at us. Chris helps me atop his.

"Want to race him?"

I laugh instead of answering, as he climbs on.

I hold on tight and enjoy the ride. The breeze bites through my clothes. The warmth of Chris pressed against my front feels safe and steady. We fly down the road, Tank at our six.

We stop at a church. My conversation with the guys about seat beliefs flashes through my mind.

Chris lifts the visor on my helmet with a grin. "Don't panic, yet. Wait here with Tank while I ask about bike parking. This is Preacher's church, I know they have a spot."

Tank leans forward, arms crossed on his handlebars. "Moving a little fast, ain't ya Keep?" He catcalls. "And without her brother, too." Chris shakes his head, as he dips inside.

"Preacher lives in the brick house next door." He tells us when he comes back out. "Bikers park behind his house."

We circle the brick house. Yeah, this is definitely bike parking. The yard isn't just full of motorcycles, there's about twenty bicycles parked here, too.

"What in the h...world have you gotten us into?" Tank asks.

"Nothing too weird," he answers. "Preacher has everything we need inside the fellowship hall."

Tank's scarred eyebrow raises. Chris just grins back leading us inside.

I have no clue what to expect, but the folding tables, set in what looks like assembly lines is not it. Tank looks even more bewildered than I feel, eyes wide.

Preacher rushes over as soon as he spots us. "I'm so glad you guys came! I'll make sure Chris and Armani are on one line, and Tank on another. I heard about the chaperoning thing. Old school, but cute. He can chaperone from across the room."

"What exactly is going on?" Tank growls.

"Care Kits. On The Lamb sponsors these quarterly. We take turns at our different churches. They're basically dignity kits for the homeless and low income families in the area. Basic hygiene products, twenty dollar visa cards, resource lists; each round is a little different.

"Today we have the flyers for both gyms and the police station self defense lessons to go in the ladies kits. Fliers for the police lessons go in the men's. The mother/child bags have information for our Treasurer's house. He stocks diapers, wipes, formula, toys, and snacks for the kids. His entire three car garage is a warehouse. His sister is an extreme couponer and there's no children in their family."

"Wow." I had no clue this was here.

"It's usually just our club, and our churches' members, but Chris shows up every time."

"I have my resources." Mischief twinkles in his eyes.

"I have to give the official opening speech and assignments." Preacher claps Chris and Tank on their shoulders. "Have fun."

Chris and I get placed on the ladies' items assembly line, next to each other: chapstick and fliers. Tank is on the row behind us, stacking and folding the fliers into mini packets.

"Thank you all for coming." Preacher greets the room. "We have enough supplies for a hundred of each bag type today. Get the bag. Add your item. Pass it on. Simple process. If the stack between you and the next person starts piling up, there are boxes under the table to stand them in. This week we have actual diaper bags for the mom and child line."

A loud cheer fills the room.

"Our men's bags have tickets for a cut and shave at Sin's

Shop, and a flier for self defense lessons at the police station. Our ladies have tickets for haircuts at Sister Mary's salon and additional fliers for other self defense options. I would also like to remind the women of our congregations to get their own fliers. These classes are free."

Another cheer.

"Now, let us pray. Lord, bless these kits and the hands that fill them. May the supplies reach those in need in a timely manner, and the resources be abundant. Amen."

"Amen." The word echoes in the rafters.

The next two hours were filled with soft conversation and laughter. Most churches fill ziplock bags. Preacher's guys didn't just get diaper bags, the women's kits have pink and purple canvas bags. The men's kits are blue and green.

I look around at the people stuffing bags–*no, assembling kits*. Stuffing bags is careless, each movement here is calculated and full of love. There are grown men counting femme products without an ounce of shame. Merely chatting with their neighbors.

The items, too, are more than I would have expected. Toothpaste, toothbrush, floss, mini bottles of mouthwash. I see goat's milk soap, rather than the far cheaper, harsher bar soap. The men's bags have wallets. The ladies have small pocket books, *and makeup*. These bags have far more than the basics.

I look for the standard slips of paper that say 'Jesus loves you' or carry some well meaning bible verse. Yet, I see no place where they would be. Unless they are in the fliers bundle. Chris and I are at the end of our line.

I try not to dwell on my past. But, there was a time, before I aged out of the foster system, that I relied heavily on the generosity of local churches. Some foster families didn't believe in spending the stipend on me. The bike clubs let me hide in their shops, fed me when they could, but that was all. I wasn't one of theirs, just a favor to a man I hadn't seen in nine years.

Those kindness bags came with little dignity. Deodorant, wet wipes, toothpaste, and a slew of Bible verses. 'Jesus loves you.' 'Repent from your sins.' 'This is just a taste of hell.'

I would have done unspeakable things for one of *these* bags.

I shake myself from that train of thought. I survived. I'm here now. Tears sting my eyes.

As the last of the bags gets passed to the end, I excuse myself to the bathroom.

Tank follows, a few steps behind. Chris doesn't, pulled into conversation with Preacher once again.

Inside the restroom, I splash cold water on my burning face, erasing any signs of tears. I dry with paper towels and realize I washed off the makeup Kami had done. It's a shame too; it was so pretty.

More tears. What is wrong with me? I haven't leaked like this since before Kyle. Before him, this was a monthly occurrence. One that stopped. A weakness I couldn't afford.

I check my monthly tracker. As I suspected, the exact middle of my cycle. Hormones, my greatest nemesis.

Deep breath. Fix my face. Deep breath. Straighten my clothes. Deep breath. Mantra. 'I am stronger than my worst days. I am lighter than the load I carry. I can and will survive.' Deep Breath. Long exhale.

Feeling more myself, I step out of the washroom. Tank is leaning casually against the wall opposite the door.

"All good?" He asks, like he knows this was more than basic needs.

"Will be," I promise. To him, and to myself.

Chris meets us just as we reach the fellowship hall. "They won't let us help clean up." He sounds genuinely upset at being denied. “Preacher said to just take my beautiful lady out to dinner. Then he called me a cheap date.”

“Shoe fits,” Tank mutters under his breath, ignoring the glare Chris shoots his way. “Before we go, I want to talk with Preacher. Join me?”

We follow. Chris takes my hand in his, twining our fingers loosely.

“Heading out?” Preacher grins, glancing at our hands.

“Shortly.” Tank's voice is so gruff that it is hard to tell if he's angry or not. “Charity rides.”

“What about them?” Preacher responds. “We join a few each year.”

Tank twirls his fingers, indicating the room. “Run one.” I realize, his voice isn't just gruff, it's full of emotion. “The Calvary would ride. And fundraise. This–this is good work.”

Preacher seems taken aback, eyes wide. He takes a half step back. “I...uhh...I wouldn't know where to start.”

Tank nods. Pulls a business card from his wallet. “Call tomorrow. Sarge, Ghost, and I will help.”

“Me too.” Chris's voice blends into mine, a perfect harmony.

“Thank you.” Preacher's voice is soft, but he waves us away as he heads back to clean up.

I expected to head back home. Maybe stop at a diner for a bite to eat. I certainly didn't expect Chris to bring us to one of the nicest restaurants in town, Agosti.

We park, and Chris invites Tank to sit with us.

“Nah. I ain't chaperoning that close. I'll save that nonsense for Boss. I'll sit over at the bar; close enough to *see*, not close enough to *watch*." I laugh. Chris's lip twitches.

I've never been here, too expensive for me. Shoot. A Wendy's biggie bag is too expensive for me right now. Even Kyle never brought me here. I look everywhere, taking in every bit of extravagance.

Something must show on my face because he leans in and whispers in my ear. "Order whatever you like. This is my treat. I'm getting Tank's too, just don't tell him."

This feels like a test, and in my mind it absolutely is. What I order says a lot about me, maybe even more than Boss's coffee theories. An expensive dish means gold digger. A cheap dish means I doubt his ability to cover *any*thing. A salad says I'm watching my figure. *What does a steak say?*

I take controlled breaths as we skip the hostess stand. She smiles at us with pearly white, perfectly straight teeth. She gives a small wave as we skip the line entirely.

Chris pauses to whisper in her ear as we pass. She giggles and nods. He grins and takes my arm.

The entire moment feels surreal.

He leads us to a semi-secluded booth in the back. We can see part of the bar, but not all of it. I half expect a panicked call from Tank, but instead the hostess leads him around and sits him in the dark shadow of the bar well.

Before we can take our seats, a server bursts through the kitchen door and tackles Chris. I step back in shock.

Out of the corner of my eye, I see Tank spring to his feet. The bartender leans over and tells him something–something that has him sitting back down with a shake of his head and a half grin on his face.

That loosens something in my chest, and I take a seat as my date rolls around on the floor with the waitstaff. I look around for menus. They must have been tossed during the tackle, because one is on the opposite bench, and the other on the floor.

I fan myself with the one from the floor before flipping it open. There aren't even prices inside. Just pretty, flowy descriptions. The steak is a 'perfectly seasoned prime cut of grass fed, grain finished beef sourced locally for a farm to table flair. Grill seared to perfection at any desired temp. Will melt in your mouth.'

I snap the menu shut, scared to look any further.

Finally, Chris stands, pulling the other man to his feet easily. They wrap each other in a tight hug and laugh.

"I was starting to think you would never stop by again," the waiter says. "Three years is a long time." He turns to me. "This man is the reason I was able to open this place. If not for him, I would still be knocking on bank doors, begging for loans."

"You would have managed." Chris's face is slowly turning pink. The wrestling didn't embarrass him, but the genuine gratitude does.

The *owner* waves his hand, dismissing the comment. "Everything's on the house for you two." His phone beeps and he checks it. "And for your...chaperone?"

"You insult my honor, Antonio. I pay, like everyone else."

"No. Tip your server. That is all." Antonio turns and disappears before Chris can respond.

I have no clue what to say. I reopen the menu, still overly cautious of the whole thing.

"Antonio and I went to college together. He had a dream; I got him a loan. He seems to think he owes me his success." He looks at the menu. Doesn't open it, just looks at it sitting on the table. "I don't know why he bothered bringing us menus. He isn't going to let us order our own food. That's why I asked his wife to not tell him I was here."

I laugh. I can't help it. The whole thing is just...ridiculous. Chris cracks a smile, but it doesn't quite reach his eyes.

"More awkward date talk?" He asks.

I laugh more. It just bubbles out of me in a way I am not used to. Luckily, I actually googled first date questions after our last date. I felt like I knew most of it, from our previous interactions. But I am not the Queen of Research for nothing.

I fold my hands and sit tall, like a job interview. "So, tell me your five year plan."

He looks startled, but his eyes actually light up with hidden laughter. No more fake smiles.

"Well, it mostly depends on who sticks around those five years. I'd like to encourage the clubs to intermingle. I'd like to put in an actual playground on my property for the kids. If I can keep this pretty girl I'm seeing around, five years is more than enough for marriage. You?"

My cheeks burn. I'm sure I am slowly turning a sunburn red.

"Well, if the guy I'm seeing plays things right, within five years, I'd probably say yes. But my real goal is to grow Armani Investigation. I'd like to hire help, offer more services. I want to create safe spaces. Domestic shelters, queer friendly spaces."

"I like your style." He grins. "I want to host a Care Kit event at the bar. Invite all four clubs, their families. But I have nowhere to store everything; before or after."

"I bet Preacher would help, but I'd worry about the experts taking over. Maybe one of the food shelters could take the afters."

A blond waitress comes over with two plates of chicken parmesan and spaghetti, two wine glasses and a bottle of something that I am absolutely certain is expensive.

"I almost expected the steaks." Chris laughs, handing the

wine back. “Can we get sparkling cider instead? I know Antonio has good stuff.”

She shrugs and leaves.

We eat in relaxed silence. Occasionally one of us would mention another idea, building off each other's enthusiasm. We barely notice the cider getting delivered.

A decadent brownie is being placed on our table by an enthusiastic Antonio, when my phone goes off.

Without hesitation, Chris says, “Answer it. It could be Kami with an issue at the office.” My heart melts. As a business man himself, he gets it.

It is in fact Kami's name and number on my screen. I show him and we share a soft smile.

“Hey, Kami,” I answer.

She wails into the phone, crying so hard I think she might throw up. She's trying to tell me what's wrong, but every time she starts hyperventilating.

Sarge takes over her end of the call. “Setting Sun Hospital. Now. Boss got shot.”

FOURTEEN

We fly down the road, leaning into turns so tight, I wonder if we will wipe out. The scenery is a blur. From speed. From tears. I cling tightly to Chris as we enter the hospital lot, spinning gravel.

He drops me at the door, throwing dust in the air as he speeds off to park. Tank is already running across the lot, but I don't wait. There are more bikers inside. They can play guard.

Inside is absolute pandemonium. Spider and Sarge are trying to soothe a frantic Kami. Lockdown is next to them, arguing with the charge nurse. Others are trying to sneak past security and into the hospital.

"Not family. Not allowed," The charge nurse barks, nose to nose with Lockdown. "I don't care about your stupid gang rules. Girlfriends and old ladies aren't wives. Gang members aren't real brothers."

My blood boils at that. Boss chose these brothers. The same as he chose me. The only difference, I have a trump card to play.

Deep breath. Smooth my hair. Good. The helmet hasn't

messed up my braid. Deep breath. Get out my ID. Don't make eye contact with any of the others. This nurse is a shark in the water. She smells blood. Deep breath. Shoulders back. Strutt.

I slam my license on the counter. “Who is in charge here? Where is my brother?” Act in charge, the others will follow.

The charge nurse sends Kami's group one more venomous look, before strutting over to me. “How can I help you, sweetie.” Her eyes roam over my date outfit, a complete contrast to the bikers clogging up her lobby.

I see Chris come in. He looks at me handling the nurse, and joins the guys.

“I got a phone call that my brother had been shot.” I slide her my card. “Damian Smith.”

She freezes, hand on my license. “Oh, honey. There must have been a mix-up. The only Damian Smith here today is...” She lowers her voice to a whisper, like what she has to say is shameful. “...a black man. Worse, he's one of them.” She waves her hand, indicating the crowd. Then she slides my ID back at me.

A feral grin blossoms over my face. I slide the ID back. “I know. I may be white passing, but I am not white.” That's a bold face lie. I may tan well, but my ancestry is whiter than fresh fallen snow.

She snatches up my ID with a sneer. Her fingers clack against the keyboard. Fake nails. Not hygienic. Probably against policy. No name tag either. Convenient.

“Room 317. Family only.” She tosses my ID at me, along with a visitor's pass.

I catch them with a grin. “Not a problem. Is there a waiting room for his friends? They aren't going to leave. Would you rather tuck them away out of sight? Or leave them here to harass you?”

She glowers. "I'll have a conference room set up for them. But they have to get their own refreshments."

I barely contain my eye roll. I do flip her the bird as soon as she turns from me, making someone laugh.

"I got his room number and a visitor pass," I tell the crowd. "Nurse Ratched is very clear on the family rule. Luckily, I play the upset sister part very well. Plus, Boss and I have the same last name."

Several eyes widen. Knowing a biker's real name is a privilege granted to very few.

"I have arranged for a private waiting area, a conference room. Send the prospects for food and coffee. Even if the nurse did bring you something, I wouldn't trust it. She is a racist. Someone get me her real name. As fun as it is to compare her to true evil, fake names don't rain down destruction."

Kami pulls me into a tight hug, crying into my shoulder. I hand her over to Sniper, knowing he is Boss's top man.

"I can't get you into the room, yet. But I can keep everyone updated."

Tears are streaming down my face. But, I push on. I square my shoulders and march past the guards, flashing my pass.

Room 317 is empty. My heart stops. The bed is messy, blood stained, but there is no other sign anyone was ever here. I start hyperventilating.

"Woah, there." Callused hands catch me as I sink to the floor, pulling me back to my feet. "Deep breaths."

I can do that. Breathe. Information. Then panic.

"I was told this was my brother's room. He was shot."

I hope I'm talking to a medical professional, not another patient's family. His dress pants and button shirt tell me nothing.

"Damian Smith?" He asks. Medical then. "I'm Dr. Peter

Curette, trauma surgeon here at Setting Sun. I was Mr. Smith's first doctor."

"Trauma?" The word is barely a gasp on my lips.

"Just a fancy and scary way of saying I'm trained to handle unusual circumstances and improvise. Nothing to worry about. I was just heading for break while your brother is in surgery with my colleagues. I'm not needed in their way."

I nod. "Can you tell me what you know first? The lack of information is stressing the family out." I give my phone a little shake. Let him think I mean our parents, or cousins, or whatever. Family for us, is the bikers in the other room.

"Absolutely. Mr. Smith was shot twice. Once in the shoulder, once in the thigh. Both bullets managed to miss anything vital, although the one in the thigh is close to his femoral artery. It's the reason for the rushed surgery. We don't want to chance disrupting it. His shoulder wound was clean. He may need some Occupational Therapy to regain full movement, but the risk of complications from that shot is low. The thigh is our primary concern right now. The Orthopedic surgeon will know more about that."

He pats my hand and leaves. I'm left standing in the doorway, mind spinning.

A nurse comes by with a handful of linens.

"Oh. I thought Nurse Viesion was preventing visitors." Her words are kind and soft. "Really hammering the family rule, that one."

I nod my head at the empty room. "My brother."

Her eyes widen. "Well, I'm just here to freshen up. No need for him to return to bloody sheets, just because Head Nurse Viesion is on one of her power trips. If you need anything, ask for Orderly T at the nurses station. I'll take care of you."

I thank her, and sit in the visitor seat. My fingers tremble as

I type out my update. Immediately my phone dings back with a million questions. Questions I don't have the answers to.

My phone hovers over the contact info for Ghost. It almost kills me to ask for help. But, my mind is not clear enough to gather information on my own.

Charge Nurse. Last name Viesion.

I don't care what he does with that information. It may be nothing. They are different clubs. Clubs that don't intermingle much, and Ghost is a reclusive man. He may have never met Boss. May not care.

I put my head in my hands and wait. And wait. And wai...

A gentle hand shakes my shoulder. I jump to awareness in a panic. I can't believe I fell asleep–actually I can. It has been an emotion packed day.

Dr. Curette smiles down at me. "I was just paged. Your brother is on his way down. Surgery went well. He should make a complete recovery."

"Can the others come see him?" I ask.

"Others?"

"His girlfriend and club members. The charge nurse said family only. I only barely managed to get them a private place to wait."

A look of rage flashes across his face, gone as fast as it came. "Motorcycle club?"

I nod.

"After he is settled back in his room, he can have up to three visitors at a time. If anyone gives you problems, tell them to page me. I can only give family updates, technically. As his sister, you can identify your other brothers, half siblings, right? I can get them passes. No more than two though or Nurse Viesion will start crying foul."

I offer a small watery smile. "Thank you."

Small problem. I don't know anyone's legal name. Other than Chris and Kami.

My phone dings in my hand. A message from Ghost.

On it.

On... oh. Nurse Viesion is going to be having a bad day soon. Ghost will make sure of it.

Ghost! He would know! Not just which brothers Boss would prefer, but legal names too. *Right*?

I fire off another message. The response comes back just as quick.

Lockdown-Jessie Baldwin

Cowboy-Wayne Oakley

I give the doctor both their names and road names.

My hands shake. I barely manage to slide the phone back into my pocket. Coldness sweeps through my body.

The nurses wheel Boss in. I clamber out of the way. There's a flurry of activity as they get everything situated. Watching them move him from the gurney to the bed terrifies me. He looks so fragile. I fear they will drop him, break him. But it's a smooth transition.

My heart races and I struggle for breath. I reach out to touch him, and freeze. My hand hovers just over his.

I don't belong back here. Kami should be back here fussing over him. Lockdown should be back here demanding answers.

But I'm the one who is, right now. Boss claimed me as a sister, and I have the name to back it up. I got in where the others were stonewalled. I played the system and won. He'll be so proud.

My hand clenches down around his. My phone is buzzing in my pocket, but I can't bring myself to pull it out. I just stand there, holding his hand in mine, waiting.

Lockdown slips into the room. He wraps me in a loose hug, like he is afraid I'll break.

“Thank you, for whatever you did to get us access.”

“Not fast enough. Doctor says once he's settled he can have three visitors at a time. I just... I barely know him. He calls me sister, we have the same name, but I don't know him.”

“You know enough.” His voice is so certain.

“Do I?” Tears well, again. “What's his blood type? Genetic history? Medical conditions?”

“They ask, you do what the rest of us do. Call Ghost. Claim our other brother keeps detailed records. You get who had what problems mixed up.”

“But he's a Cavalry, not a Cadillac.”I cry, shoulders hunching in on myself.

“And he's an amazing government trained hacker. Ghost knows everything about everybody. Probably even how many hairs are on our heads at any given moment.”

A laugh bubbles up. I choke on it.

“Where's Cowboy?”

“He won't come up. Giving his name clears him for medical decisions and updates. But he has hospital trauma. I'm genuinely surprised he managed the waiting room. Why'd you pick him?”

“I asked Ghost.”

He laughs. “Sounds right. Need a break? You've been up here a while.”

“Would...would it be awful of me to go home? I...I did my part. I got you in. Got information circling. Got visitor rights for everyone, soon. I just...it's been a long day. I...I want my bed.”

He looks at me as if he can see into the depths of my soul. As if every broken crack is visible. “If that's what you *need*, go. I've got Boss from here. But, if you're running, don't. I'm not sure I'm strong enough to stop him from chasing you.” He pulls me into a tight warm embrace. “He claimed you as his sister.

Same as he claimed me as his brother, my first day out. Once you're his, he doesn't let go. The man nearly followed me off a bridge. He does not give up."

"I'm not running. I'll even take Spider with me. That kid spends enough time here with his Gran," I mumble into his shoulder.

"Sarge or Tank, too." A tight squeeze and he releases me. "I do believe you are on a parole of your own, right now."

A small laugh. "Parole. I like it. I've been calling them my babysitters and guard dogs."

"Wardens." Lockdown chuckles. "Maybe I should suggest Warden take a turn on guard duty. For the humor. I mean it would be funny for us, but you would hate it. You would never even see a window."

He grabs a chair and pulls it to the side of the bed. Then another. I take the offered seat.

"Tell me about him? All of them?"

And surprisingly, he does.

I fall asleep to stories of bike runs, police chases and overall bad choices.

It takes me a moment to realize where I am when I wake up. There's a hand rubbing my back, and fingers playing in my hair. I freeze, and both stop moving.

"Morning, sis."

My heart soars to hear Boss awake and well. I lift my head, and his hand falls off my head. His fingers tangle in a curl, and he gives a playful tug.

Chris chuckles at my side. Kami is asleep in the chair on the other side of the hospital bed. Boss's fingers playing in her hair too.

"I sent everyone home." Chris resumes rubbing my back. "Told everyone to get back to their jobs. Clubs don't run themselves. Lockdown is on a food run, for you girls. He'll take over here when he gets back. Sadly, I have a bar to run."

"Nothing sad about it, Keep," Boss interrupts. "That bar is your baby. Can't leave it with a babysitter for too long."

Chris chuckles.

"What happened?" I ask. "Do you know who shot you? Or why?"

"I rode through some of the lower income neighborhoods, just riding to be seen. Us presidents decided that the community needs to know we are looking out for them. And whoever is hurting our community needs to know we have its back."

Chris hands him a glass of water, and he gulps it down greedily.

"Anyway, there was a young lady–maybe eighteen, probably younger. She was struggling with a car seat, an arm full of groceries, and trying to get her key to the door. I stopped to help her. Took the groceries, so that she could get the door unlocked. She kept looking over her shoulder, like she thought I would take her groceries and run. A man popped up out of nowhere, and she started screaming, trying to drag me in and close the door."

He stopped for another glass of water. Chris took the glass from him to refill again.

"The dude was hollering that she couldn't keep the baby from him. He was going to get custody because she was 'just an underage whore who had no business corrupting innocent children to her sinful ways.' That's when he noticed me. His words became even more hateful, calling her words I will not repeat. He shouted at me that 'the whore and her spawn' were his property and that I had no right to interfere with the natural order of things. Next thing I know, a piercing pain shoots through my thigh and the girl starts whimpering. Another pain shot through my shoulder and sirens started wailing nearby. Everything gets fuzzy after that."

"Adrenaline," Chris and I say in unison. Boss chuckles and shakes his head.

"Already speaking in stereo. I hear wedding bells."

"Oh, no." I plaster on a fake look of shock and horror. My hand flies up to my chest. "Better call the nurses to adjust his meds. He's having auditory hallucinations."

"Fuck." The word comes out so sharp, Chris and I both startle back. "Fucking morphine. There goes five years of sobriety. Down the drain."

"Ex-fucking-cuse me." The venom in my voice surprises even me. Chris takes a step back, eyes widening ever so slightly. "Are you saying you intentionally got yourself shot? So that the doctors could push morphine?"

He shakes his head. "No, but..."

"Did you beg the nurses or doctors for extra meds? Did you pretend your pain was worse than it was for stronger drugs?"

"Well, no, but..."

"Do you forgo even ibuprofen when you overwork yourself and ache? Because it's a pain med too?"

"No, but..."

"But nothing! You take the meds that you need. Ibuprofen doesn't break your sobriety. Doctor prescribed and administered drugs don't either. As long as you are not abusing the system to get high. You are being given the pain relief your body needs to heal. If you are worried about the meds they will send you home with, we can handle that too. Firstly, we tell your doctor your history. They will prescribe the weakest option that still works. Secondly, you give the bottle to someone you trust. To dole them out when you need them, or tell you it's not time yet. You have not broken your sobriety. You are injured and healing!"

A slow clap from the door. A small crowd gathered during my tirade. I guess I may have gotten a little loud, but my point stands.

Dr. Curette steps forward, dispersing the crowd. "Wonderfully said. I understand the temptations. But, properly monitored and dosed meds won't get you high. I will work with you."

Tears prickle threaten to spill down Boss's face. "Thank you, Doc."

I squeeze his hand. "Sleep. Get well. Listen to the doctor." I let go.

"Thank you," Dr. Curette whispers in my ear as he passes by.

"So few see things my way. Most consider that anything with *potential* breaks sobriety. You, Mr. Smith, have a wonderful support system around you. People you can trust to keep you from abusing your meds and to hold you accountable when you no longer need them. We will, of course, go with the weakest possible medication that still does its job."

"But the morphine?" Our tirades had woken Kami? "It's an opioid, right?"

"It is, but, it was medically administered, at the proper dosage. We did not get your husband high. His sobriety is intact, by my standards. I don't know his sponsor's beliefs, but this is one definition that each must make for themselves. Addiction is hard. Staying sober, even harder. I will not lie and say the coming days will be easy. But an iron will and unshakable support system can be stronger."

"We aren't married," Kami mumbles.

"Yet, you will be steadfast at his side, won't you?" The

doctor's eye twinkled, like he knew the world's secrets. “He claimed you. You're here. Old Lady may not have a legal status, but it *is* a recognized one.”

“Tell that to Nurse Ratched,” I mutter under my breath.

“I will.” His self assured grin promises retribution for the insensitive nurse. “My E.R., my rules. Unfortunately, while I can verbally reprimand her, no further action can be taken, from my end. Mr. Smith was *technically* no longer a patient of the E.R. and had been transferred to surgery.”

“Ahhh.” It clicks perfectly in my mind. Nurse Viesion used the great power of loopholes. Pity for her, she's a novice; I'm the master.

FIFTEEN

Chris drives me home. Lockdown is just a couple blocks behind us; giving us privacy. This ride is nothing like the earlier ones. Where the ride to our wonderful date–was that just this afternoon?–was light hearted and fun, racing against Tank, this ride is slow and solemn. Much slower than the breakneck speeds we did to the hospital.

I climb off the bike, tears falling down my cheeks. Chris wipes them away when he takes my helmet. He takes my hand, while he puts it in his saddlebag. A small squeeze.

He brushes a loose hair from my face; his hand ends up on the back of my neck. We just look at each other for a moment. A breath of time.

And then wie're kissing. Frantic. Desperate. Afraid to let go.

But we do.

I can see Lockdown at the end of the road.

Chris squeezes my hand again. Watching, he waits just until my hand touches the door to leave.

But inside...

Spider is sprawled over the desk in the corner. The one where I set him up to study. Blood pools around him. His papers are soaked in red. His cup, a Spiderman mug that I gave him as a joke, is busted in the puddle. Coffee mixes with blood to create the creepiest color swirl I've ever seen.

I force myself to look away.

Ember is slumped against my reception desk. Did anyone tell me she would be here? I don't remember. As I get closer, I see the blood. Spattered against the wall behind her. Dripping down her neck. A cut, deep and red, slashed across her throat. Her eyes, her pretty blue eyes, look up at me accusingly.

Where is Lockdown? He was just behind us. He should be here.

My eyes flit back to Spider. Lockdown doesn't need to see that, not without a warning. The kid is one of his.

I burst out the door, a scream teasing my lips. Nothing. No one. No sign of Lockdown. I back up slowly, back into the office.

A gun shot startles me into motion.

I run deeper into the building. I'm going to lock myself in my apartment. Where is Lockdown? I'm scared to look.

I turn the corner to the stairwell and the sight freezes my blood. Sarge is sitting at the top of the steps, head tipped back against my door. His arms are peacefully crossed over his knees. The same stance as this morning.

God was that just this morning?

But what really boils my blood–or freezes it, I can't tell anymore– is the bullet hole between his eyes.

I scream.

My throat burns, but I can't stop screaming. All I see around me is red, blood red.

Someone touches my arm. I start swinging, wildly. I have no clue if I hit anyone, anything.

I can't breathe. Am I still screaming? Can I stop for a breath? My body shakes. My face stings with tears. I can't *breathe.*

All I can hear is the rush of blood–blood!–in my ears. My heart is pounding. I hear each beat, louder than the roar of wind on the back of a bike.

Strong arms wrap around me, pinning mine down. I struggle, but have no room to break free.

My vision is still red. Nothing but red. If I could see my attacker, I could counter.

Instead, I go rock still. Lull them into a false sense of security.

Sound starts to break through the white noise. A deep voice. I can't make out words. Just the deep timber of his voice. The vibrations of it against my back.

It's soothing. A false sense of security. I squeeze my eyes shut.

I twist my arms until I can reach up around the ones on my chest. My nails dig into the flesh, but I quit fighting.

"Shhhhhhh. You're okay. Shhhhhhhh."

Is that Lockdown? What took him so long. Are we really okay?

"Shhhhhhh. Breathe. In... hold... out... Good. Again. Match me."

The chest against my back takes an exaggerated slow breath. I try to match it, but I can't. Panic wells back up.

“Shhhhhh. It's okay. You're doing great. Keep breathing.”

Sound returns to me. I hear crying. God's above. Lockdown is trying to comfort me, and Spider is dead. Just around the corner.

“Shhhhhhh. It's okay. Slow breaths.” Another exaggerated breath against my back. I struggle to copy.

More noise reaches me. I hear beeping, slow and steady. An alarm?

Another slow breath.

I peel my eyes open. The bright lights accost my vision. Spots dance, more red.

My breathing eases slightly, and the arms around me relax a little.

“Miss Smith, are you with us?” A voice in my ear. Familiar, but not Lockdown. I freeze, again. “Keep breathing.”

My vision is clearing. Boss is sitting up straight in his bed, staring at me. Kami is crying. The monitor beeps.

Another breath.

The arms let go. I spin around to face...

...Doctor Curette.

“Panic attacks and nightmares are not unusual during these circumstances.”

‘Not unusual;’ very different from ‘normal.’

My face heats. I'm certain my face is as red as my nightmare. I step away.

“Let's have the guys take you and Kami home.” Boss's voice is soft, quiet. “You'll both rest better in an actual bed.”

I shake my head. The nightmare still too vibrant in my mind.

“Where's Spider?” My voice is rough, raspy.

“He's at the clubhouse.” Boss furrows his brows. “Why?”

Dr. Curette is taking notes on Boss's file. He looks like he isn't paying me any attention, but I can feel his gaze when I'm not looking.

"Bad dream."

Kami shudders. "I don't want to go anywhere. Not while you're stuck here."

"Well," Curette interrupts. "If Mr. Smith's numbers stay right where they are, I'll be sending him home in the morning before I end my shift." He looks at his watch. "In about two hours, or so. It's 3 o'clock now. I begin discharge rounds at 5. I can start here. Everyone can leave together."

"Thank you, Doc." Boss grins. "Makes my girls feel better."

Five a.m. came much quicker than expected. Lockdown had brought Kami and I large coffees and muffins before returning to the waiting room. Visiting hours don't resume until seven, and we hope to be long gone by then.

Dr. Curette comes in with a big smile. "Great news. I got super ibuprofen for you: 1000 mg dose. This is important: no more than one every eight hours. I'm not worried about addiction here. I'm much more concerned about liver and cardiovascular function."

"Thank you, again, doc." The smile on Boss's face is filled with relief.

"Bad news: no motorcycles."

Boss groans. "How long?"

"Unknown. I have two conditions that have to be met before I can say riding your bike is safe. First, that shoulder wound needs to be not just scabbed, but scarred. No open wounds. Don't need it popping back open. Secondly, P.T. has to clear you. Muscle damage is no small thing."

Another groan.

"You got lucky. The thigh shot missed your artery. Barely. The shoulder shot is a little more than a graze."

"I turned to take cover."

"And it may have saved your life. That bullet didn't penetrate anything, missed your bones, but scraped a good bit of muscle. These muscles need to heal and regrow. I've never seen someone ride a motorcycle without using arms or legs. Sorry."

"I get it, doc. I just ain't happy about it."

"But, you're alive, so be unhappy. I'm trying to keep you that way."

SIXTEEN

I did not get to go home with Boss and Kami–not that I wanted to. Spider picked up Boss with his sidecar, Kami on the back. Instead, Sarge met me at the front door of the hospital.

The look on his face is grim. “Ghost wants to talk to you.”

“Okay.” I hold my hand out.

I've gotten used to Ghost's virtual-only quirks. I don't know why he doesn't do things face to face, but I respect it.

“At his place.” The words are icy, bewildered.

“Where?”

“Top secret. That he wants you there... It says a lot. Ghost doesn't trust easily. Something makes him trust you. Or at least, he wants to.”

Sounds familiar.

“Then, let's go.”

Ghost's place is in the middle of the woods outside of town, on the edge of Tuskegee National Forest. I'm certain the property is much larger than the short driveway and small yard imply.

Sarge knocks on the door. A specific order of raps and knocks. Ba-da, ba-da, ba-da-da-da. It creaks open, barely an inch. Sarge doesn't move, something clicks, twice, then a bell chimes in the distance. Only then, does Sarge open the door the rest of the way. He still doesn't enter. Instead he waves me forward.

"He only asked for you. Go straight down the hall, last room on the left." I raise an eyebrow at him. "That's where Ghost said he'll be. I've got some stuff to check around here for him. I'll be back for you in about an hour."

I swallow my nerves. Alone. With a man I've only ever spoken to virtually. In his booby trapped house. With no escape ride and no security. No go bag.

I follow Sarge's directions, looking over everything as I go. The old, but clean, furniture. The pictures on the walls–men in uniform interspersed with members of The Cavalry–are lower than usual. Mid-wall rather than up high.

The door is open, a table in the middle of the room, the black table cloth covered in silver *somethings*. In the corner, a man sits in front of a computer, fingers flying frantically over the keyboard. The hood of his sweater is up, obscuring his face.

"See anything over there you like?" I was expecting the usual mechanical voice. I knew that wasn't really his voice, I've heard it before. But still, the humanness takes me by surprise.

I come closer. The silver bits on the table are jewelry. A couple necklaces, bracelets, earrings.

"Is this a belly ring?"

His fingers stop. "There's a clit ring there too. Less likely to be seen, even in a basic strip search."

I choke on my next breath. "What?"

He turns his chair, the wheels coming fully into view. "This is what I have that I can put a discrete tracker on or in."

His face is covered by a half mask. His green eyes are all I can see. What little of his face that is uncovered is completely shrouded in shadow.

"You... I... a clit ring?" My face flushes with heat.

"Like I said, discrete. I also suggest something not so discrete, a decoy. You've had security on you for about a week, between the cop and Sarge. Suddenly dropping them spells trap. If they see a sudden addition of jewelry, well, two plus two is four. Their problem is, we're multiplying. Same problem. Same answer. Different sign." He wheels over to the desk. "I'm paranoid as hell. I know that."

"No, it makes sense. I'm just not so sure about piercing anything down there." Total lie. I have always wanted piercings. But between the cost and healing time, I keep putting them off, just like my leather jacket.

He shrugs. "Belly ring wouldn't be immediately noticeable. Neither would the bobby pins." He waves his hand at them.

I had originally discounted them. Too small, surely. Apparently not.

"I definitely want the bobby pins. They make a great lockpick, but I want a second discrete tracker. Just in case anyone notices them, or looks." I look over the table. The heart necklace and the charm bracelet are my favorites. But for the discrete...

"Who would do the piercing?" I don't clarify.

"Ember. She does the piercing at The Camo Bullet."

My fingers trace over them. "I'll do it."

Those green eyes sparkle. "Let me add the trackers to everything you picked. Then Sarge can take you to Ember."

He picks up a pair of tweezers and starts working. Tiny microchips get attached to each piece I picked. "These are water proof. I'm not going to bore you with the details, but know that you're safe to swim or shower with them on. Keep at least one on you at all times, preferably more. I will have live tracking on them. If Tank or Sarge can't reach you, I will send them your location. Help will be on its way."

I nod, but he's not looking.

"I suggested hourly check-ins, but Ember argued you actually need sleep if this is going to work. She talked me down to every four. I also agreed to compromise the midnight check in, if you are okay with me checking your location every night." He looks up at me.

"I assumed you would have twenty-four seven access."

"Doesn't mean I have permission to watch it. Consent is a thing."

I chuckle. "You have my permission to check my location at any time, until this is resolved. We can discuss further monitoring later. It's not paranoia if they really are out to get you."

He laughs. "I mean, it's still paranoia, it's just *useful* paranoia."

A computer dings behind him, then starts beeping. He glances at the screen, but finishes his task.

After securing my new jewelry in travel cases–and giving me the necklace to start with, he wheels over to his computers. He starts scrolling multiple screens.

"I have something. Not sure it's a bad something, but it ain't good."

"What?"

"Your new friend, Kami. She dated Kyle Dutcher. The information I have implies there was some overlap."

"Same sources that said I was still with him?" I'm not bitter, really.

"No, those sources were *his* social media accounts, where he is still posting about you and his relationship with you.

These sources had to do some digging into her history. Not to say too much, but maybe a bit of invasive digging."

I acknowledge the hint with a nod. "When?"

"Eighteen to eight months ago. At least, that's what I've found so far. Dinner at Vendotori's. Nights at Skybar. He wasn't afraid of being seen in public with her."

"Work parties?" I ask.

He turns to look at me. "Kyle's company doesn't do work parties. Lucky for pizza days. However, client and business dinners... I see no evidence of her being at any. Did he ever take you?"

"Dinners, no. But several parties that were supposedly for work. He'd assign my attire, have a fit if any of his coworkers actually talked to me, and get handsy."

"Send me dates." His voice was cold enough to freeze hell. "I'll look into them. Do you want to confront her?"

"Less of a confrontation and more of a discussion. I didn't know about her, she may not have known about me. I'll loop Boss in, too."

"Jewelry first. Just in case."

I smile at his concern. "Obviously. Before I go, I want to thank you for sending me Lockdown and Cowboy's information. Why'd you pick them."

He scratches the back of his neck. "Well, Lockdown is the VP, and err, Cowboy needed the push?" He starts strong, but turns the sentence into a question.

I nod, accepting the answer.

He puts everything in a drawstring bag, even the cases. "Sarge will take you straight to Ember." He walks, err, rolls, with me to the door.

Sarge is stacking wood on a shelf, around the side of the house when we come out. I didn't realize when we first got here that there were no stairs. Just a flat entry to the house.

Everything is at the perfect height for Ghost to reach on his own.

"Be right there!" Sarge hollers. "Just finishing up. Prospect is coming by tonight with the groceries."

Ghost growls, so low I dont think Sarge can hear it around the corner.

"Stop growling." Guess he could. Or he just knows his friend well.

Sarge comes around the corner. His shirt is soaked with sweat making it stick in all the right places. The man is eye candy, for sure. He whips it off and swaps it for one in his saddlebag.

"Where to next, princess?"

My lip curls at the nickname.

"Take her to Bullet. She needs Ember's expertise. Oh, and feed her. Hospital food is shit. Trust me." He rolls back and the door slams.

"Have fun?" Sarge asks.

"A little. It was *interesting*, for sure. I hope he lets me visit some time. I could learn a lot about cyber research from him. I'm good, but I only go so deep."

Sarge laughs. "Pretty sure he lives in the Deep Dark Web. Not exactly legal."

I faux pout. "Fine. I'll keep him as an anonymous source."

"Good girl."

I glare. He laughs. We ride.

The Camo Bullet is a really cool tattoo parlor on the edge of town. The kind that everyone complains about, yet still has a wait list six months long for appointments.

The building is a small space, but holds true to its name. The entirety of the exterior is painted in camo, but if you look close, you can see a lot of smaller designs. The name itself is written into the camouflage paint in a hidden graffiti style. So is a large bullet design. I would love to meet the artist that did this.

The door is locked, but Sarge pulls out a chunky key ring from his saddlebag.

He grins at me. "I'm one of three with keys to every business. Tank and Sniper are the others. As sergeant-at-arms, security falls to me." He unlocks the door and lets me in.

"Ember comes in at about nine. There's a bed in the backroom. The guys use it for really long sessions. Go nap."

I glare. The last thing I need is another nightmare.

"Not asking, cupcake."

My glare intensifies.

"Don't like that one either? No problem. I'll find the right term of endearment. You'll see, honey."

I shake my head. "I'll endear my fist to your face." Okay, not my best line, but I'm not exactly operating at one hundred percent right now..

"Sleep."

Before I can respond to his overbearing demand, the door opens again. Sarge whips around, gun leveled at the newcomers.

"Woah, man, just us." Tank steps in between Ember and the gun, hands raised placatingly. "Ghost said he booked Ember an early morning job. I see now why he was being so secretive about it. What're we piercing?" His grin is mischievous. But only until his wife whacks him in the stomach.

"Never you mind where." She flashes him a dirty look but turns to me with a grin. "So, where?" We all laugh.

I hand her the cases Ghost prepared for me. I don't explain. If she is as good as they say, she'll know. Her mischievous grin tells me that my hunch was right.

"Well, step on back, my lady. This is gonna hurt."

The men exchange glances, and raised eyebrows.

"Curiosity is killing me here, sweetheart." Sarge laughs as we walk away.

"I'm growling at you," I reply over my shoulder, before Ember closes the door.

She raises an eyebrow at me, cleaning her equipment, and motioning for me to undress.

"He seems intent on finding–and I quote him on this–*my* term of endearment." I curl my lip. "Hasn't found one yet."

She laughs. "That's one of Sarge's quirks. *His girls* get terms of endearment. Everyone else gets 'ma'am'." She uses her first alcohol swab.

"Yours?" She lines the gun up for my first piercing.

"Queenie." *Click.*

"Ow."

One down, three to go. Why did I choose these again? Oh yeah, I'm almost as paranoid as Ghost. Almost. Maybe. Probably not. Half as paranoid? A quarter?

My lost train of thought distracts me enough for the second piercing. *Click.*

"You can call it here." Ember looks genuinely concerned for me. I would too. Spontaneous decisions like this aren't exactly considered sane.

"We all cope with threats against our lives differently." I respond. "Keep going. Just give me something else to focus on."

"Like what?" She wipes my belly with the alcohol wipe.

"Anything."

"Uhm...Belle, do you know Belle? The hussy at the gym? Anyway, Belle tried waiting for Tank in his office, naked. She sure was surprised when he came in with three other guys to talk shop." *Click.* "Tried to claim I set her up."

"Did they fire her?" I ask.

Ember laughs, a little maniacally. "Nope." She pops the 'p' with a grin. "She's been assigned as assistant to Sarge during the self defense classes. Basically, he gets to attack her. Over and over. To demonstrate. Of course." *Click.*

"Of cour–son of a bitch!" The words come out a groan of pain. "That last one–should have started with it."

She laughs again. "I was *trying* to give you space to back out."

I force a smile to my face. "This may *look* impulsive, but I've researched these piercings off and on for the last seven years. I just never could bring myself to actually do it. The addition of nanochip trackers just sealed the deal. Security and pleasure."

It is at this exact moment that I realize: I still don't have my bug out bag. I left the black backpack at the office. A sign of trust in not just Tank as my guard yesterday, but in Chris as my date. My breathing increases, and my heart races.

I stand, abruptly, hands shaking. "I was going to tip you," I tell Ember. "With a joke about getting my dream piercings for free, but I just realized. I don't have my bag. Tank wouldn't even let me grab my wallet yesterday."

"Because even if Chris wasn't the gentleman we all know he is, my husband would never let you pay for your own dinner. And yes, these are free. Ghost covered the piercings. Something about a friend actually letting him play with his toys?"

I chuckle. Friendly wasn't the vibe I got from the paranoid hacker. Then again, I did just meet him.

"I honestly can't believe you did all four. Here are a couple bottles of saline, clean them, at least twice a day. If you need more, just ask. No playing with them or their locations"–she gives me a level look, not subtle– "for at least two weeks. After that, clean them after. Immediately."

I've done the research, but she is a professional. I let her explain it all without interrupting.

I can't help myself when she's done. I have to ask. "Do you have any?"

"Just my nips. Don't need the other, Tank has a Jacob's ladder. Besides, I would never make it a week without a *bike* ride."

"That I didn't need to know." I fake gag. "Wait. A whole week? How am I getting home?"

"I made Tank let me drive my truck. The guys will follow. Now, since you wanted to gag about my man's piercings, I'm not gonna tell you what Chris has had me pierce."

SEVENTEEN

I'm almost afraid to enter my building this morning. Between yesterday's break in and last night's nightmare, I would rather be anywhere else. I hold my breath while Tank and Sarge clear the building–even the apartment. Nothing is out of place–no new notes.

I should go upstairs and go to bed. It's Sunday; the office is closed. It's been a long week.

But my feet don't move that direction. Instead, I sit at my reception desk. Sarge takes a seat on the lounge chair, and waits. Neither of us know what I'm going to do. I don't even know what I'm thinking.

We sit in silence. Sarge watches me as I stare at the wall.

I like that he doesn't interrupt. This is part of my process. No distractions. Just staring at the wall until I get an idea. Could be minutes, could be hours.

The words 'pseudo sister' sit heavy in my mind. It's a clue, if only I could decipher it. The paint could be bought anywhere, but that picture–that came from a police file. One of

Uncle Ludwig's guys is involved. Guys I've known for a long time. Except Doe.

But, why would he attack his partner? It takes him back off motor patrol. Uncle Ludwig won't let him patrol without a partner. Unless, that was the point? Get put back on babysitting duty. Keep a closer eye on *my* investigation.

Again, why? Most of my information, he gave me. Bad information I had to sort through–and still came up short.

Where is Missy? If she isn't part of the pattern, not a victim, where did she go? Why? Is it related?

Who shot Boss? Was it random? Did the woman he was helping fit our profile? Could she have been an intended victim?

Am I seeing unicorns where there should be horses?

Lunchtime comes and goes. I keep staring at the wall. At some point, Sarge gets out his phone. Good for him.

I keep staring.

A knock on the glass. Sarge surges to his feet and rushes to the door. Preacher and a woman come in. She has an insulated casserole carrier in her hands, and a gigantic purple purse hanging off her arm, matching her purple pants suit and hat.

"We heard about Boss. Spoke with Tank. Everyone is going to meet here for an impromptu dinner." Preachers's voice is unsteady.

"My idea." Hers is not. "Boss is a friend of Preacher's. When our friends get hurt, we feed them." She glares at him, as if he's arguing. Maybe he did. "Now, my husband insists we can't take anything to the compounds–says it breaks some macho bike rules–so here we are. I was going to take it to that bar. Lord knows they all mingle there, but Preach said you were Boss's sister, and, well, this is a family moment."

She is a constant flurry of motion, like watching a human tornado, never pausing to breathe. What I thought was one casserole in a carrying case turns out to be three. She lines these up on the counter next to the coffee machine.

"Tank said something about roast chicken? Anyway, I made several sides. More to be delivered this week and next. I can do meats too, but Preach said bikers take that seriously, and I wouldn't want to offend nobody."

Out of her purse comes paper plates, plastic silverware, and even serving spoons. By the time she's done pulling things out, I am firmly reminded of Mary Poppins.

"Thank you?"

She pivots on her heels. "Oh mercy me! I didn't even introduce myself! I just came in all a flurry!" She wipes her hands on her dress before reaching one out to shake mine. "I'm Preacher's wife, Mary. And yes, I have heard every Mother Mary joke out there. They don't bother me none."

I grin. "Actually, I was thinking of Mary Poppins with that magic bag of yours."

She grins back with a wink. Then she pulls out a bottle of wine, and a sleeve of red solo cups.

She swirls over to her husband, who is in deep conversation with Sarge. "Pop this top, darling. Even Jesus drinks wine."

Preacher laughs before accommodating his wife's request. "Do remember, it's barely afternoon."

"And it's Sunday," she retorts. "A day of rest and relaxation. Just be glad I didn't send you out for fish." They share a laugh.

Another knock on the glass. Tank and Ember have arrived. They come in with arms full of roasting pans. Mary immediately rushes over to assist.

"Roast chicken and ham," Ember announces proudly. "Tank and Prospect have been at it all day."

"Chocolate pie and banana pudding," Tank adds. "Ember's been busy, too."

The dishes are added to the counter just as Boss and Kami

arrive. Kami and Ember exchange hugs and introduce themselves to Mary.

I look around my crowded office–no, crowded isn't the right word. Full. Brimming. Busy–and the lack of dining furniture. I have one small table in the corner and what is essentially a minimalist living room set.

"Why don't we eat in the conference room?" The words are out before I can think them through. "I'd hate to move all the food, but there's more room in there. And a table we can all sit at."

"Easy solution," Ember interjects. "We fix plates out here and eat in there. And by we fix plates, I mean the men fix our plates. Cavalry tradition, and they are the club with the most men present."

We all laugh.

"Except Boss. He's injured."

Mary wrings her hands. "Well, I wasn't raised for no man to wait on me. I'll fix Boss's plate."

"No ma'am." Sarge's voice is quiet but firm, just as there is one more knock on the door. "I'll get Boss and Kami's." He glances to see who Tank let in and grins. "Keep will get Armani's. Preacher will get yours. Tradition."

Ember takes her by the arm. "There is no point trying to argue."

I grab the bottle of wine, stack of cups, and Kami's arm and follow.

I pour the wine, a couple fingers in each cup. Just as I'm finishing up, Mary whips another bottle out of her bottomless bag.

"I almost forgot! Sparkling cider for Boss."

I pour his glass and the guys bring in the plates. Each of them carry two, theirs and a lady's, and take a seat. Except Boss and Sarge, who gives Boss and Kami theirs before slipping back out to fix his. Boss slides into the seat between me and Kami.

I notice Boss has a white knuckle grip on the table. I raise my eyebrow at him. He gestures to his cup. 'I really want the wine.' He mouths the words at me.

I lean close. "It's sparkling cider. Or at least yours is. I can ask Mrs. Mary to put the bottle away."

"No. If I don't have to avoid my own glass, I should be okay." He takes a cautious sip.

It doesn't take long for conversation to turn to the case. And by not long, I mean immediately.

"How's the new tracker treating you?" Ember asks with a wicked grin. "Regret it yet?"

"Nope." I grin back. "Never will, if it does its job. Any of them."

"Sarge mentioned you think there is police involvement?" Tank questions.

"I know there is." My voice is firm. "That phrase 'pseudo sister', I used it when I debriefed the squad."

"Are there any suspects?" Bless Mrs. Mary.

"They think it's James," Preacher clearly still disagrees.

"The Doe boy? Surely not." Her little gasp and hand clench is a bit dramatic.

"He's the only one I haven't known for awhile," I admit. "And when he offered to 'sneak' me some information, it was nearly useless. Lots of fake files, and a couple missing."

"He seems like such a sweet boy."

"I just don't think it's him," Preacher argues. "In my job, you learn to judge sincerity. That boy is genuinely looking into his mommy's past."

"I hate to tell you this, Preacher, but your church is full of Saturday heathens, Sunday Baptists." A little harsh, but Boss isn't wrong.

"And you don't think I know exactly which ones?" He raises his eyebrow. "I tailor my sermons to at least half of them."

Boss raises his hand in a placating manner. "No offense meant."

"Well offense was taken." I have never seen a man of God as bold as him. "But apology accepted."

"Let's look at it logically," Mrs. Mary cuts in. "Everyone on the force is suspect right now, until proven otherwise. That includes Mr. Doe."

"Officer Doe," Preacher grumbles.

His wife slaps his chest in annoyance before continuing. "*Officer* Doe is just at the forefront, because he's the one around right now. Which he was assigned, if I understand correctly."

"True," I acknowledge. "Uncle Lud, I mean Chief Ludwig assigned him here after Kyle's break in." I look directly at Kami. "Speaking of, Kami, can I talk to you, privately?"

"What does Kami have to do with your ex?" Tank grumbles.

"Talk to your hacker." I give him a sugary sweet smile. "Otherwise, that's between us."

I grab Kami by the arm and practically drag her out of the room.

"Please tell me when you say Kyle you don't mean that snot nosed, whiny, piece of shit, Dutcher."

"That's exactly who." Her grimace tells me everything. It wasn't a happy partnership. I don't think Kyle is capable.

She crosses her arms over her chest. "I dated that scumbag–if you can call it dating–for less than a year. I found out he had at least two others. The three of us got together to egg his car."

"I remember that." I grimace. "He claimed it was teenagers and that he caught them in the act. He was pissed for weeks. It was that week I resolved to leave him. One hit too many."

Her eyes ballooned out of her head. "You... He... oh, honey. I'm so sorry."

"Don't be. I'm much better off now. I needed that push."

Still, she brings her fist to her mouth and bites her knuckles. Tears well in her eyes. "I hate him," she whispers around her fingers.

I grab her other hand. "Don't waste another thought on him. We got the better deal." I gesture towards the conference room, where our men were waiting.

"We do." She gives my hand a squeeze, and we walk back in, grinning.

In our absence, conversation has lulled around the table. But all of our evidence is now on the whiteboard. Some things are in bullet point notes. Others are whole pages held up by magnets.

Looking at the information this way, it was easy to see why we suspect Doe. It was also easy to see how much was circumstantial. But, just because it wouldn't hold up in court doesn't mean I'm wrong.

"What are we doing to fix this?" Mrs. Mary demands. She stands to the side with her fists balled up on her hips. Her eyes linger on the profiles of the missing girls.

"Self defense lessons."

"More ride throughs."

"Increased patrols."

All three presidents answer at once.

"Most importantly." My voice cuts above the noise. "I have several tracking devices on me. And I'm going to be bait."

Chris and Boss frown at this. I know neither of them *like* it, but they don't protest.

Mrs. Mary, however, pivots on her heels with a fierce look

on her face. "How are you going to keep them from taking your tracker and ditching it?"

Ember laughs. Full on laughs, nearly falling out of her chair. She laughs so hard her face turns red and she gasps for breath. *Traitor.*

"Well, for one: I have trackers in places that no one would look at. And secondly, Sarge and I are going to make a big production about giving me a flashier one tomorrow."

"We are?"

"Oh, yes. At Blue's Brews, during shift change."

"The nepotism coffee?" Boss asks with a grin.

"Yep. News will fly through the station. Everyone will know that the flashy necklace is actually a location tracker."

"But if no one is involved, why would they spread it around?" Mrs. Mary asks.

"Because, I am practically the chief's niece. They are going to gossip about the protection and why I might need it. Maybe even increase patrol in this area."

She eyes me warily, but nods in agreement. "Well then, give them hell."

Preacher's gasp would be my happy thought to get through the dark days ahead. I will remember that moment the whole time I dismantle their operation from the inside.

EIGHTEEN

The next morning I wake to the sound of glass smashing. It's muffled, but near. Sarge takes off down the stairs, gun drawn, faster than I can take stock of the situation.

I grab my own gun, and follow at a much more sedate pace. Still, I'm fast enough to see Kyle mid swing, frozen, staring at Sarge's imposing form crossing the lobby. He doesn't freeze long. He turns and runs, metaphorical tail between his legs.

Sarge glances at me. “One chance to follow him...”

“Go. I'll head to HandleBars. In my car. I'll take my gun. Out the back door and lock up. Go.” My words come out disjointed and scrambled. My brain is running faster than my mouth.

Sarge takes off, jumping on his bike in a hurry. We'd been wise, parking at the side, but close to the front. Out of sight, but near enough to use in an emergency. I'm thankful for the trackers. They give us both the confidence to separate.

Kyle was still running. His car parked down the block, most likely to avoid cameras.

I quickly gather my stuff, gun tucked in my waist band. My

go bag sits ready at my bedroom door. I grab my cell, shooting Chris a message that I'm coming, and my keys.

My heart is racing. This is the first time I've been without a guard in almost a week. I almost contemplate staying here, but alone time with Chris sounds nice. No offense to my security this last week, but they've been a bit of a buzz kill.

I'm halfway down the stairs before I realize I'm still in my sleep clothes. Should I change? I've been sleeping in track pants and a loose tank, lately, with Sarge sleeping in the living room.

The bar isn't open this early. It would only be Chris seeing me like this–is that too soon? I've only known him for a week. We'd only be alone until Sarge gets back, or the bar opens, whichever comes first. I go change.

Jeans and red tee. *Warning this tee contains a smart ass.* One of my favorites. I toss my hair up into a messy bun and take off again.

I lock the door behind and slip into my car, keeping my eyes focused on what I'm doing, terrified someone might be watching me. With all my security off base at the moment, this would be a perfect opportunity for someone to grab me. I'm not prepared for that yet, but by nightfall I will be.

A blink and I'm pulling in at Chris's HandleBar. He's leaning casually against the front door, waiting for me.

“I was starting to worry,” he admits. “Park up front.”

I pull into the closest spot, grab my bag and jump into his arms. He spins me around and kisses my forehead.

“You're safe here,” he whispers it like a devotion. Like it's more than just a promise.

The door is unlocked and he holds it open for me. As soon as we are inside he locks it; the deadbolt snaps heavily into place.

“We can hang out down here, or we can go up to my apartment until nine. At that point, I need to come get everything ready for the day's operations. The choice is yours." His soft smile makes my heart race.

"I'd love an opportunity to check out your apartment. Especially, one free of chaperones."

He laughs and takes my hand, and leads me to the stairwell in the back.

"Your chaperones wouldn't be enough to stop me if you wanted something. Your every wish is my command, and my pleasure." His words send shivers down my spine.

The door swings open and the sight catches my breath. I expected a bachelor pad, something rough and rugged: bikes, rock n roll, leather. Instead, the place is cozy, warm.

The furniture is soft brown, the walls a dark blue. Even the appliances blend in, chosen carefully. This place is a carefully curated home.

He moves gracefully through the space, as if he is completely unaware of my inner monologue. But, his little smirk tells me he knows, and he likes it.

I follow behind him, letting the warmth wash over me. He leads me to the table. A moment later, he is pressing a perfect cup of coffee into my hands, and another kiss to my forehead.

I set the cup down on the table. My hands give a slight tremble as I do so, but only for a moment. I grab his hand and pull him to me, pressing my lips to him, my other hand coming to rest on his chest.

He tenses, but only for a moment. Then he pulls me tight against him. His lips brush feather light kisses over my lips. My hand fists in his shirt pulling him impossibly closer. His tongue runs along the seam of my lips. I tip my head back and let him in. My eyes fall shut and my heart races.

Eventually, he leads me to the couch, pulling me onto his lap. Our kisses stay lazy, unhurried. It would send my mind into a spiral, but the evidence of his enjoyment rests heavy against my inner thigh. We stay like that for an eternity, just trading simple, passionate kisses.

Until my stomach lets out an annoying grumble, that is.

Chris chuckles, low and deep. “Let me feed you,” he whispers in my ear. “Before I have to go to work.”

I don't want to move from my place in his lap, but he effortlessly lifts me. Placing me back down on the couch, he asks, “how do you like your eggs?”

It takes everything I have in me not to blurt out ‘fertilized’. My face reddens at the thought, and he lifts an eyebrow.

“Uhhh, cooked.” *Facepalm. Obviously.* “I mean, it depends on what else we're having or not having? Scrambled is classic. Over easy with toast, or fried hard for a sandwich. And I would never turn down a deviled egg.” *Oh, God,* I'm rambling.

Another laugh. “Easy. Got it.” He winks, before heading to the kitchen. I join him, grabbing my now cold coffee as I pass by.

Chris tops me off as I join him. We work side by side, me at the toaster, him at the stove. That's all he lets me do, butter toast. I roll my eyes, but inside I am squealing.

We eat in silence, playing footsie under the table. Like kids in school. Somehow, this has my face hotter than our make out session.

The start of the work day comes fast. I follow Chris down to the bar and start setting the floor. Chairs off the tables, from last night's mopping. Wipe down the tables. Slice lemons.

“Free labor,” I joke with a wink.

He chuckles low. “I'll pay you back for it later.” His gravely voice sends shivers down my spine.

Ten o'clock on the dot, Mikey rushes through the employee door. “Sorry, Boss.” He flies through the break room and drops his bag in the corner, before rushing back to the front.

I'd've missed the whole thing if it wasn't for a well timed bathroom break. I follow Mikey back up front. Chris leans against the bar with one brow raised. Mikey's fighting for breath.

“Sorry I'm late, Boss. Won't happen again. Probably. Things went long at the vet. Found a new momma dog with eight puppies in a ditch during my morning run. No chip, no tag, no collar.”

“And you took them to the vet?” He crosses his arms over his chest.

“Yes?” Mikey says the word like a question. “That's the only way I know to check for a chip.”

“Animal control.”

The look of absolute horror on this kid's face almost makes me break and laugh.

“And have them in a pound? No thanks. The vet checked for a chip, is helping me set up found dog fliers–minus the mention of puppies– and gave everyone a look over. They'll stay with me until their homes are found. Whether that's with the original owner or new homes is yet to be determined.”

Chris makes eye contact with me and his stern demeanor cracks, his lip twitching. “Finish morning set up. The girls will be in at eleven. You weren't even late. Exactly on time, but not late.”

“On time is late, early is on time,” Mikey mutters under his breath. Chris snaps a bar towel at him.

“Hey kid, after setting up, write me your ingredient list for orders. I hear your mocktails are a hit with the sober crew.”

Mikey gives an air punch and hollers back, "yes sir!"

Chris rolls his eyes and wraps me in a side hug. "They grow up so fast," he jokes, wiping away a fake tear.

Time flies, and I start to worry about Sarge. I know he can handle Kyle, but what if he was set up?

Noon comes and goes. Doe comes in, taking a booth in the back. He smiles and waves as he takes his seat, making my skin crawl.

Around one, Sarge strolls in. "He disappeared into private property on the edge of town. I took a look around, but didn't see anything. The place is near The Road Kings. I'll have Tank ask King to keep an eye out."

NINETEEN

The plan is overwhelming in its simplicity. There's no room for error, but then again, an error would be damn near impossible. Shift change is at three; those going in will be at the café around two. The guys coming off shift will be in around three thirty. We start our scene at two-fifteen.

Sarge and I get there early, one-forty-five. He makes a big production about a good 'defensable' spot. I nearly roll my eyes at the theatrics. But, then I remember, this is Uncle Ludwig's family–the biggest cop gossips.

He sets me up in a corner booth, in the back. One that's big enough for us to sit side by side. He has me in the deepest corner before getting our treats.

"Stay here." His booming voice carries easily through the building. "I'll get you the stupid coffee and danish, but if that door so much as looks like it might open, you drop in this seat."

Thank God he was not actually this overbearing during our week of 'probation.' I'd be even more ready for this chance at 'parole.'

I try not to laugh at the faux glare he gives me, like I've

been constantly getting myself into trouble. My face mostly holds, but my lip twitches. I swallow down the laugh as his eyes narrow at me.

"Why?" I'm not exactly quiet either. "You'll still be between me and the door."

His eyebrows furrow. "Because. If I'm focused on ordering that monstrosity you call coffee, exactly as you asked for it, then I won't be paying close enough attention to the door. You drop, and buy me time to assess the situation." He winks at me.

"Sir, yes, sir." I give the sloppiest, most disrespectful salute I can. He gives a perfect military pivot on his heels. I reward this act with a very obnoxious wave of my middle fingers.

Leah tries to hide her laugh, but a small giggle escapes. She squeaks quietly at whatever look Sarge levels at her. She knows I never order coffee here, with my convenient excuse about having my own stockpile.

"What can I get started for you today, sir?" Her customer service voice is impeccable.

"A black coffee for me." He is going to regret that choice. "And a–" deep breath here– "Half caff large skinny white mocha latte with full espresso and five shots of fully leaded sugar free cherry syrup. Made with full fat almond milk."

"Don't forget my danish!" I cheerfully holler across the shop, with a giant 'eat shit' grin on my face.

Boss would kill me for that order, full of pretentious bullshit masquerading as taste. A real life order like that, with its contradicting words, does nothing but set a 'Karen' up to complain about something. Or everything.

"Yes, that. Add a sugar free cherry cream cheese danish, toasted or whatever." He runs a hand over his face and shoots me a glare.

"Yes, sir." Leah's cheeks are impossibly pink, but she somehow manages to keep a straight face. "I'll make it exactly the way Miss Armani likes, don't worry. Total is fifteen ninety-two. Would that be cash or card?"

"Cash." He hands her a twenty and walks off.

"Sir! Your change!"

"Keep it," he growls, stomping back over to our seat.

As soon as his butt hits the seat his phone rings. I know that it's Tank, but I suspect Ghost is in the security system cameras timing it perfectly.

"Sir? Yes, sir. Right away, sir." He hangs up. "You. Stay." He gets up and walks out the door, just as Leah brings our order over. I can see him lean against the glass next to the door.

"You really don't like him, do you?" She giggles. "Fully loaded sugar free syrup?

I grin back. "Personally, I'm rather proud of the half caff with full espresso part." She shakes her head at me, returning to her spot behind the counter just as Sarge comes back in. Our first wave of witnesses file in behind him for their nepotism cop coffee.

"Freedom has been delivered!" He slams the necklace case on the table. This time he sits across from me. "Special tracking device, no more babysitter needed!" He sounds so excited I can almost believe he's actually releaved to be rid of me.

He pulls the obnoxious piece of jewelry out of the box, and begins his over the top demonstration. "The tracker is nestled in this heart pendant. It's also a panic button. You mash that, and Boss will send everyone out after your location. Other than that, location gets checked by someone every hour on the hour. If you're not where you're supposed to be, expect a call."

All a lie. Ghost has 24/7 surveillance on all of my trackers, and Boss isn't involved at all. But, no one else needs to know all that.

"So, I agree to wear this obnoxious pendant with all these little security features, and you go away? Good deal."

I feel eyes on us, but nobody is looking directly in our direction. I make a big production of snatching the necklace and slinging it around my neck.

"Bye." I stand. He grabs my wrist and tugs me back into my seat.

"Not so fast, hot stuff," he growls at me and points at my chest. "We still have to make sure the damned thing is up and running."

I see a couple officers exchange glances on the way out. Next wave should come through in about an hour. Time for dramatic stalling. These guys will gossip about the tracker before they leave the station. The next guys will be here for the official 'all clear'. But, we can't let Leah suspect that this scene is anything other than genuine.

Sarge pulls out his phone and starts tapping away at it. From my spot, I can see he is playing one of those tap for action games.

I want to laugh. I huff instead, narrowing my eyes at him.

"Is it giving you trouble?" I say in my most mocking voice, channeling all of my humor into sarcasm.

He glances up at me. "No." *Tap. Tap. Tap.*

I huff again and sit back, roaming my eyes across the café. Leah and I lock glances. She's losing the struggle not to laugh. I watch as she dips into the back room. The door doesn't quite shut before her giggles escape her.

I glance at Sarge and he grins back. It's only the two of us here right now. We can afford to let her think he has no idea she's laughing her ass off in there.

Leah comes back out just as the first of the off shift officers arrive.

"Hey Lee-Lee!" Officer Gibson hollers when he walks in. "Got anymore of those strawberry muffins?"

Leah laughs. “Not today. You bought the last one this morning. I do have some strawberry lemon scones though.”

“It'll do.” He laughs handing her a twenty. “That's my dessert tonight. I also need another bag of grounds for the house.”

He notices me in the corner, and waves. I wave back. Anthony Gibson is Uncle Lud's top pick for future son-in-law.

“Alright. Damn thing is on.” Sarge tosses the necklace at me. “Put the damn thing on and *try* to stay out of trouble.”

“Anything to be rid of you.”

He glares. I glare back. “If that thing goes off, I ain't coming. Your brother is on his own now. We're even. Tell him that.”

“With fucking pleasure.” He stomps out the door. The roar of his motorcycle can be heard over the grinding of coffee beans.

“You good?” Officer Gibson asks.

“Oh she's grand.” Leah giggles. “Been giving him an extra hard time.”

I laugh. “Yeah, my brother is worried. Pulled in a favor to stick me with an overbearing babysitter for the last few days. Now I have to wear a stupid tracker, but as long as he doesn't catch me without it, no more annoying shadow.”

“I didn't know you had a brother. Thought you were an only child.”

And everyone in this tiny town knows it.

“I am. But bonds forged in foster homes tie thicker than blood.”

“And this foster brother wants to track you? Honey, that's classic predator behavior.” Gibson slips into the seat Sarge vacated.

“Well. My brother just lost his wife and his blood sister to gang violence. So, if a little overbearingness gives him something to cling to, some sanity, it's worth the temporary inconvenience." The lies fall off my tongue naturally. It helps that I know all about Gibson's sister and her gang banger boyfriend.

"Gang violence? Here?"

"Nah." I force a laugh. "But Montgomery isn't that far, and paranoia doesn't care."

"True," he agrees. "If you need anything..." He slips me his business card, as if he hasn't already given me a hundred.

"I'll call." *Not.* I wink. "I know everyone in the department has my back. Even if I get in the way every once in a while."

TWENTY

The next week is one of the most boring weeks of my life. A few clients come in, but nobody has any exciting jobs. One lady thinks her neighbors are cheating on each other and wants proof. *Why?* Another is convinced that their neighbor is violating the HOA agreement and wants me to go over the contract. *Easy money.*

Chris comes by every morning before the bar opens. He never shows up empty handed. Sometimes he brings flowers, others breakfast.

Every day he leaves with a kiss and a compliment. The blue of my dress makes my brown eyes pop. The speed at which I handled the HOA paperwork is impressive. He loves that I don't shame the woman who wants to spy on her neighbors, even if it is weird.

Every evening, just before he heads to bed, Boss calls to check in. We talk about our days and plans. He is already talking about marrying Kami and having babies. I pick at him about moving faster than military lesbians. He just says when you know, you know.

I'm still helping Spider study, just not in person. I create assignments and study tools. Chris picks them up while he visits in the morning, and Boss gets them from him at the bar. After Spider finishes, Boss brings them back to Chris. And Chris returns them the next day for me to 'grade.' We swap papers daily, and I always text Spider how well he did, and he is doing well. The only thing that could give him trouble with his GED exam is his anxiety. I'm worried that once he sees the actual test, he'll freeze. He's been putting so much pressure on himself and this test.

It's lonely. During the last week, I got used to having people around. Sarge was always right there, and the others were constantly dropping by.

I want to scream 'I told you so' at Sarge. But I am completely aware that I haven't actually been abandoned. We're just trying to smoke out whoever has been taking these girls.

Going about my regular tasks feels unnatural. My routine has shifted, and trying to force the old one makes me feel even more alone.

I shop alone. Sarge's voice echoes in my mind, fussing about my unhealthy snack options. I grab a fruit tray to shut it up. I try not to freeze when Officer Doe slips past me in the dairy aisle. He grabs milk at the same time I'm getting an assortment of creamers.

"Friends coming?" He asks, gesturing to my cart.

"Nope, just can't decide what I want."

"Fair enough." He laughs. "Stay safe."

At Elixars the next day, Doe is two customers behind me. He has got to be the only cop that comes in here. Everyone else is loyal to Blue's. Blue backs blue around here.

"Don't tell Chief," he whispers to me as we wait for our drinks. "The stuff his niece makes is nasty."

"His niece does the best with what her mom buys. Not much fixes shitty beans," I whisper back with a snarl. "And her pastries are more than worth it."

He laughs. "Too true. Too bad I'm on a sugar cleanse, right now." He gets his sugar free vanilla latte and leaves.

Later that day, he drives down my road at least three times. He revs his motorcycle and waves as he passes each time.

I get a package that needs a signature down at the post office–new long distance camera lenses. There's Doe, mailing a package off.

"I found a cute blanket for Grams," he says.

I raise my eyebrow. "You figured out where your mom came from?"

"Ah, no." He scratches the back of his neck. "Grams isn't actually family. She and Pops are the closest I have to grandparents, though. They're the ones who found mom in the ditch, and took her to the hospital. When she was discharged *still* not knowing her name, Grams insisted she stay with them. They practically raised me while my mom was in a bad place. Pops eventually turned one of his barns into a barndominium for us, back before it was cool."

"That's sweet," I answer.

"Yeah, Grams and Pops are the best." I get my package and leave. He follows behind me.

Thursday evening is the first time I go to defense lessons at the station. I don't necessarily need any instruction, but I go anyway. I don't get to check out the motorcycle gym classes. So I'll scout here, instead. I refuse to be left out of my own plan.

There's five other women filling out release forms when I get there. Standard 'we will not be held liable' paperwork. I scrawl my signature across my waiver and hand it over.

Ludwig leans against the desk. Five minutes after the official start time he addresses the crowd. "Thank you all for coming to today's self defense lessons. All of our classes over the next six weeks will be the same, just with different instructors. Feel free to come back to as many as you feel you need. Practicing these moves more makes them more instinctual. Instinctual action can save your life. Follow me."

He leads us through the station, to the on-sight gym. The equipment has all been moved aside, and a blue mat laid out, filling the space completely.

"All set, Chief." Gibson pats Uncle Ludwig on the shoulder as he leaves. "Doe's turn to break down tonight." He waves at me as he passes by. "Have fun, ladies."

Uncle Lud commands attention, his presence filling the whole room. "I'm your police chief, Charles Ludwig. Running today's lesson, here with me, is our very own motor patrol officer James Doe."

"Welcome!" Officer Doe joins the conversation. "Today we will go over basic vigilance and how to use your size to your advantage. Most attackers will be bigger than you. They wear their size like armor. They look for smaller targets because they are easier. Don't be easier."

Uncle Lud takes over. "Our goal today is for you to leave here feeling more confident in your ability to keep yourself safe long enough for help to arrive."

Doe interrupts, "Average response time in Setting is seven minutes. That's seven minutes from when dispatch tells us there is a problem. Be the problem. Make a scene. If you can't call, give someone else a reason to."

The chief mock glares at him before continuing, "As soon as you suspect a problem, call. Everyone here today is going to get a fridge magnet with our non-emergency line number. Save it in your phone. If something feels off, call. Our staff will stay on the line with you, help you assess the situation and send an officer if warranted. And I want it noted, my staff has been trained that making someone feel safe does warrant being checked out."

Doe again. "Basic situational awareness goes a long way. Keep your hearing clear, one ear bud, max. You want to hear people approaching. Empty parking lot, but someone parks right next to you? Go get security. Alone at night and see someone on the sidewalk? Are they watching you? Be aware who is around and how close. They can't physically attack you if they can't get close enough."

"Assuming they don't have a gun," Ludwig interjects. "If they have a gun, your safest option is to cooperate until you can't. Being aware of your surroundings lowers your chances of being alone with an armed assailant, but chances are never zero."

"*Outside* of armed situations, your first step should be to make a scene. Criminals of any type usually try to avoid attention. Yell. Scream the nastiest words you can think of. Get attention."

"Unfortunately, we live in a society where 'help' isn't enough. Everyone assumes someone else will act." Ludwig appears to be playing bad cop, to Doe's informative stance, but the back and forth nature of the conversation feels less like a lecture and more like entertainment.

"Too true. Being loud isn't enough. You need people to look. Be vulgar. Be descriptive. Get attention, any way you can." Doe looks around and makes eye contact with everyone. Then in his most deadpan voice he delivers his next lines. "You overgrown cunt. Don't touch me I said go away asshole. Hey! Red shirt! Yeah you!" He points at the girl next to me. "Call the police. This overused ass wipe won't leave me alone."

"Descrptive and vulgar," Ludwig says with a low chuckle. "Now everyone is looking at Officer Doe and his unwanted companion. That attention will drive away 90% of attackers.

They want a clean out. Now I'm going to grab Officer Doe and he is going to demonstrate how to get loose, *if* he can."

"Challenge accepted." Ludwig comes up behind him and puts him in a choke hold. Immediately Doe tucks his chin as close to his chest as he can, protecting his airway. Then he grabs Ludwig's elbow with both hands.

"First protect your airway," he groans out. "Tuck your chin to give your throat some space. Get between your attacker's arm and your chest if you can. Ideally, turn toward their elbow to do this. The natural triangle made by their arms gives more space."

Doe adds pressure to the elbow in his hand pushing it toward his neck. "Use both hands and that space we talked about. Push the elbow *toward* you. I know it seems counterintuitive, driving them closer that way. But, it's actually the best way to break their grip on you." More pressure.

Ludwig's grip goes and Doe takes advantage; he pivots wide toward Lud's right arm, sweeps his leg out and knocks Lud down at the knees.

"Act fast. As soon as that grip slacks, pivot wide. Turn toward the elbow you just attacked. Swing your leg wide. Bring your arms up between you and your assailant and shove. Getting free is the priority. Once you are free, run."

He goes to take a step back but Ludwig shoots up and grabs him by the ankle. "Sometimes, they recover quickly. This is where knowing how to strike comes in. Ball shots are cheap, but there is a reason they work. A throat punch is risky. Well landed, it can put them out, but it's easy for them to get their hands on you and restrain you from there. Aim for center mass and use force. Below the ribs you can damage their kidneys, with enough force to the ribcage you can break it. Broken bones hurt, plus the added advantage of possibly rupturing an organ. Be aggressive. This is not the time to play safe." Doe address the gathered women.

He uses his other foot to step down on Ludwig's fist, executing another precise pivot. As soon as Ludwig lets go, Doe jumps back several feet.

Ludwig stands, shaking out his hand with a faux glare at Doe. "That hurt."

"Well, it wasn't supposed to tickle."

Lud rolls his eyes. "Okay, ladies, the rest of today will be sparing. Every ten minutes we will switch partners so that everyone has a chance with Officer Doe or I. That will leave two other teams of two. Each round, someone will be assigned to act as the assailant. Be loud. Get free. Avoid being grabbed if you can. Let's go!"

The rest of the class is indeed spent sparing. I get a good look at each girl's face, taking note of who looks most like me. All five of the other girls could be potential victims. We all look just enough alike.

I leave, tired. But I don't go straight home. The car needs gas, and I ate all the fruit already. It was good, so I stop and grab more.

Back at my office, I notice a paper taped to my door. I pull a rubber glove from the side pocket of my go bag before touching it–I'm not stupid. There are substances that can be added to paper that will drug a person and make them an easy target.

I carefully unfold the paper, tipping it away from me. I don't need any suspicious powders billowing up in my face. *Clear.*

It's a copy of today's sign in sheet at the station defense classes. All six of our names. In red ink across the bottom is a scrawled message.

Thanks for the shopping list.

TWENTY-ONE

Everyone panics when I send a picture of the note to the group chat. Boss demands I come stay at the compound, and Kami begs for the same. Tank assures me that I'm not as alone as I feel. Sarge promises his gym's sign in list is under lock and key, and Boss claims his is, as well. Preacher prays, well he actually types out a two paragraph prayer in the group chat. Everyone responds with 'amen.'

Chris messages me separately.

You good?

I'm fine. Thank you for checking! 😍

Mikey has gotten good here. Date tomorrow?

Yes, please.

Dress to ride. 😉

The morning sun paints the sky red and orange. *Red skies at morning.* I shake the thought away. Today is going to be a good day. How can it not? I'm going out with Chris, and this man is an absolute genius. He's taking me to an escape room, but not just any escape room, a murder mystery themed escape room. It's a perfect date, catering to my interests. Watching Chris solve clues is hot, too.

Afterward, Chris brings me home on his bike, flying through the streets. We're both high off the adrenaline from the escape room, and it's making me giddy. He walks me to the door, waiting patiently while I unlock the door. He peaks in the office, eyes roaming over the lobby. All is clear. Nothing out of place.

"Sleep sweet." He whispers in my ear before bringing his lips to mine in a heated kiss that takes my breath away. Just as soon as I think this is going to go further, he steps back. "Dream of me." He winks.

My knees are weak. He waits with a grin, while I lock up behind him. I watch through the glass as he drives away, before heading upstairs to my apartment.

I float in a live filled daze to the stairs, sobering instantly as I turn the corner. What I find in the stairwell turns my blood to ice. Officer Gibson is leaning against my door, twirling a knife in his hands. "How cute. Too good to let him in your bed?" He sneers.

"How did you get in here?" My hand shakily flies to cover my mouth, heart pounding.

"A little birdie loaned me a key. You really should be careful who you trust with things like that."

Shit. I knew I should have changed the locks after Doe showed up. I trusted that he gave it back to Ludwig. I forgot my first lesson. Trust but verify.

"So you and Doe cooked up a little scheme together. Trouble getting girls on your own?" Should I be antagonizing him? Probably not. But this is me, it's going to happen. Might as well weaponize it.

He laughs. "Something like that, Amy." He stands and stalks down the stairs.

I refuse to make it easy for him. Getting taken might be part of the plan, but I will not go down easy, not without making him earn it. I pivot and run for the door–the door I just locked. *Shit, what do I do*? I crash through the glass, brushing my fingers over the edge. The hidden panic button comes off in my hand. I press it repeatedly as I run. Gibson is on my heels, but I run and I scream. I glance around for Chris, but there's no sign he hung around.

"You want me? Come get me! You ugly ass excuse for a pig." Gibson gains ground quickly though. I may be in shape, but so is he. In his plain clothes he runs faster than in a normal foot pursuit. Still, I make a racket. "What's the matter, pork chop? Too many donuts? Does chasing girls make you feel like a man?"

He grips me by the hair and yanks me back on my ass. He grabs me at the scalp, wrapping my hair around his fist. I shriek in pain, scalp burning. As he drags me to his car, I have to scramble to crab crawl, trying to keep from getting road burn.

"See how your mouthy ass likes this." He snatches the pendant necklace off my neck and throws it toward the rain drain. Then he pops the top off an aerosol can before shoving me in the truck with it. My last thought is of attempting to kick out a brake light, but I never get the chance.

I come-to slowly, refusing to open my eyes. My head is pounding, and my scalp burns where my hair was nearly ripped out. The cold concrete beneath me does little to help. Neither does the metal pipe I am apparently hand cuffed to. I can hear soft whispers, but I'm still too out of it to make out any words.

The room is freezing and smells like shit. Literally like someone or something took a massive dump under my nose. I can't help but try holding my breath.

Something scrapes the cement next to me. "I can tell you're awake." A soft voice cuts through the fog in my mind. "Your breathing changed. I know the drugs are rough, but can you open your eyes?"

I slowly blink my eyes open. The room is full of women handcuffed to anything and everything. Some have little to no clothes on. It's easy to tell where the feces smell comes from. They've been left in their own filth. My own shirt is missing and my pants are torn.

Wynonah is handcuffed across from me. She offers me a weak smile. "Crazy ride, huh?" There's blood pouring down her face, and her eyes are a little hazy. I'm fairly certain that whatever caused that gash on her forehead gave her a concussion.

The blond woman next to me scoots closer–as close as her cuffs allow. She looks me over, best she can. "I'm Krista.

Wynonah and I are the only ones here who talk much. Stockholm or survival or whatever. These girls are terrified."

My head tips back. "Krista Trussell, younger sister to Kami Trussell. She's been looking for you." I shake my head trying to clear the fog. "I'm here for a reason," I murmur.

"Yeah," Krista agrees. "You're here because you caught the attention of a psychopath."

"I never expected Anthony Gibson. I've known him for years," Wynonah agrees. "He thinks he's a big shot, bragging every time he comes down here."

"And you keep running your mouth and getting hit," Krista growls.

"Keeps his attention off the others." Officer Wynonah grins. Her mouth is full of blood, giving her an unhinged look.

"I got caught on purpose," I tell them. "Put up a convincing fight, and dropped my security team earlier this week."

"Doe mentioned you were under lock and key," Wynonah chimes in. "Started with problems about an ex? I think."

"Yeah. Then we noticed all the missing girls have a similar profile," I tell them. "Every last one of us looks like we could be sisters."

"Kami!" Krista gasps.

"Is safe. I got her put up with a security team as soon as I realized. My friend Boss is handling it. She *never* goes *anywhere* alone."

"Caught on purpose?" Wynonah chimes in. "What good does that do us? Brady bragged about ditching your fancy tracker jewelry."

"Jokes on him. I have extras. We made a public show about that one so nobody would think to look for more. Back up is most likely already on the way."

"He tossed your bag in a ditch on the way," Kami says. "Something about not chancing extra trackers."

I brush my hand over my chest. "They're a *little* more personal than that."

I dig a couple bobby pins out of my hair and make quick work of the cuff lock. I uncuff Krista and Wynonah and give them each a few pins.

The other girls are all weak. Some are drugged to the nines, while others are broken and beaten. There is no way I can get all of them out of here.

"We have three choices. One, we release the others and all try to leave together. That means herding these girls through this place without getting anyone's attention. Two, we leave them knowing back up is on the way and you come with me now. Three, I get out of here on my own, and you stay to help and watch over the other girls. Either way, I promised I would make haste and get out as soon as I could. This location has been tracked. Help is coming."

"We can't move them." Krista and Wynonah speak at the same time.

"I'm staying," Wynonah adds. "To serve and protect."

"Me too," Krista agrees. "As much as I want out of here, you stand a better chance on your own. I can help keep these girls calm. Been here a while."

"Okay," I don't argue. They made their choices as fully informed as we are capable of being. "Here." I pull the pin with a tracker from deeper in my hair. This one is slightly bigger at the bent end. "This pin has a nanotech tracker on it. In case they move you after I leave. Back up is coming in the form of a swarm of bikers. Leather vests are friends."

The girls in the back exchange looks and shake their heads. I don't think they believe help is coming.

TWENTY-TWO

Slipping out of the basement is laughably easy, almost too easy. The window latch is rusty, but once it opens, there's plenty of room to climb through. It is a little high from the inside, but there is plenty to use for climbing. Krista helps me move a metal shelf, picking it up *just* enough to keep it from scraping the ground. Don't need extra noise drawing attention.

My mistake was assuming that my escape from the basement would set the tone for my escape off the property. News flash: it didn't. I barely have the window shut behind me, when someone rounds the corner.

Immediate pandemonium.

I shoot off into the dark shadows, and drop low to the ground. He had a decent look in my direction, but he's searching the area at my height. Instead, I army crawl under some bushes and watch as he runs past, yelling his head off.

Once the area is clear, I stay crouched down, but I slowly make my way out from the shadows and towards the woods.

Bark. Bark. Bark.

It sounds like at least five dogs have been let loose to track me; I have to move fast. I can see headlights in the distance on what I assume is a county highway–not that I would flag someone down here. I do, however, keep the road just inside my line of sight. I'm being tracked by more than just dogs, and that road is my ticket out of here.

Wizz. Bang.

A bullet flies past me, lodging into the tree to my right. I lean forward and keep running, thankful I wore boots on my date earlier.

There's a fallen tree up ahead that's lodged itself in the vee of another. I scale it like I'm part monkey. From the branches, I can see both the road and the hunting party. These guys have beagles chasing me! Beagles!

I nearly fall out of the tree laughing. They have my scent, sure, but come on. Those guys get distracted by squirrels. Chances are the handlers will think it's a squirrel in this tree. Still, I'm not taking chances. It's a drop from here, but the first thing I learned when I started learning to fight was *how* to fall. I jump, land, and tuck straight into a roll. Once I'm back on my feet, I'm running again.

Bullets fly in the distance. They're guessing. *Goodie.*

Up ahead is a creek and I have only a moment to decide: am I getting wet or jumping over it? Getting in would slow me down, but the dogs would definitely lose my scent. I'd stay in the creek aways before getting out. Or jump over and there's less chance that they lose my scent.

I jump. Slowing down isn't safe, and I don't want to get too far from the road anyway. I have to trust that Ghost is following my jewelry. That he realizes the pin is where I broke cuffs and my piercings are where I am. I need to trust that my new friends won't let me down. Help *is* coming, this time.

My legs are getting tired, and it's getting harder to catch my breath. I pause to listen. The dogs are in the distance and so is the shooting. I don't have long, but a moment to breathe now will keep me alive later.

I walk slowly towards the road, staying completely in the shadows. There's a convenience store up ahead, which looks to be about a mile away. Can I afford to chance the workers being in league with the criminals down the road? It's clearly a bigger operation than I had expected.

The roar of motorcycles makes my decision for me and I run again. Less frantic this time, more even paced. About twenty bikes file into the parking lot. Everyone is jumping off and spreading out.

“Armani! It's us!” Sarge's voice echoes through the trees as I burst into the light.

“Shut up,” I hiss. “They're tracking me. With *beagles*.” A laugh bursts out. “Fucking beagles. Great noses, but little legs and so easily distracted by wild life.” I'm laughing uncontrollably now, tears streaming down my face. “Beagles.”

Chris whips his jacket off and wraps it around me before pulling me into his strong arms. He holds me tight, tucking me into his chest. He buries his nose in my hair and takes a slow deep breath.

“I've got you,” he whispers. “You're safe now.”

I lose myself in his arms as the discussion flows around me. Barks echo around us. Eventually everything is decided. Chris will take me to the station, while Tank and the others will mount a rescue.

I climb on the back of Chris's bike, grinning wide. The ride to the station settles something deep inside me, adrenaline fading. Uncle Ludwig has been working nights lately. I'm going to tell him everything. It's over. Finally over.

I race through the station. It's oddly empty tonight. My stomach drops, heart picking back up. *Where is everyone?*

The blinds on Uncle Lud's office windows are shut, but the

light is on inside. I can see the general silhouette of someone inside with him. I knock anyway, shaking slightly–I'm not sure if its adrenaline or something else.

He slams the door open with a glare that softens as he notices me. “I told everyone to get–oh, Angel. Sorry, I'm in an important meeting right now. I'll be with you in just a moment. I have to handle this.”

Before he can shut the door in my face, I see Officer Gibson in the room with him. I freeze, blood turning to ice in my veins.

“It's important, Chief.” My eyes dart past him hoping he catches on.

“Always is, Angel. Just give me five.” The click of the door closing echoes in the hall. I haven't told *anyone* that Gibson was involved. Damn my scattered brain.

“Angel?” Chris questions.

“Yeah. It was my dad's nickname for me. Armani Celeste; warrior of the Heavens; Angel.”

“That's cute.” Chris wraps his arms around me.

“Yeah, and my uncle is in there with the guy who kidnapped me.”

Chris stiffens. “Not Doe?”

“No, Gibson. But there were so many people there. Doe could still be involved.”

Whack.

I never heard the door open. Chris goes slack, his arms slipping from around me. He drops to the floor.

“Anthony? What are you doing?” Uncle Ludwig is furious.

Gibson snatches me back by my hair. “I ain't going down for this alone.” He drags me through the station. I kick and scream, but there is no one else here. Which worries me, but I don't have a chance to focus on that oddity. I feel cold metal press against the base of my neck.

He drags me out to the alley behind the station. Usually

there's a few shops back here, but tonight it's totally empty. Literally everyone is gone.

I bet when my alarm went off, Uncle Lud showed up. Finding my mess he panicked. He has everyone out looking for me.

"I ain't gonna be the only one going down in this mess, Chief. I go down, the whole department goes with me."

"It'll be a stain on their reputation." I agree, going limp. I force him to use his energy to hold me up. If he's going to kill me, it won't be easy. "But Uncle Lud will recover. You and Doe won't win."

Uncle Ludwig's lip twitches. Even in this high stress situation, he has my back.

TWENTY-THREE

A motorcycle roars into the far end of the alley, the sound echoing loudly and grabbing everyone's attention. They only pull halfway down the lane. No colors are visible; their visor pulled down over their face. I can't tell who it is. It could be back up, or it could be Doe.

Ludwig glances back and a grin slowly covers his face. “She's right,” Ludwig agrees, pulling his gun. “My station can withstand a few hits. Breaking a major case like this will garner back some of the goodwill that busting dirty cops will diminish. Rescuing all seven of Setting's current missing people? And several others from surrounding towns. Bringing our missing persons caseload down to one? That kind of attention, it brings funding.”

“Seven?” The word falls out of my lips in shock. I only had six files. I only *showed* him six files.

Gibson shoves me to the side, pointing his gun at Ludwig instead. “I go down, this station burns to the ground with me.” Spit flies from his mouth, fury filling his eyes.

"Seven!" My words are intentional this tim. "Seven missing girls? I thought it was six?"

"Whoops," Ludwig deadpans, turning his gun on me. "I may have buried a few files while helping Doe look for his poor pitiful momma. Couldn't have hers be the only one missing. *That,* you might have noticed." He grins, wild and feral. "Yeah, I knew he was planning on sharing. He's not subtle, and will never make a good UC. Not that it matters, the kid has his heart set on death patrol, I mean motor patrol. I made sure to throw in lots of extra fake cases too. Thought you might spend a little extra time chasing your tail."

"But you told me only twelve cases in Setting. You were quite proud of it." My head spins. Nothing is making sense to me right now.

"And look how quick you were to jump to distrust. Your eyes were on Doe, instead of my operation right under your nose. I am sorry, Angel. If you had dropped that whore's case when I told you to, we wouldn't be here right now." He waves his gun at me, glaring. I've never seen such hatred in his eyes as I do right now.

"You lost the right to call me Angel when you had me kidnapped," I growl.

Gibson starts laughing. "Only then?"

"Honestly, I probably lost the right to call you Angel the day I paid a teenage Anthony Gibson to ram into the side of your daddy's truck."

"You what?" Just when I thought his betrayal couldn't hurt me more. He called me daughter. Said he understood that he would never replace my dad, that uncle would be an honor. And all this time, *he's* the reason they're gone.

"I never got that full payment, either." Gibson throws out with a manic laugh. "I thought I was adding your momma for free. Turns out the old man wanted her for himself."

"But, Aunt Mindy?" I choke out through my tears.

"Was never who I wanted." Ludwig shrugs, like he isn't completely shattering my world view. "She was sick and needed insurance. Your mom had already married your dad. I could afford to make his sister's life better in a way he couldn't."

"No one ever told me they were siblings."

"I don't think your daddy ever knew. But, I did my research. Turns out your granddaddy had a wild hair, liked the ladies. Use them and lose them. Left behind a half sister, quite a few actually. That is what flowed in your daddy's genes. I had to get rid of him before he broke your momma."

"Instead, I did!" Gibson doubles over in laughter. "He wanted your daddy out of the way. Instead, they're together forever!" Ludwig loses his cool at this, swinging his gun around toward Gibson instead. He levels his gun directly in Gibson's face and pulls the trigger. Thrice. *Pop. Pop. Pop.*

"Your momma was never supposed to be in that car. She was never supposed to be with him at all! I saw her first, I flirted with her first, but he bought the first round of drinks that night. He flashed his money, and she followed. She should have been mine! You should have been mine! I could have provided a much better life! Because I wasn't throwing my money at every whore who wanted to suck my dick!" Ludwig shakes with rage as he screams at me, gun once again aimed in my direction. I take a hesitant step backwards and my back hits a wall, trapped.

The man on the motorcycle pulls closer. From here, I can see his hands trembling. Ludwig may have thought this was his back up, but this person is infuriated with what is being said.

"You fooled me." Officer Doe flips his visor up, revealing his face. There are tears and hatred in his eyes and voice. "I thought you were the epitome of a perfect cop. You have your guys' backs. You work hard to protect the community. But it's all a ruse, so you can fuck us over instead?"

"You are not the biker I expected," Ludwig mutters.

"So instead of telling me you don't want a motor patrol, you find me a partner and frame me for her kidnapping!"

"Something like that. But, it's all going to be fine. I've never had a problem getting rid of officers who don't fall in line for me." He turns his gun on Officer Doe. "I'll just tell everyone you transferred to the city, they had a motor patrol position open. You couldn't resist."

Another motorcycle pulls into the alley. A moment of hope flashes across Ludwig's face before he realizes it's not who he expects either. Preacher sits proud on his bike, no helmet. He pulls his phone out of his pocket and turns it toward us. A live stream of the alley from Doe's point of view is playing on the screen. "But can you make a whole congregation disappear?"

Ludwig lunges at Preacher, his face red. Before anyone can move, Officer Doe casually pops off two rounds, center mass. Ludwig clutches at his chest. His knees hit the ground first and his eyes meet the muzzle of the gun before he completely collapses to the ground before him.

At that exact moment, Spider spins around the opposite corner from Preacher and Doe. Gravel flies. Behind him and his side car, a huge black truck pulls in. Boss climbs out of the truck and effortlessly catches his cut, thrown to him by Spider, while approaching. "Nice shot. Wish I could've done it. Pity I can't carry a gun. Well, *I can*, but my club can't. Don't want any legal trouble here today."

Officer Doe approaches Ludwig's body, gun still drawn. "Thanks. The paperwork for this is already going to be a bitch."

He reaches to roll him over, but Ludwig swipes at him with

a switch blade. Boss immediately stomps on his wrist, the crunch echoing through the alley.

“Hey now, that's my move.” Doe grumbles.

“Oops.” Boss tosses him a grin.

A laugh bubbles out of me. This entire situation is insane. I'm going to wake up any minute still rattling around in the trunk of Gibson's car.

Officer Doe pulls Ludwig to his feet by the broken wrist. He screams as Doe spins him around and cuffs Ludwig's hands behind his back. I can see his bullet proof vest through the holes in his shirt. I hope he broke a rib. Or two.

TWENTY-FOUR

I trust that the men have this situation handled, but Chris is still outside Ludwig's office. Hurt. I fly back through the station, feeling as if my feet don't even touch the ground. I gasp in relief as I turn the last corner. Chris is sitting up–hand to his head, but up. His eyes are unfocused, but he smiles when he sees me.

"Wha' 'append?" His words slur.

"A lot," I choke out, crying. I drop to my knees next to him and take his face in my hand. "You're okay." It's both a question and a reassurance.

"Miss Armani?" I jump at Spider's voice. He has a phone to his ear as he watches me. "Boss says the EMTs are on their way, and Tank checked in. Things didn't go one hundred percent, but they thought you might like to know that the girls are headed to the hospital."

I nod.

"Boss also says he and Officer Doe have 'contained the scene' for county and state officials, who are also on the way. He asks that you secure the chief's office as well."

I glance at the door behind me and back to Chris.

"M'ine," Chris slurs.

"I'll stay out here with him. I am *technically* a felon–sealed juvie records, but still, not a good look."

I crack a small smile. "Thanks, kid."

I slip into Ludwig's office. Apparently the meeting he was having with Gibson was about their little operation, because the desk is covered with files. I don't touch them, but by the seals I can tell that they come from county records as well as local.

The sign in sheet from the other day is there, a star next to the date. I see his meticulous handwriting across the top, and it makes my blood boil. Tears fall freely down my face.

Kyle, any of these will do.

But a first name is not enough to implicate my ex, legally. Ludwig's phone is there too. I know his pass code, but I can't bring myself to look.

I hear the EMTs outside. Spider, too.

"Hey, Mr. Keep, sir. I'll follow on my bike. That way I can ride you back to your place. They won't let you drive with a concussion. Boss can bring your bike in the back of his truck."

God bless that kid.

"Miss Armani." His voice is soft when he pokes his head around the door. "Pretty certain he just has a mild concussion, but they're taking him to the hospital to check. I'ma ride behind. Take him home after. Are you okay? Do I need to send someone?"

"I'm good, Spider, just overwhelmed." I wipe my face. "I thought I knew him."

I am so excited when Uncle Lud picks me up from school early. He doesn't do it very often. Mommy always fusses about my education, but Daddy just laughs. Uncle Lud is Daddy's bestest friend ever.

I skip to the cruiser, waving at the kids on the playground. Uncle Lud wanders behind me, slower than usual, but when I turn around he smiles. Maybe he's tired? Daddy always says being a policeman is hard work.

"Where're we going today?" I hop around impatiently while Uncle Lud opens the front car door for me. I don't always get to ride in the front. Today must be extra special.

He ruffles my hair and buckles me in. His voice sounds funny when he answers. "We need to go to the station. There's some people there to see you, Angel."

"Is Daddy going to be there?" I ask twisting in my seat to watch him get in his side of the patrol car. "Daddy says don't talk at the police station without a grown up."

Uncle Lud sighs a big sigh. "I'm your grown up at the station today, Angel."

I love when he uses my special nickname from Daddy. He doesn't do it a lot. No one at the station does. Mostly they call me "Little Detective."

I smile when Uncle Lud turns on the lights and sirens. It's my most favoritest way to ride. We go so fast! But that means my ride is shorter.

When he opens my door, I race right to the front door. I bounce and bounce as he walks so, so slowly to me. The door is too heavy for me to open on my own, but Uncle Lud has super muscles. They might even be bigger than Daddy's!

Inside is really quiet, except for someone crying. There's nobody at the front desk, which is weird. Someone always gives me a police badge sticker and tells me I need my identification.

I try looking around for somebody, when Uncle Lud takes my hand and leads me to the back. We pass lots of crying people on our way. I want to give them all big hugs to make it better, but Uncle Lud just tugs me away.

He takes me to Chief's office. Chief's eyes are extra shiny today.

Uncle Lud closes the door behind us. I've never been in Chief's office without Daddy, or my badge. I sit in the chair, like at the principal's office, cause Mommy says Chief is Daddy's principal.

"Oh, Armani." Chief's voice sounds funny today, too. Maybe my ears are growing? "I asked Officer Ludwig not to tell you, to let me have the dishonor. I hate to have to tell you this."

He takes a big shaky breath. Oh no! Am I not allowed to be their Little Detective anymore? Mommy says one day I'll be too big. But Daddy says never.

"Your parents were in a car accident this morning. The car rolled many times after it was hit, and the other car drove away."

"Are Mommy and Daddy at the hospital? Am I gonna stay with Uncle Lud and Aunt Mindy while they get better?" I turn to Uncle Lud, excited to stay at his house.

But, he shakes his head at me as a tear drips down his face. I reach over to brush it away, because it doesn't belong. He grabs my wrist and pulls me into his lap.

"No, Angel. Mommy and Daddy aren't coming home. The car accident was too bad." Uncle Lud squeezes me tight. "They were both killed on impact, sweetie. We are waiting on Social Services to send someone to decide where you will go."

I'm crying now too. "Why can't I stay with you?"

"I hope so, but it's not up to me."

There's a commotion outside the door. Someone is yelling. Chief slams his door open with a glare at whoever is out there.

"Reynolds! Back room, now. Ludwig, come uncuff Big Mike. Does no one read department memos? I sent notice that he would be working in town today."

"Of course, I attempt to buy off an undercover cop, rather than get information on sales," Big Mike answers.

I peek out the door to watch Uncle Lud take his cuffs off. Big Mike is a huge guy that rides a motorcycle. Daddy says–said–he's the best of a bad lot. Mommy says–said–that because he isn't in a club, he gets special privileges. I wonder what kind of club he could be in?

A pretty lady in a tight skirt demands attention, and I slip back out of sight. Her voice is sharp and makes my growing ears hurt. Uncle Lud strolls past the door, pausing with a smile. The lady yells again, and he shakes his head.

Big Mike joins me in Chief's office, leaving the door open. "Ludwig just told me about your Daddy, sweetheart. He will be missed." He sits in the chair that Uncle Lud left empty. "I'm betting that screeching harpie out there is here to figure out where you go."

"I wanna go to Uncle Ludwig's house."

"I know." He takes a slow deep breath. We sit there, quietly, waiting. Raised voices echo down the hall.

Uncle Lud comes back before Chief. "I've got good news and bad news, kiddo. They say you can stay with me and Aunt Mindy until after the funeral. Only until the funeral. Your social service agent will pick you up and take you to your new home then. They won't let us keep you. We aren't blood family. I'm so sorry."

I throw myself into his arms, sobbing.

Big Mike kneels next to us. "I know it's scary, kid. It's a big world out there, full of good and bad people." He pulls something out of his pocket. "I try to give these patches to as many lonely kids in the Southeast as I can. Bikers everywhere know me. If you're ever in trouble, take this to the closest one, and they'll either help you or call me. I'll come as fast as my bike can carry me." He hands me a patch that says 'protected by Big Mike' on it.

"She's too young " Uncle Lud argues. "Don't be pulling her into your leather clad nonsense."

"Good point." Big Mike gently takes it back. I grasp desperately at it. Safety gone that fast.

I gasp when something settles over my neck. "There ya go kid–a leather necklace. Now you can keep it with you always, even as you grow."

Uncle Lud uses his angry eyes at him, but doesn't take it away again. I grasp the cord tightly in my hand, crying in my uncle's arms.

"Hey, Angel!" Chris yells from the gurney, pulling me from the memory. "His loss."

TWENTY-FIVE

Reinforcements arrive in a timely manner. After the EMTs take Chris, I spend my time leaning against the door. Everything in this office makes my heart hurt.

My high school graduation picture, where he drove across the state to be there for me in my father's stead, sits on the shelf behind his desk. I want to smash it. My office key, that I trusted him with, lays on the desk. I guess Gibson did return it. Even his trench coat hanging on the rack. He jokingly bought it 'so we could match' when I opened my business.

The state troopers and county sheriffs aren't quiet as they make their way through the building. They argue over jurisdiction. Setting spans both Macon and Lee, so I'm guessing a joint investigation is in their future. I'll give them everything I have, and I'll testify, but I hope they leave me out of it otherwise.

I give my statement in a haze. One of the deputies tries to pat my shoulder and I flinch. Hard. I start crying all over again. They offer to drive me home, but I decline.

Boss sits in the waiting area near the office. He doesn't say anything, he just sits and waits, eyes watchful as I'm questioned.

One officer asks why I was chosen to secure the office, when I'm clearly connected to both the case and the perpetrator.

“Maybe because Officer Doe was the only police officer on the whole damn property! He had an actual murder scene to secure. As a certified private investigator, I actually know how not to contaminate evidence. No matter how badly I want to smash things.” If my head wasn't spinning so fast, I'd have much more to say to his smug face.

“Sir!” Another officer holds up Ludwig's phone. “Gonna need IT to crack this. It's locked.”

“Give me a glove.” I hold my hand out expectantly.

“What? Don't have your own?” The officer questioning me teases as his partner complies.

“Did you miss the part about me being kidnapped and not having any of my things on me?” I snap.

He rolls his eyes.

I glove up and hold my hand back out for the phone. They exchange a glance but accept my silent offer. I type in the pass code with ice in my veins–the date of my parents' deaths.

He always told me it was his personal reminder that life was short. And that by typing in that number every day, it reminded him to take a moment to honor them. I thought it was morbid, but very cop-like. To hold close to something like that.

Now I don't know what to feel–what I am feeling.

I look the man questioning my place in the face. “The code is the date of my parents death. Give me a moment, I can change it to swipe to open.”

He snatches it out of my hand. “And contaminate the evidence? Just tell me.”

I glare, no longer feeling very cooperative. "It's public record. Look it up." I turn to walk away.

"We ain't done here." He grabs me by the arm, and Boss jumps to his feet.

"Yes, we are." One of the state troopers intercedes, before my brother can. "And, we have lead, since both counties have equal claim." He hands me a card. "Call me if you remember anything else."

"I'd offer you one of my cards, but it's been a shitty day and I have no clue what was done with my things. Google me if you need me. Only P.I. in town."

Boss wraps his good arm around me and pulls me tight to his side. "Here." He hands over a few cards. "Me and the other two motorcycle clubs' presidents that were involved today–these are our cards. Thought you might need them. And I have one of Armani's." He digs in his wallet and pulls out the card I gave him the day we met.

"Can I take my sister home now?"

The trooper looks over all four cards. Two with the same last name on top. "Yeah, we're good here."

I don't remember walking to the truck. I don't remember getting in or buckling. I remember noticing Chris's bike in the bed of the truck and choking on a sob.

"Everyone is heading to HandleBar," Boss tells me. "Tank is bringing the girls. Spider has Chris, and Preacher said he was going to fill in King."

I nod, numbly. Doe is behind us. When did that happen?

He opens my door when we arrive and offers me a hand. "State says they have that compound locked down. Tank and his guys were cleared to bring the girls home. I've been ten-sevened for the night, possibly longer."

"Ten-seven?" Boss asks, getting the door.

"Out of service," I whisper. "He's been sent off shift." My voice sounds foreign, hollow.

Kami rushes me, squeezing me tight. "Tank and Boss have been keeping me posted. Oh my God, Armani, are you okay?"

"I...no."

"Come, sit. I've ordered the kitchen to do a big fry up. Several Newcomer's Specials. Boss's orders. I have all the guys in there cooking."

"These girls are going to need food. You too," Boss tells me.

Ember sits on the other side of me. "I've also ordered soup from damn near every restaurant in town. Some might not feel up to solids."

"Did they get checked out? EMTs or hospital?" *Did someone already tell me that?*

"EMTs took them for a quick check. The girls who survived are all being brought here after discharge. They want to stay together." Kami starts biting the end of her nail. "No one has told me if Krista is one of them."

"She was good when I crawled out," I tell her, before her words sink in. "What do you mean 'who survived?'"

"The guys chasing you opened fire when Tank's crew showed up." Boss answers softly. "Spray shots down the stairs at the whole basement. Killed most of them trying to escape. The ones who survived stayed to the back. Best we can tell they wanted to verify who was coming in. The others just wanted out."

"How many?" The words stick in my throat. "There were at least twenty girls down there."

Officer Doe steps forward. "According to the Troopers, five girls made it out. Identities withheld. I asked specifically about Krista," He tells Kami. "They wouldn't tell me anything. Sorry."

"For now, no news is good news," Boss declares, kissing the top of her head.

"She is smart," I agree. "She was helping Wynonah. I'm certain the two of them were at the back."

Just then, the door slams open. Spider and Chris come in.

"Wasn't allowed close enough to get any names, but they were releasing the girls right after us," Spider says. "Tank's crew should be here shortly. I wish I could say I recognized Miss Kami's sister, but they all kind of looked like sisters."

"Thank you, Spider."

We sit in silence after that. Chris doesn't join us, but rather heads to the kitchen. Ember follows him, trying to convince him she has everything handled. Boss joins Mikey at the POS. Probably making some sort of payment for the food, without Chris trying to stop him.

Eventually the door creaks open again. Sarge holds it open as everyone enters. All five girls are wrapped in blankets.

Krista spots her sister immediately, dropping her blanket and running at her. Both girls are crying and grasping at each other like they can't believe the other is there.

Wynonah wraps the blanket tighter and drops herself in Doe's lap. "They bragged about framing you," she mutters. "Thought it was funny."

He wraps his arms around her briefly, before she slips into her own seat. "I know," he answers. "Who all did you see there?"

"I gave a full rundown to the troopers," she responds. "They told me about Chief Ludwig. I never saw him, that floored me. At least half the department was there. If I didn't see Ludwig, who else didn't show their faces?"

"ACAB, am I right?" Boss says, slipping into his seat.

"Absolutely," Doe and Wynonah respond in unison, startling a broken laugh from me.

Kami ushers the girls to the next table, sitting them behind Wynonah.

"It all started with Ludwig's obsession with my mom. We noticed everyone looked a bit like me, but they look even more like my mom. Found out he ordered a hit on my dad, and hated him. I never saw it coming. I thought they were best friends. Turns out Gibson killed them both."

"He spilled his guts on camera," Doe adds. "Not that he knew I was recording. I hope that doesn't make it inadmissible."

"Alabama is a one party consent state, and there is no expectation of privacy at a police station," I respond on autopilot.

Everyone looks at me. "What? Research is my bitch, and I wield her like a knife. I use one party consent laws to cover at least ninety-five percent of what I do. It was the premise of my last big case. I testified the day Kyle broke in–the day I met most everyone here."

"I almost forgot about that." Doe bumps his shoulder against mine. "My first babysitting job."

"He might have been involved. I saw a note in Ludwig's office. No last name, but still suspicious."

"You thought I was involved."

"Looked suspicious, too," I countered. "Showing up everywhere I went. Bringing false documents. And I have to ask. You never mentioned dating Alivia Bennett. She was missing too."

"Alivia? My ex? Last time I saw her, she dumped me. I figured not seeing her around was by design. She disappeared too?"

"File says mystery boyfriend never came forward. Seeing your connection to her made you look extra sketchy. I never, ever would have suspected Ludwig. New guy, though? Easily."

"I get it," He responds, with a shoulder shrug.

"Just remember to stay on her good side," Chris says, placing platters of food on both tables. "I've seen her spar."

"That's right!" Krista pipes up from her spot in her sister's arms. "That woman right there is an angel of chaos."

"No, she was an angel of freedom." One of the others chimes in.

"An angel of death." Another mutters.

"She's an angel of care." Kami says.

"Personally, I think she's an angel of destruction." Wynonah laughs.

"Nah," Sarge says with a grin. "She's just Angel."

TWENTY-SIX

It doesn't take long for the night to devolve into what basically amounts to a party. Preacher and his guys show up first, their wives riding with or bringing trucks. In a matter of moments, Mrs. Mary has a beautiful buffet set up along the bar.

During the commotion, Ember's delivery drivers arrive. Mrs. Mary is quick to set up a table for just soups.

Slowly The Road Kings trickle in. The rescued girls start to get a little nervous at the influx of people, of men. Mrs. Mary notices, and suddenly they are surrounded by church ladies.

Food flows freely, all four clubs enjoying the fare. This is exactly the vibe Chris has been aiming for with his monthly Family Nights. If only it didn't take a literal nightmare for it to happen.

I snag Chris at one point. “How much for me to plan the next family night for you? I think we can maintain these vibes.” I hip check him with a smile.

“Five thousand?” He answers, questioningly.

“Okay.” A bit steep, but doable. “It might take me a bit, but I can do that.”

"I'll help." Sarge tucks me under his arm.

Chris looks back and forth between us, lips pursed and eyebrows furrowed. "I meant the budget is five thousand. I'm not going to *charge* you to work for me."

"Speaking of Family Night." Sarge winks at me and climbs up on a table. With a sharp whistle, he has everyone's attention. "I'd like to propose an idea to all four clubs. I thought I'd do it now while everyone is here. Chris has taken care of us for a while now. HandleBar has been a safe place for all bikers, regardless of colors. We have all taken advantage of his hospitality. We go to Family Night, but never cross the lines that divide us. I'd like to encourage all four clubs to honor Keep with his own protection patch. Take it to Church. Vote on it, and get back to me."

He climbs down to a smattering of applause.

"You didn't have to do that," Chris tells him.

"Yeah, I did."

Over the next couple weeks, I put my research skills to the test. I start with surveying all four clubs about what they'd like to see at Family Night. Then I coordinate the food–Mrs. Mary is a big help with that. No more separate bar-b-ques. I put The Calvary in charge of meats, and distribute sides and deserts amongst the others. If this goes well, each club can take a turn at the grill.

Finally, Family Night arrives.

Mrs. Mary and I direct everyone to put their food on the buffet we set up. Tables are spread across the lot with nice teal and navy table cloths, colors I carefully picked–not in any of the clubs' patches. I look up at the HandleBar sign with a grin. The teal tablecloth matches the neon sign perfectly–a small detail that fills me with pride.

Activities are spread out too. New things for the kids to do: a coloring table, a bubble station, and a scavenger hunt. There's a couple corn hole stations set up. I even found a giant Jenga set, and a huge Connect Four game.

The night is a hit. There are no cliques. No lines of division. Everyone mingles. I can tell not everyone is happy about it, but no one actually voices any displeasure.

After everyone has eaten, Sarge calls for attention. "Just a couple weeks ago, I proposed something to the clubs. Over the last few days, everyone has gotten back to me. Keep, Armani-Angel, will you join me?"

I don't know what he wants me for, but I stand proudly by Chris's side.

"Everyone has voted." Sarge pulls out a beautiful vest. Instead of colors, the patch is a replica of the HandleBar's neon sign. He turns it around to show the protection patches. All four displayed proudly on the front. "I was honored to finally get Keep the protection patches he deserves. I was even more honored when he reached out to me with a little venture of his own."

Sarge pulls out a beautiful leather jacket with a pair of drop dead gorgeous silver wings across the back. Angel is written in beautiful calligraphy above them. My heart jumps to my throat. It's so pretty. "Angel, the clubs have voted. Not all of us feel close enough to you for club protection patches. Instead–" he turns the jacket around. "–we have individual protection patches for you. And we left room for Big Mikes."

They are beautiful. Simple, but beautiful in their meaning. Boss, Sarge, Tank, all have their protection on me. It makes my eyes water.

He hands something to Chris.

"Armani, Angel, you have been a blessing sent from above. You showed up and changed my world and forever made my life better. Would you do me the honor of accepting the title of my old lady? You are it for me, and while this isn't a proposal, it's a promise. Forever?"

"Yes."

He adds his patch to the spot that was already prepared for it, directly above my heart. 'Property of Keep.' Not a declaration of ownership, but of value.

The yard fills with the sound of applause, but I don't care. I'm lost in Chris's arms and his kiss. "Let's give it up for Angel and her Keep!"

EPILOGUE

It amazes me standing here, surrounded by the hustle and bustle of Chris's HandleBar, how even though I've had Big Mike's patch nearly my whole life, even though I've been surrounded by biker clubs every turn, just right now it finally hits me. That feeling Big Mike spoke of when he gave me this patch, the feeling of belonging, of finding where you fit in the world. All those other Clubs, over the years, they watched over me with respect to Big Mike. I never belonged to them, not like I belong right here. They protected me, sheltered me, and helped me through so much, but I was never theirs, just a temporary loan. But here, now, these are my people. I didn't need one club, I needed four. These four.

If I'm going to throw my hat in with this lot, I'll have to put my skin in the game, or rather, my leathers. There's so much to this lifestyle that was kept from me, wasn't yet meant for me. So much that I still have to learn. But, that's okay. *Research is my bitch.*

ACKNOWLEDGMENTS

I'd like to start by thanking my husband, Shane, for always being in my corner and being a huge support during this whole process. I'd also like to thank my mom, Chris, for encouraging me every step of the way and being an active Beta reader. Another big thanks to Nicole Anderson for dredging through my second draft and giving amazing editor level feedback at such an early stage. My actual editor, L. M. London, would have had a lot more work to do if my early readers had not given so much quality feedback. Thank you, Lara, for the inspiring feedback and constructive criticism–your notes were exactly what I needed.

I would also like to extend my acknowledgement of thanks to two very supportive author groups: The Author Cult, a supportive chat on TikTok, and The Indie Author Revolution. Without these two groups, I doubt I would have ever been able to make myself start that first round of edits, let alone finish a publishable story. H. R. Justice came in clutch, helping me find the perfect wording for my last major edit.

Thank you K. L. Thorne, for amazing cover art and other designs. I love the page break image you developed for me, and cannot wait to show off your other works as well. The bar sign and club logos turned out amazing.

ABOUT THE AUTHOR

Photo credit: Barbie Winfree

Kelly Kata Winfree grew up in Michigan, moving to Alabama in high-school, where she met her now husband, Shane. Writing has always been one of Kelly's passions, as has reading. Throughout school she dominated every reading and writing contest available. All she ever wanted to be growing up was an author.

At age 33, Kelly began her debut novel, Angel's Keep. Despite many personal surprises that year, she proudly presented her book to the public less than a year after beginning. She now has multiple projects in the works and can't wait until they are ready to share.

Kelly spends her days homemaking and homeschooling

her children. Well suited to life on a farm, she is quite proud of her Australian Cattle Dogs and her husband's Simmental Cattle operations.

www.ingramcontent.com/pod-product-compliance
Lightning Source LLC
LaVergne TN
LVHW091301150826
845673LV00006B/1497

* 9 7 8 1 9 6 8 7 0 0 2 3 2 *